Heavenly praise for the novels of NIKKI HOLIDAY

HEAVEN KNOWS BEST

"A true pleasure, a clever, amusing, and satisfying story filled with deftly drawn characters I cared about . . . Can't wait to see what Mr. G is up to next."
Kay Hooper

"How can you go wrong? The concept of ghosts coming back to life and doing good works, especially Quentin and Mia, is extremely exciting. Do we dare to hope for more? . . . Don't let these two pass you by. They are great."
Rendezvous

HEAVEN COMES HOME

"Every page is a delight. You literally won't be able to put down this heavenly fare."
Affaire de Coeur

"A great book, which I dearly loved . . . It hit me with all the emotions."
Rendezvous

"A wickedly funny, rollicking read . . . Holiday's view of the hereafter is so creative and entertaining that it really would be a sin to miss it."
Romance Forever

Avon Books are available at special quantity discounts for bulk
purchases for sales promotions, premiums, fund raising or educa-
tional use. Special books, or book excerpts, can also be created to
fit specific needs.

For details write or telephone the office of the Director of Special
Markets, Avon Books, Dept. FP, 1350 Avenue of the Americas,
New York, New York 10019, 1-800-238-0658.

HEAVEN LOVES A HERO♡

NIKKI HOLIDAY

AVON BOOKS ◆ NEW YORK

This is a work of fiction. Names, characters, places, and incidents either are the product of the author's imagination or are used fictitiously. Any resemblance to actual events, locales, organizations, or persons, living or dead, is entirely coincidental and beyond the intent of either the author or the publisher.

AVON BOOKS
A division of
The Hearst Corporation
1350 Avenue of the Americas
New York, New York 10019

Copyright © 1997 by Nancy Wagner
Inside cover author photo by Debbi DeMont Photography
Published by arrangement with the author
Visit our website at **http://AvonBooks.com**
Library of Congress Catalog Card Number: 97-93014
ISBN: 0-380-78798-9

First Avon Books Printing: September 1997

AVON TRADEMARK REG. U.S. PAT. OFF. AND IN OTHER COUNTRIES, MARCA REGISTRADA, HECHO EN U.S.A.

Printed in the U.S.A.

WCD   10   9   8   7   6   5   4   3   2   1

This one's for Tom, specifically for having the wisdom to diagnose my tunnel vision, and most especially, for loving me.

With special thanks to Eric, for the name; to PJ's Coffee and Tea of River Ridge, for the second home; and to Keith, for the swift read and constant support.

1

Some days you never know what might happen.

That refrain charging through her head, Mia Tortelli leaned back in her uncomfortable folding chair, arms crossed, foot tapping, unable to believe the words Quentin Grandy, her husband of one month, three weeks, and six days had just uttered.

The rest of the people gathered around the large oval table in a studio rehearsal room apparently shared her reaction. The production designer, the art director, the film's stars, Francine May and Hal Cormoran, and the first and second assistant directors, to name only a few of the cast and crew assembled for the first read-through of *Permutation*—all looked as stunned as Mia felt. Even the screenwriter, Jeffrey "Beetle" Leonard, sitting at the end of the table, stopped scribbling in the notebook he held.

Heartened by this shared reaction to Quentin's announcement that they were shifting at least two weeks of production out of the studio and into the mountains above Santa Barbara, Mia turned to Quentin. Gazing into the brown eyes of the man she loved more than life itself, she said, "Over my dead body."

Quentin whistled softly through his teeth. In a low voice, he said, "I should have discussed this with you before announcing it, but it hit me only this morning. You know I have my best ideas in the shower." He gave her the boyish grin she found so appealing under other circumstances.

Whispers ran around the table. One or two chairs scraped as the more seasoned members of their production team chose to refill their coffee cups. Mia groaned inwardly, hating to have this debate in front of everyone. But as producer, she had the budget for *Permutation* finely honed. Two weeks on location, even in Santa Barbara, which was only two hours away, would kill them.

"Anything we can do there, we can do here," she said, refusing to ask Quentin why he considered the move so necessary.

"Think so?"

"Absolutely."

Quentin shifted in his chair, cocking a quizzical eye at her. "Don't you even want to know why I think it's important?"

She set her jaw and shook her head.

"I see."

"Good." Mia lined her papers and pen in a neat parallel. "Then let's get started."

"At least you accept my judgement."

"Wrong." Honestly, how could he be so stubborn? Mia felt like a principal lecturing a child in trouble again for the same thing three times in one hour. "We have a budget. We have a shooting schedule. We have commitments of time from all these people. Two weeks in Santa Barbara will ruin us."

She ticked off the arguments on her fingers. "It's not just the same two weeks we have scheduled in the studio; it's two weeks plus time to find locations, time to work the deals to secure them, time to shift the production, time to light, time to worry over the weather." There, she'd proved her point. Satisfied he'd have to listen to reason now, she faced him, eye to eye, trying to check with her peripheral vision how the others were taking this little discussion.

Quentin sat there, looking too smug for Mia's comfort. He wanted her to ask why Santa Barbara, but she'd be darned if she'd break down. Of course, her curiosity rivaled her determination to stick to budget, but the last thing she would do now was ask why.

"Time," Quentin said, "isn't always the most important element."

The production designer, sitting beside Quentin, nodded. "He's right, you know. A quick pic without heart'll be death at the box office. I agree we don't have the time, but somehow the idea of shooting the biker camp outdoors appeals to me. There's a great spot on one of those mountain roads above Santa Barbara, a dump called the Cubby Hole. All the local Harley riders hang out there."

Quentin's grin grew broader.

Mia's heart sank. "You've been there, haven't you, Quentin?"

He nodded.

"When?"

"Last Friday."

Friday. She'd spent the day in the office, over-seeing details. Details, the story of her life. Well, as producer, details were her job. There'd been some problems with Francine May's medical in-surance coverage, something about a weak heart. Mia had anted up for a higher premium to insure completion of the production, feeling a bit guilty for not sharing the information with Quentin. But the last thing Quentin needed was any more am-munition for his argument to dump May and sign Portia Goodhope, another source of their ongoing differences of opinion over this production.

Mia sighed. They hadn't always disagreed so much, but now that they were married and worked together as producer and director, they seemed to spend their days debating.

Quentin and the production designer were carrying on about the rustic delights of the Cubby Hole. Around the table, heads began to nod. "So much more authentic." "Great color potential." "Use the local bikers, rather than extras playing bikers."

The phrases flowed around Mia. In her mind she saw dollar signs and balance sheets, all the reasons they shouldn't shift production at such a late date. But the biggest reason she objected had nothing to do with dollars and cents.

It had to do with her heart.

If only Quentin had consulted her first. Sure, she'd been gone when he'd gotten out of the shower that morning. But he could have whispered his idea to her before blurting it out. He should have shared it first with her.

With his wife.

The buzz grew louder as the excitement for the idea grew. They were making a movie most of Hollywood had turned down, a film Oscar-winning director Quentin Grandy had declared he just had to do. Working with Quentin amounted to taking risks, risks that so far had turned to rewards of gold. If Quentin was for it, who were they to object?

"How 'bout it, Mia?"

Quentin spoke softly. She knew him so well, she could tell he regretted springing this news on her. As well he should. "It may be brilliant," she said slowly, "but our budget won't stand for it."

"Tell you what," he said, disappointment clear in his brown gaze, "let's long-and-short it."

Mia looked at him in shock. They had a tradition of pulling straws or sticks or whatever was handy to settle minor differences. Usually they'd laugh, win or lose, and accept the decision. "Long-and-short a decision this expensive?"

"And this crucial." He nodded. Reaching across the table, he snagged two wooden coffee stir sticks and broke a piece off one. Leveling off the tops, he hid their lengths behind his hand.

"I don't think we should do this," Mia said,

feeling like a spoilsport as others around the table began laying odds on the outcome.

"Come on, what have you got to lose?" He winked. "It's fifty-fifty, like always."

Mia gritted her teeth and yanked one of the sticks from his grasp.

He opened his palm, revealing the unbroken one. She looked down at the jagged end of her shorter piece and wondered why what used to be such a fun game didn't feel so jolly anymore.

A week later, her skin warm, her lips love-swollen, Mia lay with her cheek resting on her husband's chest, her flushed face cushioned by his thick mat of golden brown hair. A wayward strand tickled her nose and she circled a lazy finger around it, drawing it back into the fold and thinking how impossible it was for her to remain upset with him.

He'd apologized more times than she could count for springing the Santa Barbara announcement on her, sincere in his belief that she'd understand his need to shift production. In all the movies they'd done together, they'd thought in unison, making whatever adjustments were necessary for the best quality film possible.

When they'd finally made it home that night, Mia had found a bouquet of roses awaiting her.

She sighed. If only their days were as perfect as their nights!

Through her lashes, she studied the face of Quentin Grandy. The world knew him as the brilliant young director who'd already garnered two Academy Awards; Mia knew him as the man who once a week took time from his hectic schedule to visit Mrs. Klopfenstein, the crotchety widow who lived alone in the house next door. Quentin had even been known to down Mrs. K's noxious fresh-pressed vegetable juice.

The world knew Quentin as the charmer who'd finally fallen in love and settled down. As the object of his affections, Mia basked in his love but worried despite her own love and trust in him how long his love would last.

And lately, with the way the two of them had been arguing like a Persian and a Pekingese over every detail of production of their current film, Mia worried even more.

"We've been married for two months and six days today," Mia Tortelli whispered half to herself, half to her husband's chest. Here in their private world, with the light of dawn not quite intruding into the special world of their lovely new bedroom, Mia forgot to worry. Here, nestled under the covers with Quentin, she felt safe, loved, and very, very sexy.

Mia felt his smile as his lips moved against her forehead. "You keep track of everything, don't you?" He nibbled on her neck, taking any sting out of his words.

"That's who I am," Mia said.

"And I guess that's why you're the best producer Hollywood has ever seen."

"Gosh, thanks—but I can think of more than a few who'd differ with you on that."

Quentin pulled her even closer. "But they've never been in bed with you, Mrs. Grandy."

"I should think not!" Mia snuggled against him, hugging the only man she'd ever loved. He knew she'd come to him a virgin. Quentin, on the other hand, had been well on his way to making headlines as a Hollywood playboy when Mia and Quentin had experienced their first amazing encounter with the afterlife. And it was thanks to that miracle that Quentin had finally realized Mia his best friend was the woman he loved, the woman he wanted to be his wife.

"And now we're married," Mia murmured.

Quentin drew back slightly and looked into her eyes. "Not thinking of changing your mind?"

Rather than answer the question with words, Mia eased her body, a few teasing inches at a time, until she lay cradled atop him. Her heart beat faster and she tossed back her head, casting a naughty smile. For a rather shy woman, she opened up beautifully with the man she loved, a gift Quentin had given her, a gift that made her love him even more.

"It's a good thing I'm still a young man."

"You're not even thirty," Mia said, and wrapped her hands around his shaft, swollen and eager once again.

Quentin lifted her around the waist, raised her above him, then began to lower her slowly, oh so slowly.

Mia squirmed with pleasure. The time she spent making love with her husband was pure paradise. The rest of the day might give her headaches, might find her arguing with her talented director husband in a way she didn't recall them doing in all the movies they'd made together before their wedding, but now, just for these special secret moments, none of those problems existed.

Quentin held her so close to him she could almost feel him straining to enter her, yet he held back. He tweaked a nipple with his lips as she squirmed and tried to lower herself to mate with him.

He shook his head and moved his mouth to her other breast. "Remember," he said, before capturing the hardened tip, "we like to wake up nice and *s-s-l-o-w.*"

Mia panted with pleasure. When she thought she'd melt completely, she felt him begin to enter her. She cried out greedily, but he lifted her away from him again.

"Please, Quentin," she said, not caring that she begged for what she wanted.

He smiled, making a facial expression she could only describe as delightfully wicked, and lifted his hips as he lowered her body.

And then the phone rang.

Quentin made a noise that sounded a lot like a growl as he claimed her, filling her with heat and movement.

Two rings.

For once in her busy, responsible life, Mia ignored the telephone, the instrument that dictated so much of her existence.

The ringing stopped.

Then the phone rang again, just twice.

"Quentin—"

He groaned and slowed his body . . .

Two rings meant they had to answer the phone. Only their parents and Mia's trusted personal assistant had that number.

"Maybe it's a mistake," Mia whispered, even as she reached for the phone. Her parents wouldn't call unless someone had taken ill. Quentin's parents would phone only in the event of a crisis. Surely nothing had happened to any of them.

Still lying on Quentin, she raised the receiver to her ear. *Please let it be the film,* she said to herself. *No matter what goes wrong with a movie, it can be fixed . . .*

"I'm sorry to call you, Mia." Her assistant's voice came clear and strong over the line and Mia breathed an instant sigh of relief.

She knew Quentin felt her reaction, for he smiled slightly before mouthing, "What's wrong now?"

What's wrong now? Mia mumbled a few words to the effect of, "Of course it's okay to call," thinking that they should change the name of their current film from *Permutation* to *What's Wrong Now.* So far, it seemed if they could experience a problem, they did.

"It's Francine May. She's had a heart attack and they've rushed her into surgery."

Unconsciously, Mia formed the sign of the cross over her bare breast, fighting a wave of guilt as she thought of the insurance doctor's report she'd neglected to mention to Quentin. Francine May had been her candidate to play one of the lead roles in *Permutation*, a choice hotly contested by Quentin. "Is she expected to make it?" she asked. She mouthed "Francine May" to Quentin.

He grabbed the receiver from her hand.

Mia toppled to the bed, setting up a side-to-side wave in their waterbed. "Hey," she cried, "I'll handle this."

Quentin glared. "Get her agent on the phone," he said into the receiver, then hung up. Pushing back against the headboard, he said, "A heart attack! What next?"

Mia hugged her arms to her chest. "Honestly, Quentin, have a little sympathy. Francine's a woman of advanced years. She may not live through this."

"We should've signed Portia Goodhope."

"Are you going to start that discussion again?" Mia glared and pulled the comforter around her. She and Quentin had gone round and round over the casting of the lead role in *Permutation*. As producer, she felt entitled to the final call. As director, Quentin held exactly the same opinion. With the exception of the dismal failure of Quentin's college production *Sew-Sew and the Hand Grenade*, she and Quentin had agreed on major production issues. They worked together like a bobbin and needle in a well-oiled Singer. But, ever since they'd

returned from their paradise of a honeymoon on
Maui, Mia'd felt as if every day brought a new
question for which each of them had a different
answer.

Or maybe she only felt that way because on her
wedding day she'd promised herself she'd make
the best wife ever for Quentin. After all, if she
were perfect, he'd never, ever leave her.

Then they'd rehash something like the Francine
May–Portia Goodhope choice and Mia, launching
in with both feet, would debate until she'd run out
of breath.

And begin all over again to worry whether
she'd drive Quentin away.

If it weren't for their nights together, when
work got left way, way behind, Mia thought she'd
probably go nuts.

What was a woman to do?

Sighing, Mia realized she wasn't sure she knew
the answer to that question, but she certainly understood the duties of a producer. Francine May
had been perfect for the role of the biker/fairy
godmother. Portia Goodhope, a grande dame of
Broadway who'd never stepped foot behind a
camera in her fifty-plus years on this earth, would
have been a disaster, one more catastrophe in a
production that couldn't bear another splinter, let
alone a fallen tree trunk crashed across its path.

"What are you doing?" While she'd been lost
in her thoughts, Quentin had leapt from bed.

"Going to see her agent, get out of the deal . . .
then I'm flying to New York and signing Portia

Goodhope." He stuck his arms willy-nilly into his bathrobe, a beautiful monogrammed robe Mia had purchased for a welcome-home-from-the-honeymoon present. She hated to admit to it, but she was secretly sentimental.

Mia drew herself up to her full sitting-up-in-bed height. "I don't think so."

Quentin scuffed his feet into his slippers. He dashed a hand through his hair, hair she'd dragged her fingers through only moments ago, during their impassioned lovemaking. "This time," he said, "I'm doing it my way. I'm sorry, Mia, but this film means too much to me to screw up now. And Portia Goodhope isn't the kind of woman you can sign over the phone."

"Aren't you jumping to conclusions?" Mia sprang out of bed and donned her own robe, a chenille favorite she'd owned for years, and which, she knew, had another two or three years' wear in it. She didn't mind spending money on presents for people she loved, but she sure hated wasting it on herself.

Quentin turned to face her. Slowly he shook his head. "When a woman as old and fat and out of shape as Francine May has a heart attack and goes into surgery, what other conclusion can I draw?"

"Quentin, that's mean!" Mia straightened from pulling on her slippers. "She's a sweet woman who's had a long life. Give her some respect."

He flashed her a quick grin. "You sound like your mother talking." Then he stepped to her side and gave her a swift kiss. "Can't wait to finish what we'd started," he said, "but I'm racing for the shower, then I'm going to see her agent. Come to New York with me. We'll talk to Portia Goodhope together."

Mia set her jaw. "We should wait to see the prognosis on Francine before acting."

"I guess that's a no." He headed out of the room and into the master bath. At the doorway, he turned. "You know," he said, looking at her with those great big brown eyes that always turned her heart to mush, "I hate it when we disagree."

Then he whisked out the door. Mia heard the water gush forth in the shower.

"*You* hate it," she said, striding out of the room, taking the spiral stairs down to the kitchen two at a time, her body on automatic pilot as she headed for the coffeemaker. If she had to be up and about before five in the morning, she needed caffeine. "You think I like it?"

Measuring the coffee, Mia fumed over Quentin's determination to recast the role. He could go to New York alone. Even if she went with him, he wouldn't listen to her. He had his mind made up, and if he could persuade Portia Goodhope, *Permutation* would be stuck with her.

Mia sighed and poured the filtered water into the coffeemaker, switched on the unit, and leaned back against the counter to await the steaming drip, drip, drip that she loved to hear and smell early in the morning. Routines could be a comfort in a time of confusion.

And confused she was. Some things were beyond reason, and why she and Quentin were fighting one another this way ranked right up there with the biggest mysteries of her life.

She nibbled on her thumb and wondered why Quentin had said she sounded like her mother. Then, instead of fretting over his words, she let go of it, knowing suddenly what she had to do.

In the shower, Quentin let the water beat down on his shoulders and watched the steam fill the room. Usually he jumped in and out of a shower as fast as you might expect a cat to, but he couldn't think of this morning as anywhere near normal.

Never in his life had he let anything interrupt sex.

Reaching for the soap, Quentin pictured Mia cuddled on his body, teasing him like the little minx she was, something she hid from the world very well. He grew hard just thinking about her. Damn, it was all he could do to work beside her morning, noon, and night and not pull her into a closet a couple of times a day.

But since they'd begun *Permutation*, Mia had made it clear that during the day, business came first. She thought the cast and crew should see them as director and producer, not as two horny honeymooners.

Well, at work they sure didn't act like honeymooners. Take this Portia Goodhope thing. Quentin knew in his gut Portia would be the best thing to happen to *Permutation*. But Mia, operating as any good producer did, recited all the reasons Portia would be nothing but trouble.

He'd given in finally, not because he agreed, but because if he hadn't, they'd never have gotten where they were today: two days away from the start of principal photography.

But it hadn't made him happy to sacrifice on a point he felt so crucial.

Quentin dropped the soap. He kicked it to the back of the shower and watched as it slid toward the drain. Again he knocked it with his toe and watched it follow the same path back.

Just like people, he thought, leaning to pick up the bar. Predictable. Behaving the same over and over again. He could predict he would act on his creative instinct while Mia would seek to follow a logical, orderly path toward solving any problem.

She would also, he knew, always be a perfectionist, a trait that he suspected was behind her worrying over the state of their marriage. Only the other day she'd asked him if he thought everything was okay between them.

Quentin, who couldn't be happier, hadn't taken the question seriously. He'd held out his arms, kissed her until neither one of them could breathe, then promptly forgotten the question. He knew he loved Mia, knew she loved him.

He threw some shampoo on his hair, determined to quit puzzling over why Mia would be concerned about their love life and get on to problems he could solve.

He wanted to reach Francine May's agent in time to make a morning flight to New York, and the best way to do that was to pay a visit to the hospital. May had made her agent a rich woman, and Quentin figured the ten-percenter would be hovering beside the hospital bed. He hated to make Mia unhappy with his choice, but he had to do what he had to do.

Ducking his head under the stream of water, Quentin wondered how it was he could be making a movie that was all about the possibility of change and still be so goddamn set in his ways.

2 ⁓

Mia found her mother making angels for the church Christmas bazaar.

The front door stood ajar, the world held at bay by the wrought-iron security screen. Mia peered through, smiling at the sight of her mother bent over her work. Somehow that familiar picture steadied her.

She tapped on the door. "Ma?"

Without looking up from the styrofoam form she held between her stubby fingers, Eireen Tortelli said, "Don't stand there like the Fuller Brush man, Mia. Let yourself in."

Mia turned the handle. Sure enough, the security door wasn't locked. Even though her parents had moved out of the deteriorating East Los Angeles neighborhood of Mia's childhood to the relative serenity of Alhambra, Mia didn't want her mother taking risks.

She stepped into the living room, the words on her lips cut off before she could say them.

"And don't tell me I ought to have locked the door." Eireen did at last glance up, and Mia found herself reassured at the fire in her mother's expression. She counted, more than she realized, on her mother's steady strength.

Eireen's dark eyes, echoes of Mia's own, wore unfamiliar shadows beneath them. Her thick brown hair had long since been overcome by gray, with her mother refusing to bother with rinses or dyes. A touch of lipstick softened her lips, but most of the color seemed to have been chewed away, a sure sign something was bothering her.

Forgetting the troubles that had sent her across town to seek her mother's counsel, Mia dropped her purse on the sagging sofa and crossed the room to the dining table where her mother's craft materials were spread. She pulled out a chair and seated herself, careful not to comment on her mother's apparent agitation, suppressed though it might be. Eireen didn't stand for fussing.

"There's coffee on the stove," her mother said, before storing several straight pins in the corner of her lips.

"Thanks," Mia said, but made no move to rise. Her mother liked to take care of her family, but she didn't respect too much nicey-nice, as Eireen phrased it. In a few minutes Mia would get the coffee, but she'd let her mother remind her first.

Being needed made her ma happy.

Her mother fastened two gauzy wings to the styrofoam angel, stabbing them in place with straight pins. Reaching for the next form, she said, "Your sister and brother are healthy. Your pa's asleep. So that leaves you. Are you here to tell me you've gone and married the wrong man and now you want to move back home?"

Mia sat back in surprise. She toyed with one of the precut angel's wings. "What makes you say a thing like that?"

Her mother pushed a lock of hair out of her eyes and tucked it behind her ear. "Mia Tortelli, I gave birth to you. I watched over you for eight years of grade school and four of high school, and never once did you miss a day of class. And I don't suppose since you've started working in the movies you've ever not been at work at nine o'clock in the morning." She held a scrap of gold fabric against the form, then discarded it. "Not on a weekday, leastways. So, I figure there's something troubling you."

Mia had to smile. "I'm that predictable, am I?"

At that her hardworking mother smiled, too. "You've always been one to stick to a routine, that's for sure. If there ever was a rule, you'd follow it. Not like your brother, oh, no, not Michael." Then she frowned and bent back over her angel.

Mia recognized that look and sensed a clue to her mother's state of mind. "What's Michael done now?"

Eireen pinched her lips and glared at Mia in a way that sent a shiver down to her toes. "He's talking divorce. Thinks he can waltz out on his wife and kids because he's taken a fancy to some chippy in his office." She sniffed and stabbed another pair of wings into place.

"I think I'll get that coffee now," Mia said, and

walked the few steps into the kitchen. The Alhambra house was small, so she had no problem hearing her mother mutter under her breath, "Marriage is for life, make no mistake about that."

Mia poured a cup of coffee and stirred in some sugar. She knew her mother's words were meant as much for her as they were a comment on her brother's situation. She gave herself a moment's pause, leaning against the edge of the sink, noting that as usual, not a speck of dirt showed on the linoleum, nor did a dirty dish rest in the sink. Mia didn't have to wonder from what source she'd inherited her own compulsion for perfection.

It was that very same drive for perfection she brought to her marriage, naturally. So it was no wonder her current state of affairs with Quentin drove her nuts. With a sigh, Mia pushed away from the counter and rejoined her mother at the table.

Eireen shot her a quick glance. "Your brother's not getting a divorce. He'll come to his senses and Katie'll take him back. She's a good wife." Then, to Mia's surprise, her mother didn't reach for the next styrofoam angel. "You want to tell me what's eating at you?"

"Quentin's going to New York this morning to cast an actress who's all wrong for the part. It'll mess up the entire production, run us over cost, and make Quentin a laughingstock with casting agents." Mia's words tumbled out. "He's wanted this person for the role all along, but I insisted on someone else, and now she's had a heart attack, so Quentin's racing off to get his way."

Her mother picked up the angel, turning it this way and that. "And my son-in-law went to New York without asking you to go with him?"

"Oh, no. He asked me. I said—"

"Don't say it." Mia's mother slapped the table and the angels danced. "Don't tell your ma you told your husband you weren't going to New York with him."

Mia nodded, indignant that her mother should take such a tack. "I'm the producer, and I know what I'm doing."

"Producer-smoosher." Eireen wielded a pair of scissors, then carefully trimmed a loose thread from a pair of wings. "He's your husband and you're his wife, and you shouldn't be sleeping three thousand miles apart when you've only been married a couple of months."

"But Ma, he's wrong." Mia felt like a child scolded for something someone else had done. "He's wrong to butt in and take over."

"Hmmph. Didn't you say this other actress had a heart attack?"

Mia nodded again.

"So it's God's will." With that, her mother smiled. "And that's something even *you* can't argue with."

Mia opened her mouth to do exactly that when the memory of her encounters with Mr. G stopped her. She'd never quite figured out who in the galaxy of heaven Mr. G actually was, but she'd known ever since the accident that had landed her and Quentin in the state between life and death, that Mr. G definitely fit in there somewhere. That knowledge had edged her back into the comfort of believing in something bigger than herself, a belief that had framed her life as a child in a Catholic household.

But neither faith nor Mr. G had anything to do with her argument with Quentin over Portia Goodhope. She felt her mouth settle into a stubborn line. Her ma might be right, but she saw no reason to give in so easily.

"What are you waiting for?" Eireen rose, pinched a stray thread from her faded shirtwaist dress, and leaned over to give Mia a rough pat on the shoulder. "Go find your husband."

Knowing she'd get no sympathy from her ma, Mia rinsed her coffee cup, kissed her good-bye, something her mother didn't much like, then left her bending over yet another angel.

It wasn't until she was halfway back home that she remembered guiltily she'd left before asking her mother if there was anything she could do to help with her brother's situation. Not that Mia wanted to meddle, but knowing her mother, she'd worry herself in circles over her brother's plans for divorce. Mia slowed to a crawl on the Hollywood Freeway. The last thing her ma needed was another one of her offspring to fret over. Sighing, giving in to the inevitable, Mia knew she'd be the good child.

She'd send her parents a postcard from New York. Her mother wasn't one to call to check on her children, so at least this way she'd know Mia had done the right thing.

Mia the wife would join her husband.

But Mia the producer would give the Portia Goodhope decision one last argument.

Portia Goodhope's agent remained firm. Her client couldn't possibly chat with Quentin Grandy until the next morning. Didn't the esteemed Mr. Grandy understand that on Mondays the lady didn't even talk to him?

Mondays were Portia's beauty days, and no one, not even the Queen of England, nor the *Times'* theater critic would have been granted an audience.

Left to kick his heels for the afternoon, Quentin checked into the Sherry-Netherland Hotel. The first thing he did was call Mia. To his surprise and concern, she hadn't gone to the office. Not at home, either. Puzzled, he hung up.

Never one to sit still for long, Quentin headed out to Fifth Avenue. Mia refused to spoil or pamper herself, a trait that made buying gifts for her a special treat. He'd stop at Tiffany's and see what he could find for her. And, too, he was honest enough with himself to admit he hoped a gift would soften the sting when he returned to LA with Portia Goodhope in tow.

He felt oddly bereft, as if he were walking out on a rainy day without his umbrella, or calling for the cameras to roll before the slap of the clapper board.

But, he supposed, his gaze fixed on the sidewalks rather than on the faces of the people he passed as he loped at a steady pace toward Tiffany's, there was no mystery about why he felt that way.

Mia had been by his side day and night now for the two-plus months they'd been husband and wife. And for the year prior to their wedding, once he'd come to his senses and realized the woman who'd worked with him for years was the only woman he would ever truly love, Mia had been with him.

Day and night.

Regretting once again his hasty vault from their bed earlier that morning, Quentin continued to walk and began to kick himself mentally. In his book, as well as in many others', Mia merited the title of best producer in Hollywood, and he'd had no business at all grabbing the phone from her hand. And more important, as his wife, Mia deserved his respect.

Not to mention his loving.

Wondering how best to apologize to her, Quentin entered the monied world of Tiffany's. A suited man appeared at his side, murmuring polite greetings. The obsequious behavior secretly amused Quentin. He hoped, no matter what fame and fortune brought to his life, he'd never let his head get so swollen he didn't consider himself an ordinary joe.

He restrained the quirk of his lips and found himself wishing Mia were next to him, snuggled in the curve of his arm, strolling rib to rib as they surveyed the riches Tiffany's had to offer.

Knowing Mia, though, she'd have a fit over the Fifth Avenue prices and whisper to him they'd best save their money to put into the production of *Kriss-Kross*, a film they both wanted to do but had yet to convince the studio heads to finance. But he'd win her over, and rather than whisper back, he'd nibble on the lobe of her ear and soon they'd forget all about jewelry and end up back in the hotel room . . .

"Yes?" The clerk had obviously been waiting for a response for some time, yet he maintained that patient look that communicated how difficult the nouveau riche could be.

Quentin snapped out of his reverie. "Sapphires," he said, his voice catching. If he got any harder, he'd burst. Damn it, but he couldn't believe Mia was clear across the country. She felt so near to him he could picture himself reaching out, touching her, first here, then there . . .

"We have quite a nice pair of earrings in this setting," the clerk said, presenting atop a swatch of white velvet a pair of dark blue stones set in silver cusps.

"Not earrings," Quentin said, picturing Mia lying naked beneath him, wearing only a necklace sporting one perfect sapphire set in a circlet of diamonds. Only, of course, his mental image didn't dwell too long on the gems. He saw, instead, the dusky nubs of her nipples, hardened, puckered, begging to be kissed.

"A necklace, perhaps?"

"Yes!" Quentin shouted, then lowered his voice. He had to get control of himself. One afternoon away from Mia shouldn't turn him into a quivering bowl of Jell-O.

"Very good, sir," the clerk murmured, then pulled out the most magnificent sapphire Quentin had ever seen. Surrounding the oval-cut stone was a double ring of diamonds.

Swallowing a pant, Quentin said, "I'll take it."

"*Very* good, sir," the clerk said. He held out his hand, and Quentin fished in his wallet for his platinum buy-anything credit card.

The man seemed to approve, as he nodded reverentially and proceeded to arrange the necklace in a blue Tiffany's box, closed sweetly with white satin ribbon. He handed Quentin the charge slip, checked the signature, then turned the purchase over to him.

With a hint of a smile, the clerk said, "*Dino-Daddy* may have won the Oscar, Mr. Grandy, but *Quetzalcoatl's Overcoat* will always be my favorite."

Surprised, Quentin gave a slight shake to his head, then sketched a quick salute to the clerk. "We do what we can," he said, slipping the box into the pocket of his linen blazer. "Every film is a new child."

"Ah," the clerk said, "I gather from what I read about *Permutation* that not every film is a godchild."

"Don't believe everything you read in the papers," Quentin said, forcing a cheerful smile, then quickly exited the store.

Rumors could bury a movie before the film was even in the can. Not a godchild? He'd show that clerk. Quentin chose the movies he wanted to make and if people would just shut up and leave his crew alone, *Permutation* could be every bit the success *DinoDaddy* had been.

If Quentin couldn't see his way through to the purpose of a film, he wouldn't take even the first step toward standing behind the camera and living through the agonizingly slow process of bringing the story to life.

Not a godchild? He dashed across the street, barely missing a cab, holding his hand protectively around the jewelry box resting in his pocket. At moments like this, when doubts might set in, he yearned for Mia. Despite their different points of view on a few production issues, she stood firm with him in believing in *Permutation*.

It had been Mia who'd brought the film's screenwriter, Beetle Leonard, to his attention. At that point, every other major director in town had turned down Beetle's script, but Quentin knew the first time he read it that the story held such possibilities that he'd feel less a man, not to mention less a director, if he didn't tackle it.

And now, of course, in order to prove that he and Mia were right on their hunch about Leonard's script, he'd taken on not only the studio, but Mia. But somehow, he thought, breaking into a whistle as he walked up Fifth Avenue, everything would work out okay.

Stranded at that moment in Chicago's O'Hare airport, Mia didn't feel at all optimistic about the way anything would work out.

Staring through the bank of windows at the angry sky, watching the thunderclouds pelt the grounded planes with blinding rain, she counted her mistakes and wished herself anywhere but Chicago.

First, if she and Quentin had gone to New York together, they could have taken the MegaFilms jet. Second, if she hadn't let her mother work on her conscience, Mia might have stayed home. Third . . . Mia traced the pattern of the raindrops slashing the opposite side of the glass and decided to quit counting.

She had tried to call Quentin at the Sherry-Netherland, where he always stayed. He'd checked in but wasn't in his room. Somehow that bothered her, and she knew that was silly. Late afternoon in New York would probably find Quentin buying drinks for Portia Goodhope's agent.

And it wasn't as if Mia had anything to worry about with Quentin going off to woo a woman nearing her sixtieth birthday. Now, if it'd been someone like the bombshell actress Chelsea Jordan in her heyday of hoydenism, Mia would have commandeered a plane to get to New York.

Her flight wasn't due to leave for at least two

more hours. She should settle down and do some work, but for once her heart wasn't in it. She moved away from the window, shifted her laptop to her left hand, settled her purse more firmly on her shoulder, and slung her garment bag over her right arm. She'd walk the length of the concourse.

Mia made her way through the milling crowds of grumpy, travel-weary men, women, and children. She stepped around a screaming youngster who'd just dumped his scoop of ice cream on the floor. To her dismay, she saw the woman with him slap the child and tell him to shut up.

She paused and turned back to say something to the woman. It was none of her business, but couldn't the woman have a little sympathy for the child? Mia walked on, the child's cries ringing in her ears. When she spotted the ice cream vendor a few feet away, she stopped and stared at the pictures of banana splits, malts, and shakes. She pictured the lonely scoop of chocolate the boy had dropped on the floor.

Impulsively she approached the counter.

The child's tears had slowed to a snuffle when she found him, after somehow juggling the double-dip chocolate cone with everything else she carried. To the cross-looking lady, she said, "Do you mind?" Then, before the woman could say no, Mia handed the ice cream to the little boy.

His tears stopped instantly. He looked at her as if he'd seen an angel. Mia smiled at him, then cast a glance at the woman she assumed was his mother.

"You didn't need to do that," the harassed woman said, but not in a mean way.

"I know," Mia said, "but there are few things worse than having something special, then losing it."

The woman looked her sharply in the face. "We're on our way to his granddaddy's funeral." Then she turned away, and Mia saw her shoulders shake.

Mia stood there for a moment, feeling helpless, and also sensing the woman preferred to be left alone. Slowly she backed away and let herself be drawn away by the surging crowd of travelers. As she walked, she thought of her own words. What would she do if she lost Quentin? Her world would be meaningless. And yet she'd let him leave for New York without even saying goodbye.

In front of her she saw a sign that read "Chapel." Mia stopped. She felt sort of silly even considering stepping inside. But she needed to say a prayer, a prayer for her marriage, a prayer that somehow she and Quentin would figure out what was wrong and fix things between them.

She pushed on the door and halted half in and half out of the dimly lit room. During college she'd grown away from the faith of her childhood. But even as she'd acted on impulse to buy the ice cream for the boy, she knew she needed to follow this instinct.

And even if she no longer had a clear and simplistic view of who God might be, she knew she had a friend, an otherworld cohort who'd rescued her and Quentin more than once before.

Inside the small carpeted room, Mia piled her possessions beside one of the two pews. Already feeling much less burdened, she knelt and clasped her hands.

Closing her eyes to the sterile gray walls of the nondenominational chapel, Mia pictured Mr. G as she'd first seen him, resplendent in his billowing crimson robes in the red velvet confines of Purgatory's Second Chance Room.

He'd worked a miracle then, and she needed one now. What with the way she'd been acting, how else could she live up to her vow to be the best wife ever?

"Mr. G," she said aloud, "we need to talk."

3 ⌒

"Rats!"

From her perch on the scaffolding she'd erected in the oldest church in one of the oldest sections of New Orleans, Amity Jones gazed down, way down, at the paintbrush she had just dropped on the outstretched wooden arms of St. Benedictus.

The knock that had disturbed her concentration sounded again, much more sharply. Rap-a-rap-rap! The wooden door of the church shuddered against the impact and Amity winced. Poor thing, didn't people know buildings had feelings, too?

"Hold your horses, I'm coming," she called over the crooning saxophone filling the church from her boom box. When the racket began again, she lowered the volume, then repeated her message.

Glancing down to where her paintbrush had fallen, Amity muttered another "Rats." Before beginning work on the ceiling mural, she should have blanketed the place with dropcloths, but Amity had been so full of her vision of the finished masterpiece she hadn't wanted to take the time.

What had the sisters at the Crescent City Foundling Home told her over and over again? *Preparation and patience, Amity, these along with piety are the keys to success.* Swiping a carmine-streaked finger across her nose, Amity made a face. A gypsy of the soul, she had little use for the three Ps of the sisters' trinity.

Amity danced her way to the edge of the scaffolding, wondering who it was this time disturbing her work.

The rackety metal stacks rocked and swayed. She had collected the pieces of scaffolding from unsupervised construction sites and was pretty darn pleased with the job she'd done spot-welding them into a structure that allowed her to reach the ceiling of the church, soaring some twenty feet above the pews. There was one joint she needed to tighten, but she'd forgotten the tool she'd meant to bring along with her that morning.

Again the pounding interrupted her thoughts. She made a face toward the door, but began to descend. Partway down, she turned for a look upward at her handiwork. When she did, a cascade of her long fine hair escaped from the purple turban designed to protect it from the paint. She might not shroud St. Benedictus, but her gorgeous hair was quite another matter. Pausing to tuck the unruly blond strands under the turban, Amity pictured the ceiling as it would look upon completion.

Coming together from the four corners of the chapel—and, figuratively, the world—loomed four naked rainbow-hued personages sporting both male and female anatomies. Honestly, Leonardo da Vinci had never done anything so challenging!

Amity had painted only one figure, but so clearly did she envision the finished mural, completing the job would be almost as easy for her as following a paint-by-numbers kit. Her hardest task was battling the constant crick in her neck.

Taking the last four feet in a light-footed drop, Amity laughed gently at herself, thinking that painting was the only easy thing about her life. But never one to dwell on her problems, she pattered to the door, the floor cool against her bare feet.

Cracking open the door, she peered out into the reddened face of a priest she'd never seen before. But standing beside him she saw Father Peter. "Hey," she said, "where y'at?"

The young priest blanched at her local slang greeting, quirking his head toward the short, red-faced man who accompanied him. "Miss Amity," he said, "this is Father O'Riley. From the *Archdiocese*."

His emphasis was hard to miss. Amity winked, then scooted one hand through the opening in the door. "Pleased to meet you," she said.

Father O'Riley's face grew even more crimson. "So you're the young lady who is painting the mural for our holy chapel."

She nodded.

"I would like to check your progress." He harumphed importantly. "And your artwork."

"Oh, I'm afraid that's not possible." Amity shifted her weight against the door. She'd dealt with authority figures before; it always paid to be one step ahead of them. She had a feeling this humorless man wouldn't quite see the beauty of her creation.

"Er," Father Peter said, with a deep clearing of his throat, "it might be best if we just took a quick little peek."

"But you promised I wouldn't be interrupted!"

O'Riley smiled a big, fake smile. "Oh, now, I'm sure Father Peter would never say such a thing." He grasped the large iron handle of the church door. "We'll just take a look-see."

Amity braced her body against the door. She'd always been taller and stronger than the other girls in the foundling home, and she prided herself on staying in shape. She'd be damned, and yes, she meant the words, before she'd let this bully have his way.

But one thing she'd learned early was to use words as weapons whenever possible. Careful to keep her body braced against the door, she said, in a sweet voice that any of the sisters from the foundling home would have known to take as a warning sign, "But Father O'Riley, he did promise, and when a priest promises something, he has to stick to it or it's a mortal sin, isn't that right?"

That stopped him. He dropped his pompous hand from the door and swung around to Father

Peter. "Tell me you didn't give this creature free reign in the chapel."

"Oh, but I did."

Amity threw another wink at the younger priest and slammed the door shut. She hoped he didn't get in too much trouble, but she and the others who found shelter and comfort in this crumbling chapel would make it up to him.

Through the door she heard Father Peter fumbling with his explanation. "But—but—but," he said, then trailed off.

Amity's curiosity got the better of her and she leaned an ear to the door.

"But what?"

"Well, she has a way of appealing to one's sense of—"

"Dishonor?"

Amity made a face.

"Oh, no," Father Peter said, "rather one's sense of the possibility of humanity. Of a greater good."

"Hah. She's a sweet young thing with a body designed to tempt men. Go ahead and confess you gave in to her from a weakness of the flesh and I'll assign your penance."

"But it was nothing like that!"

"No?"

Amity almost swung the door open. What a rude, insensitive, crude, and belittling man Father O'Riley was! But she knew the younger priest could stick up for himself. It had taken that kind of courage for him to minister to the motley crew of this Bywater neighborhood.

Their voices died away before Amity could make out Father Peter's reply. Her blood boiled as she scooted from the door and back toward the scaffolding. What a dirty old man Father O'Riley was. She frowned and fumed. She'd show him. Her masterpiece would become world famous and Father Peter would be known as a patron of the arts.

Dipping to the floor beside St. Benedictus, Amity collected her paintbrush, then dabbed the streak of red acrylic from the statue's nose and hands with the tail of her lavender-and-rose-striped painter's smock. When she turned away, one of the flowing sleeves caught the head of the statue. Pious St. Benedictus swayed alarmingly and Amity lunged to save him.

"Oh, rats," she muttered, then added, "You know, Amity, you really aren't the best person to be left alone in a church." She laughed a little, somewhat sadly, as she heard the echo of years of the sisters' reprimands in that comment.

The commotion roused Spike Jones, the pooch who was her favorite among the five dogs, four cats, and as of last month, three newborn kittens that comprised Amity's self-made family.

Spike Jones made a grab for the brush, leading with his nose, his sightless eyes seeming to follow but falling short like a shadow lacking sun.

Amity tousled his short, curly fur. Spike's pedigree was a hundred percent mutt, with strains of collie and terrier and possibly a smidgeon of boxer. He carried real strength in his compact body, a strength that had challenged Amity to learn how to help protect him from himself as his eyesight had waned and finally disappeared.

Now he rested on his haunches, his tongue hanging out one side of his mouth, his body quivering, prepared as always to wait for her attention.

"You got all the patience in this family, Spike-o," Amity said, fishing in a pocket of the smock for a dog biscuit. "Here you go, little one."

The biscuit disappeared instantly and Amity turned to climb the scaffolding again. She'd taken only one step up the makeshift ladder when a grumble of thunder sounded outside the church. Amity groaned. But it wouldn't be a summer afternoon in New Orleans without a good storm to unload moisture from the Gulf and sweeten the streets.

Spike Jones whimpered. He hated thunder. Amity moved to his side, gave him another pat, then turned to climb back to the ceiling.

As she did, another knock, so soft and tentative she scarcely heard it over the thunder, sounded at the door.

Maybe if she ignored it, whoever it was would go away.

A louder tapping followed.

With a sigh and a resigned glance up toward her waiting masterpiece, Amity returned to the door, once again peeking out through an opening only a few inches wide.

When she saw the young woman who stood there, she forced her welcoming smile into a stern line. "Breeze, what are you doing here?"

"Visiting?" Her friend looked at her, obviously in search of a blessing on her unexpected arrival.

Unexpected and unwelcome. Not that Amity didn't enjoy her friend's company. But Breeze, a talented musician who could make a trumpet swing and a saxophone sing, never seemed to grasp the concept of artistic work ethic. Only yesterday she'd promised Amity to work more diligently at her music.

"Aren't you supposed to be working on those songs for your demo album?"

Breeze lifted one skinny and golden tanned shoulder. Her designer shorts outfit showed off her figure in a way Amity could only dream of for herself. "It's much too nice a day to stay inside."

Amity pointed a finger toward the rapidly darkening sky. "Not for long."

Breeze repeated her careless shrug, shifting her glossy black hair off her shoulders. "Can I come in? I won't bother you. I need to talk."

Amity stared at her friend and almost laughed. Only Breeze could say those words with that earnest look in her eyes, that sincere tone in her voice, and truly believe she wouldn't be bothering Amity if she only talked to her while she worked. Breeze, child of plenty, did not grasp reality as well as she might.

But Amity loved her nevertheless.

"Boy trouble again?" Amity asked, without letting the door inch open even another centimeter.

Breeze nodded, twisting the ends of her hair, her blue eyes filling with glistening tears. "Girl-friend, how did you know?"

Amity gave a shrug of her own. With beautiful Breeze, it was always boy trouble. And with Amity's own miserable track record with men—so far, every man she'd backed had proved a loser—it amazed her that her friends insisted on asking her for advice.

"It's Bubba. He wants to marry me."

"Bubba?"

Breeze nodded, continuing to twist the strands of her hair around her perfectly manicured nails. Her tears had magically evaporated.

Glancing down at the paintbrush she still held, Amity figured the paint had evaporated by now, too. She'd listen for a few minutes, because she couldn't help herself, but then she had to hurry Breeze along or she'd never get her work done. And she wouldn't put it past that pushy Father O'Riley to come sneaking back.

"So Bubba wants to marry you?"

Breeze nodded.

Bubba was the lawyer who owned the coffee-house where Amity and her friends hung out. He liked to come around, playing it cool, but Amity had long since detected a tendency in him to work hard, earn lots of money, and save most of it. Breeze could do a heck of a lot worse in a hus-band.

"Do you want to marry him?" Amity waited for her friend to consider her answer, wondering whether any man as sane and steadfast as Bubba would ever ask her to marry him.

"Oh, I don't think so," Breeze finally answered, letting go of her hair and smiling up at Amity. "Bubba's too much like my father."

"Oh." Amity couldn't think what to say to that answer. An orphan, she'd never be able to compare a prospective suitor to her own father. And for the slightest of seconds, she experienced the old, familiar prick of envy, a feeling she thought she'd long since outgrown, as she digested Breeze's casual dismissal of any man like her father not being quite right.

Breeze's father, unlike those of Amity's other friends, kept Breeze not only in rent, but in designer clothing. Breeze pretended to be as poor as the rest of their gang, but unlike everyone else, whenever Breeze felt a bit out of sorts and wanted a few days at the beach or had a hankering for a new dress, she had only to call her daddy.

In any other woman, these childlike tendencies might have been a true pain in the tush, but no one could hate Breeze. Especially not Amity. The time Fleezer had been hit by a car, it had been Breeze who'd rushed him to the vet and paid for the operation to save his life.

A smile had returned to Breeze's face, reminding Amity of how the New Orleans afternoon sky would clear just as soon as the still-threatening storm passed over.

"Gosh, I feel better," Breeze said. "Thanks for talking to me."

"Happy to help," Amity said, wondering whether she had.

As Breeze swung around and stepped away, Amity gave a little wave. She'd almost closed the door when Breeze paused. "Sure you don't want to grab a coffee with me?"

Amity smiled and shook her head. Before Breeze could dream up another diversion, she shut and bolted the door once more.

Coffee could wait. Only dabblers and dreamers lounged about the bars and coffeehouses, dreaming and bragging.

Artists painted.

And Amity the artist put her work first.

She stopped before climbing the scaffolding to give Spike Jones a pat on his head. Eager to return to her mural, she hoisted her skirts to ease the climb back up.

As much as she wanted to comfort Spike as the approaching thunder grew in volume, she didn't have time to pause for long. Father Peter would try to hold off O'Riley for as long as he could, but she had a feeling the older priest wouldn't stand for it much longer. She knew from experience most people's curiosity got in the way of their patience. And she didn't want anyone interfering with her vision. Where would Michelangelo have been if he'd had Father O'Riley looking over his shoulder in the Sistine Chapel?

Granted, Amity hadn't been the father's first choice of artist, but she had been available, and for the right price. "Free of charge" spoke volumes. The old church served as a gathering place for the artists, musicians, writers, and street waifs who inhabited Amity's neighborhood, a wedge of the city tucked against the Industrial Canal and known as Bywater.

Far less commercial than the famous nearby Vieux Carré or French Quarter, Bywater was also much more affordable. The cheap rents drew the artists who lived from commission to commission; poverty-friendly prices might attract them, but the sense of community kept them there, some remaining even after they'd made a name for themselves.

It was for the community that Amity, nonbeliever that she was, had volunteered to paint the mural on the chapel ceiling.

Too, she admitted, having reached the top of the scaffolding, she liked to cause a sensation and this mural just might make her famous.

Or infamous.

Once more atop her scaffolding, Amity cranked the volume on the local jazz station. The other reason she'd insisted she must paint alone was her sure instinct that the priest would never let her blast her music in the church. And the music helped her work.

Brush poised in her teeth, she framed with her hands the section she was painting. She liked to focus on her work.

Amity knew some people scoffed that she was merely another untalented self-taught primitive painter; others lauded the originality of her creations. And Amity didn't care. She loved her art, often thinking that all the pain and loneliness she'd endured in the foundling home had been worth it, since that was where she'd met Sister Mary Margaret.

Sister M & M, as Amity had christened her, stood barely four feet tall and looked younger than the ninth graders she'd been told to instruct in French and art.

Amity, unruly and bored as always, had been prepared to heckle Sister M & M the way she did all the other nuns.

That was, until the sweet-voiced sister had leaned over Amity's sketch and explained to her how working with perspective, rather than fighting it, would improve the work.

She'd grasped immediately the good sense of the advice. Where her art was concerned, Amity remained open-minded. Never before had the home given her instruction; she'd learned on her own, following her instincts.

Sister Mary Margaret had changed her life.

Of course, Amity still refused to study French. Until one day the nun offered to take her to the New Orleans Museum of Art, provided Amity passed French I.

After that, Amity made straight As in French and in art.

The last time she could remember crying was the day Sister M & M had been sent away to another school.

Amity blinked and stared up at her mural. Sister M & M had never laughed at her dreams. Sister M & M had taught her to envision, plan, and focus. In her memory, Amity intended to paint the most striking religious mural ever created.

Tapping her toe softly, she swayed into position and imagined the Being's crimson leg coming to life, sensed the musculature, ligaments, flesh. When she could feel them, her hands warming to the touch, she began to paint.

As the limb took shape beneath her brush strokes, Amity remained dimly aware of the thunder knocking the heavens. As high up as she stood, she imagined she could feel the vibrations rumbling through her own flesh, and she paused, distracted by the question of how she would paint thunder.

Questions like that occurred to her a lot. The nuns had been forever punishing her for daydreaming, or for doodling when she should have been calculating square roots. But Amity would rather envision how she'd create a prime number. Understanding someone else's definition held little interest for her.

Spike Jones had hunkered down at the foot of her scaffolding, his nose buried on the stone floor of the church, his paws shielding his sightless eyes from the horrors only his ears could detect.

"You know, most people would be more concerned with what they were going to do with the rest of their lives, rather than worrying over how to capture thunder on canvas," Amity said aloud, echoing the voices so dominant in her childhood.

She talked out loud a lot, telling herself her voice comforted Spike Jones, but Amity was honest enough to acknowledge she did it because she spent too much time alone. "Too damn much," she muttered.

As if to agree, the heavens sent a streak of lightning arcing across the sky, causing the stained glass window of the church to shimmer and dance with so much life Amity knew she had to try to capture the effect on paper.

She grabbed for her sketch pad at the same moment the thunder opened fire directly overhead. Spike Jones leapt up and bolted, barking wildly and driving his frightened and very strong self straight into the statue of St. Benedictus.

Amity might have survived, had not the smiling saint crashed smack into the rickety scaffolding.

The loose joint in the metal legs gave way and the support swayed as if dancing with the storm. Then it began to topple ever so slowly toward the floor twenty feet below.

For the tiniest of moments, Amity laughed. She was flying free. Then she screamed. The sketchbook still clutched in one hand, she grabbed at the tumbling metal platform. Her paints slid with her, splashing her and the floor below.

Spike barked wildly. She heard him along with the screech of metal against metal right before she slammed against the floor, her body tangled in the

4 ⁓

Bone tired from her delayed flight to New York, Mia at long last pushed open the door to Quentin's suite, thankful the hotel staff knew her well enough to hand over the key with no questions asked. By the clock in the lobby it was well past midnight. From the darkness that greeted her, she assumed Quentin had turned in.

Anxious to see him, unwilling to wait for a bellman, she'd carried her own things to the room. Quietly she settled her purse, laptop, and garment bag in the entryway and tiptoed through the sitting room.

The bedroom door stood ajar. Mia peeked in. By the light of one bedside lamp, she studied her husband. He lay atop the covers, still in his dressing gown. His chest rose and fell, and along with it, so did the telephone propped there.

Mia smiled. She knew, in the way she understood Quentin, that he must have fallen asleep trying to reach her by phone. Touched by the image, she felt all the tensions of the day dissolve. She'd done the right thing by coming to New York.

Still smiling, but this time with a hint of mis-

chief that belied the fact that ten minutes earlier
she'd wanted nothing more than to drop into
sleep undisturbed, Mia began to ease out of her
suit. Feeling brave and daring and incredibly sexy,
she let her primly cut jacket slide to the floor.
Humming softly, she shimmied out of her skirt,
noting as she did that her nipples had gone hard
as gum drops. They also strained against her lacy
bra as if begging to escape, a feeling that egged
Mia on as she began to unfasten the buttons of
her sensible white silk blouse.

The frenzied agony she experienced as her body
fought to be naked and wild and free to go to
Quentin both frightened and exhilarated her.
Casting her tongue over her upper lip, she forced
her eager hands to move slowly. Taking a step
closer to the bed, still wearing her heels, nylons,
and blouse, she studied Quentin again.

He slept on. His chest continued its rhythmic
rise and fall, though to Mia's discerning eye, it
seemed to be moving at a quicker pace. But his
eyes remained firmly shut. This emboldened her.
One slow twist at a time, she freed a button, then
scooped her breasts under her hands. Lifting, raising, offering them to Quentin, she swayed close
to the bed. Then, in a move she could scarcely
believe came from shy little Mia Tortelli, she tilted
her head down and flicked her tongue across the
flesh swelling above the lacy cups of her bra.

Quentin stirred, and Mia came quickly back to
herself. Whatever would he think! She slipped her

blouse off, kicked off her shoes, and skimmed her pantyhose off.

Then, feeling a bit like a scaredy-cat who's run away from its own shadow, and also incredibly aroused, Mia lifted her hands above her head and twirled beside the bed. Oh so slowly, she slipped the straps of her bra off, and swaying just a bit, picturing Quentin's pleasure and arousal if he could see her just at this precise moment, she unclasped the hooks and freed her breasts.

Moving slightly from side to side, Mia lifted a cautious hand and edged Quentin's robe open. He slept naked, and she gasped in pleasure as she saw he might be asleep, but his body was more than awake for her.

Leaning over him, letting her nipples skim his chest, she lifted the telephone and set it carefully on the bedside table. Then she lowered her panties inch by inch, knowing for certain she'd go up in flames if she didn't wake Quentin soon and fill herself with his loving.

He stirred again, and Mia slipped onto the bed next to him. With a sure hand, one that had grown to love pleasuring him, she stroked his shaft and smiled with the sheer feeling of power his reaction to her provided.

He lifted his hips, pushing against her hand, and she lowered her mouth to claim him.

Quentin stifled a groan and accepted the gift of Mia's loving. He knew every ounce of blood in his body was straining to explode right at that very second. Was there ever any man as lucky as he was in his choice of wife, lover, mistress, and scamp? Lying there, watching her enter the room, he'd been so taken that she'd come to him in New York, he'd been about to call out, go to her, take her in his arms.

And then the minx had started slowly removing her clothing, and Quentin had lain as still as a mouse trying to outfox the family cat. Once or twice he knew he'd almost given himself away, but the beauty of watching his shy but sensual wife pleasure both herself and him was more than he could bring himself to disturb.

And now, as she brought him to the brink of crazed and fiery eruption, all he could do was stroke the back of her hair and wonder what he'd ever done to deserve such a wonderful, precious, sexy siren of a wife.

"Mia," he said, somewhere between a whisper and a groan, "you're the best thing that's ever happened to me." When she raised her eyes to his, full of love and loving and life, he smiled back, then gave himself up with a cry.

Later, snuggled against his side, Mia asked him in a sleepy voice, "Just when did you wake up?"

"Let's put it this way," Quentin said, casting a careful glance at his bride before reaching to turn out the light, "I heard you drop your garment bag and put down your laptop."

She bolted upright, the covers falling to her waist. Quentin admired the way her full breasts offered themselves above the snowy white sheet. Breasts made for fondling, kissing, for driving a man—no, not any man, only him—wild.

"Come here," he said, and reached for her.

He knew she blushed by the way she clung to the sheet. "Then you saw me?"

"Perform that striptease?" He grinned, then realizing she really was embarrassed, said gently, "That was the best gift I've had since that very special one of our wedding day."

"Which present was that?" Mia edged down beside him again, letting the sheet drift to her curvy hips.

He kissed one breast, then the other. "You," he said, and eased her over till she cradled his body beneath hers.

Mia still blushed a bit, but the warmth of her skin quickly fled her cheeks to filter lower, inflaming her body as Quentin performed his miracles again, kissing her in a manner that took away not only her breath but her senses. No matter what other uncertainties appeared in her life, she knew she'd never, ever doubt her love for this man.

"Oh, Quentin," she murmured at last, through lips puffy from his kisses, "whatever must you think of me?"

He lifted her up, holding her carefully by the shoulders, and seemed to contemplate his answer. "For an amateur," he said, "that was one fine striptease. So can I respect you? Yes, but I won't object if you want to practice once or twice a week."

After such a silly answer, Mia fell back against

him and forgot, for once in her life, all about being shy or embarrassed.

They slept very little that night in their wonderful bed at the Sherry-Netherland, and Mia arose with joy in her heart, joy that began to fade when they arrived at Portia Goodhope's co-op to learn the imperious actress had instructed her maid that Quentin must walk her precious pedigreed pooch while she completed her morning toilette. Only then would she deign to talk to him.

Now, out on Madison Avenue, watching the actress's schnauzer tug at the leash Quentin held, Mia frowned, upset with herself as much as the hapless canine. She'd promised herself, at some point during last night's lovemaking, to try not to pick a fight with Quentin again, no matter the provocation. And yet here she was, acting against her best intentions.

"What kind of woman takes a perfectly self-respecting animal and saddles it with a name like Mr. Pish?" she heard herself ask, in a voice that clearly begged to provoke a quarrel.

"Portia Goodhope." He said the name with reverence.

Stubborn to the end. Mia didn't know whether to admire or despair over Quentin's stalwart defense of the grande dame of Broadway.

"My point exactly," Mia said. Then in a low, determined voice, with her back turned, she said, "The last thing we need on the set of *Permutation* is a prima donna. With all the problems we've had, we need an experienced workhorse."

Quentin walked around till he faced her, then fixed her with a stare. Behind those sexy aviator glasses he sported, he'd be glaring at her. At her, his bride of only two months and one week!

Mia set her jaw. As producer of the eighty-million-dollar production, she owed the director the truth, even if the director was her husband, or especially so.

As she stared back, catching her reflection in Quentin's glasses and noting her angry body language, Mia thought that last night's passion might never have happened between them. They faced off, Mr. Pish's trembling silver body between them, staring one another down.

In front of the Frick, the dog yanked at his leash and Quentin muttered something under his breath. Ignoring the well-dressed Manhattanites surging by them in front of the impressive building, Quentin stooped, face to face with the schnauzer.

"Look, pal," he said, "making Portia Goodhope happy means a lot to me. I need her for this film—"

"Do not."

Quentin threw an exasperated look over his shoulder. "Do too." He turned back to the dog. "I wouldn't walk a spoiled mutt like you for just anyone. But your mistress asked me to walk you to the park and back, and by damn, you'll go along with the program." He rose.

The dog cocked his head, muzzle quivering,

whiskers dancing. Mia could have sworn the animal gave Quentin the evil eye.

"Let's not quibble over Portia Goodhope anymore," Quentin said. "Please." He wiped the back of his free hand across his forehead. "New York in August with this dog in tow is bad enough, but when we—"

The dog had lowered himself over the marble steps of the mansion Mia had admired.

Quentin grabbed the dog around the middle. "Not at the Frick, you snarly mutt," he yelled, and carried the dog to the curb.

Mia smothered a smile. Quentin looked so very chic in linen trousers, a collarless shirt, and a brushed cotton jacket as soft as silk and as expensive as a union crew on double overtime. She'd scarcely recognized him when he'd dressed that morning at their suite. She wrinkled her nose, considering the changes she'd witnessed in this man she had married only a short time ago but had loved for so long.

Today Quentin looked like a movie star.

But now, holding out the struggling dog and cursing, he seemed a lot more like her Quentin. Of course, on the outside, she no longer resembled Mia, the worrywart who'd grown up in East Los Angeles, penny-pinched her way through school, and only last year stopped having her hair done at Supercuts.

Mia smoothed the skirt of her own linen suit and straightened the chain on her Dior bag as she bit her lip and hoped that fame and money didn't change them beyond recognition.

But even more than that, she hoped marriage didn't wreck their partnership.

"Let's go," Quentin said. He picked up his pace and the schnauzer whined but kept up until they stopped at the light at Fifth Avenue. Then he plopped down and flattened his muzzle to the steamy sidewalk, the picture of obstinate dejection.

Mia, feeling sorry for both Quentin and the dog, offered, "We could just turn around now."

"Oh, no." Quentin scooped up the struggling dog and tucked him under one arm. "Good try, but I'm not losing out on this coup because I didn't go that extra step."

They moved across the street, then left the rushing cars and blaring horns behind as they passed into the shelter of the park.

Mia still couldn't understand why casting the woman meant so much to Quentin. True, Portia had won a bouquet of Tony Awards. True, she'd steadfastly refused to do a film. True, if she appeared in *Permutation*, the movie would benefit from the press on her screen debut.

"If only Francine hadn't had that heart attack, this never would have come up," she murmured, keeping in step with Quentin and beginning to feel the effects of the August heat.

Quentin smiled. "Looking for a sense of meaning in life still, my dear little worrywart?"

"I'm just trying to find a sense of purpose in

this needless jaunt to New York." Mia knew she'd spoken more sharply than she should have. Quentin was just as frustrated as she by the delays in *Permutation*.

Everything that could go wrong had gone wrong. But worse than this latest disaster of Francine May's heart attack—worse than the summer wildfire that had eaten with a fiery breath one of their prime locations only last week—worse than the temblor that had brought the second unit crew out of their trailers at dawn only two days before—

Worse than any of those problems was the way she and Quentin disagreed.

The dog stopped to sniff the base of a tree and Quentin paused.

"She probably won't say yes, you know," Mia said, stubbornly continuing her attack on Quentin's choice.

"If we get this dog back alive," Quentin said, in a voice Mia could only think of as a growl, "she'll say yes or I'll choke it out of her."

Mia shook her head. "Look at you, you're obsessed. It isn't like you, Quentin, to worry this much over one role."

"It's not simply a role, Mia." Quentin waved his arms, then quickly lowered the one holding the leash. "Beetle Leonard has written a brilliant script, all about the possibility of change. What better subtext to bring to that film than casting an older actress who, for the first time in her life, has agreed to change, to try something new?"

Mia stared up at Quentin. He'd never expressed this reason to her; he'd simply insisted Portia Goodhope was perfect. Now, suddenly, his insistence made sense. And she felt pretty darn foolish for resisting him as hard as she had. She worried the edge of her lip with her thumb.

"Mia," Quentin said, propping his dark glasses atop his head, then gently lifting her own shades.

She gazed at him, drinking in the gentleness and concern in his dark eyes.

Looking very serious, he studied her face, then lifted his hand and traced the outline of her lips. "I hate it when I make you unhappy."

Mia melted. "Me too," she cried.

"Good." He opened his arms and she moved into his embrace. He lowered his lips to hers, and Mia anticipated the rush she always experienced from the heat of his touch.

But instead of that pleasant rush of feeling, she was jolted by Quentin breaking free, arms flailing.

The schnauzer, having seized its moment of opportunity, skittered away, leash trailing. Across the path, a squirrel flicked its tail and ran, Mr. Pish hot in its wake.

Holding onto his glasses, Quentin bolted after the dog, shouting, "Come back here, you goddamn mutt! *Permutation* is an eighty-million-dollar film, and I won't have it sunk over a runaway dog!"

Mia started to laugh, then quickly sobered. The pampered pooch wouldn't last an hour on its own in the park. Breaking into as much as a run as she could manage in her heels, she followed Quentin.

She couldn't help but notice as she jogged that no one seemed to take any notice at all of her, Quentin, or the runaway animal. Thinking of how much this day meant to Quentin, she worried how soon Portia Goodhope would begin to fret over the absence of her darling dog.

"Looks like a busy night." Mr. G blew air from his cheeks. As usual, he talked to himself. That way, he liked to say, he had only himself to complain to if he didn't like the conversation.

"Too busy." The cavernous hall known as Central Receiving was lit up like a switchboard on a call-in radio show. From his perch on the balcony overlooking the floor bustling with people scurrying to and fro, he surveyed his domain. Beneath the balcony railing, the giant clock struck the hour.

Purgatory.

All things considered, not a bad territory.

"Face it," he muttered, "you'd be miserable with those angels upstairs, and this place is a lot cushier than the other choice!" Not to mention cooler.

Far across the hall, he spotted a red speck moving rapidly in his direction. Mr. G blinked and turned the unlit cigar hugged between his teeth. His vision cleared, or rather, the red speck blossomed into one of his crimson-jacketed rollerblading emissaries moving with particular speed.

"Emissary" in this case serving as a pretty grand word for "flunky."

Mr. G coughed, then pounded his chest. When the spell passed, he wedged the cigar more firmly in his teeth, wondering what shape he'd be in if he ever smoked the things, rather than simply using them as thinking aids.

The youth, breathing only slightly fast, swooped to a halt some thirty feet below. Looking up, he called, "Sir, I've got a message for you."

His hands planted on the railing, Mr. G leaned over and glared down at the youngster. "And I s'pose you have to shout it from there?"

The boy pointed to his feet, sheathed with those in-line skates, then shrugged.

"What's the world coming to?" Mr. G remembered when his flunkies wore robes and sandals. Those guys could climb stairs, or mountains, if the need arose. Well, he held himself partly responsible, what with trying to change with the times.

He sighed. Next thing he knew, the kids'd be wearing rocket-powered skates, much too busy whisking about at the speed of light to bother learning the protocol of delivering messages.

"So what's your news?" Mr. G asked, even though he already knew. One of the burdens of being the guy in charge, he reckoned, was always knowing too much.

The youngster held out his red-clothed arm, revealing a handheld message monitor. After clearing his throat, he read in a steady monotone: "Mr. G, we need to talk. Once upon a time you helped

Quentin and me back to life, and now we need help figuring out how to live the life we're making together. Or at least, *I* need help . . ."

When the boy started to read more, Mr. G waved an impatient hand. "Never mind, I get the gist."

"But, sir, you don't know who it's from."

"Mia Tortelli." Mr. G rubbed a hand over his jowls. He was getting too old for this job. Once he'd have leapt into action, his mind brimming with schemes, turning over how he'd use Subject A to inspire Subject B, thus influencing Subject C. Once he'd been excited about his work.

But now, standing over the bustling Central Receiving Hall, only half paying attention to the sycophantic red-jacketed Purgatory guide, all he felt like doing was paying a quick visit to Earth to knock a few heads together. Namely, the fine, normally intelligent heads of Mia Tortelli and Quentin Grandy.

"Awaiting instructions, sir."

"Whatever you do, don't keep making the same old mistakes over and over again."

"Yes, sir. I mean, no, sir!"

Mr. G nodded, absently smoothing the cuffs of his red velvet smoking jacket. Muttering aloud again, he said, "Running Purgatory is a lot like being a parent. Even when your kids grow up and move away, you still have to pull 'em out of hot water."

Turning his back on the youngster below, he trod with heavy steps toward the Central Receiving computer terminal, thinking of Mia Tortelli. Her prayer for help had come from the heart, and curmudgeon though he might be, he couldn't ignore a plea like that.

He'd see who'd checked into Purgatory that day, then amble over to the Second Chance Room.

Amity Jones patted her arms and legs and passed a tentative hand over the bump on her head. She glanced around her, wondering how in the dickens she'd gotten from the church in Bywater to the park.

Squinting, she checked for some telltale markers, tried to spot the snowball stand or Peristyle, two landmarks that would confirm that for some strange reason, she'd abandoned her project and ambled off to City Park, her favorite green space within New Orleans.

She looked around her, taking in the joggers foolhardy enough to run in the midday heat. This was not the City Park she knew and loved.

Then she remembered the fall from the scaffolding.

What had happened after? Had someone carried her here, thinking fresh air would help?

Then she recalled a vision of a grumpy old man in a crimson velvet smoking jacket, a vision she'd experienced before opening her eyes to the lush trees and summer-dry grass beneath her bare feet.

She must be dreaming still.

Amity shook her head, then winced.

She might be dreaming, but that darn bruise, swelling rapidly, sure felt real.

And the wild-eyed silver schnauzer bolting toward her, its tongue hanging halfway to its paws, sure hadn't sprung from any dream state.

Amity called softly to the dog. Just as she spotted the trailing leash, the leather strap caught on a root and yanked the dog to a halt.

"Come to Amity, frightened one," she crooned, and stepped slowly forward. Dream or not, she'd never once in her life turned her back on an animal in need of help. She'd been rescuing cats and dogs since she'd been old enough to filch food for them from the foundling home kitchen. And she most certainly knew better than to rush up to a spooked animal.

Something the man hurtling toward her, shouting, "Get back here, Mr. Pish, you damn dog!" had obviously never learned.

Amity offered a paint-streaked hand to be inspected by the trembling schnauzer. The dog lifted his eyes toward her, brows quivering, then sniffed.

"Hey, boy," she murmured, inching closer. She didn't think he'd bolt again after the painful way his leash had jerked him to a stop, but she wanted him to feel safe. The man in the fancy white suit would be upon them soon, and Amity wasn't about to have him scaring the poor thing out of his wits again.

People who frightened their animals didn't de-

serve to have them returned, excuses notwith-
standing.

The noisy man in the white suit raced up to her.
She noted his athletic build and the fact that he
wasn't a bit out of breath.

Amity faced off, holding the leash in a hand
held firmly behind her back. If this man thought
he could continue abusing his dog, he was wrong.
Dead wrong.

"I'll take him now," the man said, swiping at
sweat rolling from his forehead.

Amity said nothing.

The man held out his hand.

She lifted her brows. Behind her, the dog
whined.

"I don't think he likes you," she said.

"I don't care if he likes me or not," the man said
in an exasperated voice. "I promised to walk the
dog in Central Park. The dog's had more than his
share of fresh air and fire hydrants, and now I've
got to get him back where he belongs."

"Central Park?" Amity couldn't place a park by
that name in New Orleans.

The man stared at her as if she'd said something
stupid. He pointed around them. "You know,
Central Park, where Manhattan gathers to enjoy
nature?"

"Manhattan, as in New York? Very funny.
Don't think you can distract me from saving this
dog," she said sternly. "There's no way you'll
convince me to hand him back over to a nutcase."

"Nutcase? *Me*?" Quentin looked around him.

Mia had almost caught up to him. He was sweating like Old Faithful due to erupt. It occurred to him he had no idea how he could explain his heated, rumpled appearance or the dog's lathered condition to Portia Goodhope—if he could persuade this ditz in a purple turban to hand over the leash.

"Yeah, you." The woman stroked the dog's ears and said a few soothing words Quentin couldn't make out, before turning to glare at him. "Don't you know dogs have feelings, too? Don't you care what it must be like to be chased across a park, being shouted at? I mean, how would you like it if someone held up a megaphone and yelled out all *your* faults?"

"Lousy, I'm sure." Quentin stared at the woman's outfit. He considered himself fairly cosmopolitan and generally open-minded, and that the way this New Yorker dressed could amaze him said something about the lady.

A purple turban sat sideways on her head, with long blond tendrils escaping in disordered array. Her tall body was garbed in a rose-and-lavender-striped smock with flowing sleeves that seemed to float about her, every so often providing teasing glimpses of a sheer chemise barely hiding a curvaceous body. Her feet were bare and on her left ankle she wore a delicate silver chain with a tiny bell on it.

As he watched, the woman patted the front of her smock and to his amazement, produced a dog biscuit. "Here you go, sweetie," she said, bending to offer it to the shivering schnauzer. "You've had a hard day, but Amity's here to take care of you now."

"Amity?" Quentin wondered whether he'd stumbled across a representative of some animal rights group. Just what he'd need, bad press to go along with the other production problems of *Permutation*. Any more bad luck and his latest project might never rise above it.

"This isn't my dog," he said.

The woman glared at him. "I don't care whether it is or it isn't. You were chasing him and frightening him, and I've a good mind to call the police."

"And tell them what?" She'd started to irritate him.

"That you're dognapping." She smiled sweetly and smoothed a few crumbs off the dog's muzzle.

"You're the one who's nuts," he said, and reached for the leash again.

"Oh, good, you've got him," Mia said, arriving at his side and patting her brow. Then she looked around. "Who were you talking to?"

Quentin wiggled his brows. "One of New York's finer specimens of womanhood."

Mia glanced behind Quentin. "I hope you thanked her before she left. It's a rare person who bothers to get involved."

Quentin realized he'd been too busy arguing with the blonde to thank her. "I'll take the dog now," he said, then added, "Thanks for your help.

It was kind of you to stop him, but I'm sure his owner is getting concerned."

"Quentin, who are you talking to?" Mia sounded more puzzled than annoyed, but Quentin definitely detected an edge to the question. He couldn't blame her; he'd dragged her through the park on this chase and her feet, encased in those sexy but pointy heels, must be killing her.

"She's the woman who stopped to help."

"My name is Amity," the woman said, holding out a hand to Mia. When Mia ignored it, a flicker of surprise crossed the woman's face. "The paint's dry," she said, then wiped her hand on the side of her dress.

"That's a painter's smock." Quentin felt like an idiot for assuming the woman dressed strangely. "You're an artist?"

She nodded, eyeing Mia with a look of distrust. "Doesn't the lady care for artists?"

"Stop," Mia said, fanning her face with her hands. "Quentin, something very odd is going on here. You're talking to thin air and Mr. Pish is standing there calmly with no one holding his leash. Now, I ask you, what's wrong with this picture?"

Quentin glanced from Amity, who'd cocked her head to one side and stood watching him with birdlike interest, back to Mia. Surely she was pulling his leg. Before they'd married, she'd suffered bouts of jealousy over his playboy past. Perhaps she pretended not to see Amity, a woman Quentin could describe in all honesty as a blond Amazon capable of attracting any red-blooded male.

"Mia, please," Quentin said, "don't make believe you can't see this woman. I can't help that the only person who stopped to help us is a dynamite blonde with a body to die for. Please say hello and good-bye. We've got to get back to Portia Goodhope."

"A body to die for?" A mutinous glint in her eye, Mia shook her head, but after a long moment during which Quentin held his breath, she said, "So pleased to meet you."

Amity stood four feet away, watching the two of them with a curious look in her dark eyes.

"Happy now?" Mia asked.

"Yes. Can we go?" He held out his hand for the leash.

Amity shook her head. "If you think I'm letting you take this dog away from me, you're definitely the nutcase."

Quentin could tell by the angle of the woman's chin and the grasp she had on the leash she was dead serious. "If you won't give me the dog," he said slowly, "you'll have to come with us."

"Nobody tells me what to do."

"Are you ignoring me?" Mia said, in a rather strained voice.

Quentin rolled his eyes and started to laugh at his predicament. "Can the three of us please just stroll back to Portia Goodhope's apartment and sort all this out later?"

Mia looked at him with worry in her big eyes. "Do you think the heat has gotten to you, Quen-

tin?'' She smoothed his hair back from his forehead and lay the back of her hand gently against
his skin. Her touch felt so good he almost forgot
she continued to play her silly game of pretending
she'd not seen the woman who'd caught Mr. Pish.

He started to play along, to humor the woman
he loved. What harm did it do that Mia wanted
to deny the existence of the good-hearted rescuer?
It was more than likely she was behaving this way
because Quentin had described her as a woman
to die for. That Mia, despite her love for him, still
didn't trust him not to return to his philandering
ways suddenly disturbed him very much.

Such thoughts could only lead to problems for
their marriage so recently solemnized, an event
that meant too much to Quentin for him to jeop-
ardize.

He shook his head, ever so slowly, and said to
his wife, ''The heat hasn't done a damn thing to
me, Mia, but until you assure me you trust me
enough not to be jealous of a total stranger, I'm
not budging.''

5 ～

Mia kept her chin held high. How could she be worried about someone who'd passed in and out of their lives in less than a few minutes?

She wasn't jealous, was she? Surely she'd gotten over those silly feelings and learned to trust Quentin.

Remembering her promise to herself to try harder, she figured she might as well start by humoring him. Though she saw no one else in sight, other than an old man sitting on a nearby bench, tossing peanuts to a couple of squirrels, she said, "It was kind of you to rescue our dog."

Then, turning on her heel, Mia said over her shoulder, "You've really been working too hard, Quentin. The pressure's getting to you." But Quentin had worked equally hard in the past. Only now, after their wedding, everything seemed too, too difficult. Mia had assumed life would be easier, somehow blessed by the beauty of their love, rough times smoothed by the magic of their caring for one another. Because she sparkled, she expected the rest of the universe would.

Only things weren't turning out that way. And

worst of all, she and Quentin argued over these stupid, stupid details, and even when she promised herself, during the deep magic hours of the night, that tomorrow would be different, she'd arise only to repeat her behavior.

Each of them, Mia reflected, turning to see why Quentin hadn't followed her, wanted to be right. And proving that to the other had taken center stage. If only she could take the simple perspective of her mother, her life would be easier. But then, she'd never been her mother and wasn't about to start now.

Thoughts of the flaws in the fabric of her wedded bliss halted as she stared at the schnauzer's leash. Of its own accord, it had jerked away from Quentin's hand.

"Give it back," Quentin said.

Mia walked slowly in his direction, trying to understand what she saw.

Or rather, what Quentin must be seeing.

"What do I have to do to convince you I won't hurt the mutt? I told you, it belongs to an actress and I'm only taking it for a walk."

Mia licked her lips. She knew, as clearly as if she could see the woman Quentin had described, an invisible woman *did* stand there, grasping Mr. Pish's leash. A sinking feeling settled in her tummy. An invisible person appearing in their lives could mean only one thing.

"Quentin?"

"Yes?" He looked rueful, and hot and bothered, and all of a sudden she felt sorry for being upset with him. And just wait till he realized that he, Quentin Grandy, could see the woman he was speaking to, and neither Mia, nor, if her guess was on target, anybody else in Manhattan, could see her.

"Remember on our wedding day, when I wished myself invisible?"

He snatched at the leash, without success. "Hmmm?"

"Ask her if that's what she's done."

"Why would I do a thing like that?"

Mia knew the instant Quentin understood. He paused. He stared at the end of the leash, then down at the dog. And then he faced her. "You really can't see her, can you?"

Mia shook her head.

He reached for her hand, turned it palm upward, and kissed her gently. "Forgive me," he said. "I was an ass to yell at you for not speaking to her."

Mia smiled, her heart lifted. Then her smile worried itself into a straight and rather tentative line.

"Don't worry," Quentin said, dropping her hand and making another grab at the leash, "it's probably just my overactive imagination. Or maybe the lox and bagels I had for breakfast." Turning away from Mia, Quentin said, "If you've never been to Central Park before, where is it you think you are?"

Amity gave him another one of those "you're nuts" glances. "New Orleans, of course. I live here, in Bywater." She rubbed the back of her head, tilting the purple turban. It slipped loose and landed on the ground. Before either one of them could retrieve it, Mr. Pish had nabbed it in his mouth.

"I can see that," Mia said, wondering just what kind of woman could carry off such a bright purple fabric. And in a turban!

To Amity, Quentin said, "You wouldn't happen to know an old geezer named Mr. G, would you?"

Amity paused in fingercombing her silky, flowing hair, hair Quentin couldn't help but admire.

"G?" She considered the question. "What's he look like?"

"Short hair, thinning. Big nose. Likes to wear red. Has a bad cough."

"Oh, him! I never forget a memorable face. Do you know where I can find him? I'd like to do his portrait." Amity danced one hand in the air and Quentin imagined she was mentally sketching Mr. G. He wondered whether the old guy would be pleased with the results.

"Hey, wait a minute." Amity dropped her hand. "I thought I dreamed up that man." Again she rubbed her head. "After I fell from the scaffolding . . ." She trailed off, then glanced around her. "Where did you say we are?"

Despite the August heat, Mia felt goosebumps prickling the air on her arms. Quentin's asking about Mr. G could mean only one thing: for whatever reason, she and Quentin had been plunged into another one of their adventures brought to them courtesy of the boundless Mr. G.

The time of their near-death experience, only a little over a year earlier, it was Mr. G who'd greeted them in Purgatory and sent them off on an Intervention assignment. The prize—a second chance at life.

Two months and five days ago, on their wedding day, Quentin's cold feet and dillydallying had brought Mr. G to call. That assignment, turning around the life of multimillionaire A. G. Winston, had carried with it the bonus of Mr. G taking a tuck in time. Not one of their five hundred wedding guests had ever known Quentin had been over an hour late for the ceremony. And of course none of them had ever known the bride and groom had spent a week in Arkansas while everyone else's lives stood still.

To explain it to anyone else would be impossible.

Mia glanced over at Quentin, seriously carrying on a conversation with a being only he could see.

Oh, yes, to share with anyone else their adventures would bring not only a laugh, but a man in a white jacket!

Stifling a sound somewhere between a laugh and a sigh, Mia wondered what in this world, or any other, would happen to them next.

But she wasn't one to sit around waiting passively. She tugged on the sleeve of Quentin's jacket. "What's she telling you?" Not being able to see this person was already driving her bananas.

Quentin flashed her his quick smile. "Her life story."

"Seriously." Mia gripped his arm more tightly. "It's Mr. G, isn't it?"

"Yeah, and with everything else we've got to deal with, that's just what we need!"

A growl of distant thunder sounded, oddly out of place in the sun-soaked sky.

"Behave, Quentin," Mia said. "Ask her if she has a message for us from Mr. G." Mia couldn't imagine why Mr. G wanted them for an Intervention now. Before, he'd appeared only when she and Quentin were in trouble.

"Okay, okay, but let's get going first. If we don't get this dog back to Portia Goodhope, my life won't be worth saving!"

He tugged on the leash. It tugged back.

Starting to retrace her steps, Mia furrowed her brow, thinking hard. She well knew Quentin's penchant for passing off the miraculous as mere coincidence. But Mia knew from the tip of her spiky hair to the bottom of her now-aching feet that Amity's appearance could not be easily explained away.

Mr. G had to be behind it. But why?

Amity had started to back away from Quentin, the schnauzer happily moving in unison with her.

"Oh, no, you don't!" Quentin grasped the leash. "I don't particularly care whether you're one of Mr. G's cohorts or simply another schlub caught between life and death, but you're not going anywhere with Portia's pooch."

Amity fastened him with those eyes of hers, eyes he realized with surprise were a deep shade of violet, the look in them clearly a challenge.

The schnauzer had settled on his haunches, snuggled against his savior's leg. He seemed to be smiling.

Studying that contented expression, Quentin knew what he had to do.

"Look," he said, in a far gentler tone than he'd used yet with this ditzy blonde, "help me out and I'll do whatever I can to get you back to New Orleans."

Her face lit up. "So I can get back to my mural?"

Wondering what Mia would think about him promising something he knew had to be beyond his control, Quentin nodded. "Right away."

"Just tell me what I have to do." Amity took a step toward Quentin, the pockets of her purple smock sagging with goodness knew what other oddments, Rapunzel-like hair escaping from the turban she'd recaptured from the dog, face and hands streaked with red paint. Very much, Quentin thought, a black comedy version of a fairy-tale princess.

"Are you coming, Quentin?" Mia turned from several yards away.

"Now I am," he said. Both of them holding the leash, he and Amity fell into step behind Mia. Watching Mia's careful posture and the way she didn't slow down to join him started a warning message in Quentin's brain. But so help him, he would do whatever it took to sign Portia Good-hope. Speaking softly, he told Amity exactly what he wanted from her.

"If he's harmed one hair on my precious Mr. Pish's head, he'll never take out the trash in this town again!"

Portia Goodhope's voice, a contralto that had brought Broadway audiences to their feet night after night for thirty-some years, rang through the apartment as her maid opened the door to Quentin, Mia, Mr. Pish, and the invisible dog tamer.

"Who is at the door, Claudette?"

"Mr. Grandy and Ms. Tortelli, ma'am." The uniformed maid smiled at them, then said, "And your dog," almost as an afterthought.

To Mia's delight, the maid winked at them.

Portia advanced into the foyer. Mia blinked at the vision the older woman presented, clad in black tights that clung to her legs like a car hanging for dear life on the edge of a cliff. The tights were topped by a silky wraparound blouse that exposed cleavage a woman of any age would be proud to claim. The actress swayed on high-heeled mules topped with fuzzy black balls. Her inky coal-black hair had been swept into a chignon and diamond studded cat's-eye reading glasses hung on a rhinestone chain around her swanlike neck.

Her famous emerald eyes blazed with fire. "I have been worried sick!" She placed a hand against the gap in her blouse. Then, as she saw

Mr. Pish happily rubbing his muzzle against Quentin's linen trousers, the fury left her eyes.

"He likes you!" She darted forward, her arms opened, as much to Quentin as to the favored canine.

Quentin gave the actress one of his slow and easy grins Mia loved so much. "Why, Miss Goodhope, I should hope so." He ran a hand lovingly over the dog's ears. "Mr. Pish is a veritable angel." He slid a wink in Mia's direction.

Mia wondered just how close the invisible woman had to stand to Quentin to accomplish this miracle of man and beast bonding. Too close, she was quite sure, for Mia's wifely comfort.

Quentin thanked his lucky stars Mia couldn't see Amity. At that moment, the artist had herself wrapped around him like an oyster fashioning a pearl, doing an ace job of fulfilling her part of the bargain.

As he stroked the dog's ears, Amity's hand joined his. As the dog nuzzled his leg, Amity kneeled between Quentin's legs, urging the mutt to follow the hand she rubbed up and down Quentin's leg.

The artist might be invisible to others, but she sure as life felt like flesh and blood to the distracted Quentin.

He slipped the leash from the dog's collar, trusting it would dash to Portia Goodhope and Amity would be able to give him some breathing room.

"Come to Portia," the actress said, dipping to her knees and holding out her arms.

Quentin caught the maid suppressing a smile. He, too, started to smile, but lost all sense of humor as the mutt stayed glued to his side.

Portia straightened, casting her chin at a regal angle. "My, but he does like you."

Quentin shrugged.

"I guess you've found a friend, Mr. Pish," Portia said, advancing on Quentin. She tucked her hand under his arm, spared nary a glance for Mia, and led him into her drawing room, cooing, "Why don't you come in and tell me what you wanted to see me about?"

They swept from the foyer, the dog never budging from Quentin's side.

Mia managed a half-smile for the long-suffering maid, who had picked up Mr. Pish's leash.

"Miss Goodhope's a fine lady," the maid said in a low voice, "but she does cotton to men who've just started to strop a razor."

Mia stifled a groan, then laughed despite herself. Now she had both invisible artists and lecherous actresses to deal with. Loving Quentin took a strong heart!

6 ⌐

"California, here we come," the man called Quentin said, rubbing his hands together, surveying the sidewalk in front of Portia Goodhope's building and smiling the way Kitty Cassatt did when she caught a mouse.

Amity blinked. He hadn't said a word about California when he'd promised to help her get back to New Orleans.

"She could have said yes right away and saved us a couple of hours," his wife said.

"Stars like to be coaxed and wheedled. You know that."

"That one likes to be wined and dined and no doubt bedded."

Quentin rolled his eyes.

Mia was obviously the more serious of this duo. "Quentin," she said, "something happened to change Portia's mind. I'm positive she intended to turn you down."

"Sure you're not projecting your own wishes—"

"Absolutely not! Seriously, remember when that funny little man delivered that telegram?"

Quentin nodded.

"It was after that that she started warming to the idea. I wonder why?"

"I can answer that," Amity said.

Quentin turned toward her. "You can?"

"Sure. I read the telegram after she dropped it on the floor."

Mia's eyes never left Quentin's face as he carried on his one-sided conversation with Amity. Feeling just a little bit sorry for the dark-eyed woman, knowing she'd be as frustrated as the dickens not knowing what someone else in a conversation was saying, Amity said to Quentin, "The telegram was from someone named Mortie Gold."

"Her agent!"

Amity shrugged. "Whatever. Anyway, it said her show had been canceled early and she should sweet-talk Grandy before he learned she needed him as much as he wanted her."

"Well, I'll be d—"

"Don't say it." Mia clapped her hand over Quentin's mouth.

He smiled, something Amity could tell by the light in his eyes as he removed his wife's hand, giving it a gentle squeeze.

Watching the two of them, Amity had to laugh. For two people who gazed at one another as if they wanted to gobble each other up, they sure could dicker.

"Well, that may be what brought her around, but I know she's used to being courted and she naturally expects to be flattered."

"Shall I add that into your job description?"

"If that's what it takes to keep her happy, the answer's yes." Pulling Mia away from the doorman, Quentin said, "Thanks for going along with me. I promise you'll see she's right for the part. Not just right, but perfect."

Amity didn't know much about acting, but two hours spent in close quarters with Portia Goodhope hadn't impressed her. First, the woman clearly never threw away anything related to her career. Her drawing room, as she'd called it, was papered with framed pictures and articles all relating to her career, along with a gallery of people so famous even Amity, who spent most of her time with her head behind an easel, recognized.

Portia Goodhope did score one point with Amity. She liked her dog. She dressed him in a silly sweater inside the bone-chilling apartment, but she did dote on him.

Amity glanced over at the man and woman she'd met in the park. She didn't know whether to think of them as rescuers or the other way around. Without her help, Mr. Pish probably would have chewed Quentin's ankle in two, so she guessed they owed her.

"Never mind about Portia," Mia was saying. "What are we going to do with *her*?"

Ooh, Amity had heard that tone of voice before. Several times the sisters in the foundling home had told her to pack her bags; she was going to go and live with a nice family. None of those visits had lasted longer than a couple of months. Within a few weeks, the foster parents pulled their hair out and sat around their kitchen tables, asking each other, "But what are we going to do with her?"

She began to edge away. Even if the guy had been telling the truth and she had ended up in New York by some weird means, she'd get herself home. She didn't need help from anyone. Not Amity Jones, no sir.

"Take her back to California with us."

"Oh, look!" Staring at amazement at the herd of dogs heading their way on the sidewalk, Amity forgot about her troubles. Kneeling, she clicked her tongue gently and whistled.

An elegant wolfhound broke from the pack first, galloping straight toward her. Behind him, leash flapping, hurtled a dachshund. The young man who'd dropped the leash grabbed at the rest of the leads and called in a very cross voice, "Get back here, Wentzel! And Waldorf!"

Amity let the animals nuzzle her. What beautiful dogs they were. "You must be very lucky, having so many wonderful animals," she said to the man when he caught up to her and the two dogs.

To her shock, the man snatched the leashes and without a word, hauled the pack of animals off down the sidewalk.

"Well, of all the rude people!" Perhaps they were in New York. She couldn't imagine anyone in New Orleans treating a fellow animal lover that way. Why, in New Orleans, they had their very own Mardi Gras parade for canines, with two special dogs crowned each year as queen and king of the Krewe of Barkus.

But it was ridiculous to think she'd been magically transported to New York. No, this man must have recently moved to town.

Still on her knees, Amity felt a gentle hand on her shoulder. She looked up to see Quentin standing next to her.

He offered her a hand and she got to her feet. "What an unfriendly man," she said. "I only wanted to greet his dogs."

"Oh, those weren't his dogs," Quentin said. "He's a dog walker."

"A what?"

"Someone who gets paid to walk other people's dogs because they're too busy or they're out of town," he explained.

"Oh. That's nice, I suppose, but he didn't have to ignore me."

"I don't think he could see you."

"There weren't that many dogs."

Quentin shook his head.

"Don't you think we should figure out why she's here in New York before we simply dive in and whisk her off to California?" Mia, looking fairly cross, stood tapping her foot on the sidewalk.

Quentin nodded.

"I'm not going to California. You told me if I helped you out in there, you'd help me get back to my mural."

"I know I promised to help if you'd keep Mr. Pish happy with me."

"How did she do that?"

"Do what?"

"How did she get a dog that plainly didn't like you to cozy up to your leg that way?" Mia looked worse than cross now; a hint of crimson tinted her olive-toned cheeks.

Amity couldn't blame her. If she were married, she wouldn't want some other woman curled between her husband's legs.

"Come on, Mia, you saw her just now with those dogs. She's a natural with animals."

"With men, too, I bet," Mia muttered.

"Oh, no," Amity said. "Feel free to tell her, since she insists she can't hear me, I always strike out with men. First I pick the wrong ones, always impulsively, and have to backpedal my way out of the worst situations. You see, they always turn out to be flakes. You know—writers, artists, wannabe directors. What I wouldn't give to meet a nice stable accountant or banker someday!" She sighed. In her circles, that would never happen. Except for Bubba, who was a lawyer, which was close, but he was in love with Breeze.

"I see," Quentin said dryly. "You've nothing to worry about from this woman, Mia dear, she's sworn off men."

"Hey, I wouldn't go that far," Amity said. Then she saw Quentin throw a wink at her. "Gotcha," she said. Why make his wife worry?

Of course, she'd have to be blind not to notice

Quentin was enough to speed a beating heart. He ranged equal with Amity's leggy height, and some quality in his piercing brown eyes, deep set beneath craggy brows, signaled to her artist's soul. This man was no average bloke. Amity had pieced together the information that he was a fairly famous film director, but she couldn't find any resemblance to the deranged artists, flaky musicians, or never-get-around-to-it novelists that peopled her world.

But for all her bad luck with guys, Amity didn't mess with married men. And even if she had, she'd have known better than to waste her time on a man who gazed at his wife with a desire Amity found herself coveting. Had any man ever looked at her in such a way—with that blend of longing, attraction, love, and, let's face it, a pretty healthy dose of good old-fashioned lust?

Amity shook her head. Lust, yeah, she'd experienced plenty of that. But what man of the many she had known had ever gazed at her with such tenderness?

Her heart twisted. Would she ever meet a man who would look at her that way?

Pulling her thoughts back to her present quandary, Amity tuned out Mia and Quentin and studied the men and women scurrying past, most of whom were dressed in black despite the August heat, and began to worry that perhaps she really was no longer in New Orleans.

Certainly at home no one would walk so fast. New Orleanians knew how to pace their steps, knew better than to defy the heat by rushing about. They were pros at finding shelter from an overhanging eave or a leafy tree.

How could she not be in New Orleans? The City That Care Forgot, the Crescent City, the home of the French Quarter and Mardi Gras was her only home. That she'd even consider the idea that she might have been transported to New York made her think she must have hit her head harder than she realized.

Amity looked askance at the sexy man who insisted she'd encountered him in Central Park. Central Park, as in New York City. The borough of Manhattan, to be exact. Amity might not have traveled much beyond the boundaries of Bywater, but she knew her geography. One of the sisters at the foundling home had groomed her for the Geography Bee, only to give up on her in disgust when Amity had persisted in sketching the pictures the place-names suggested to her.

Even now, trying to deal with what was happening to her, Amity mused, relying on her imagination would serve her in good stead. Something strange had happened to her, something well beyond the bounds of logic.

Take the way the dark-haired woman insisted she couldn't see her. Amity had never taken well to being ignored, and this instance was no exception. The woman didn't strike her as the snobby type, and other than blatantly pretending Amity didn't exist, she seemed an okay person. And the way she looked at Quentin with her heart in her eyes made Amity catch her breath.

"Ask her," Mia was saying, as Amity turned her attention back to their debate.

"I don't care if she has the name of her Intervention assignment written in gold leaf, we can't miss production to help her." Quentin glared as he began picking silver dog hairs from his trousers.

"I'm the producer, Quentin. I'm the one responsible for the schedule. I'm not suggesting we delay; I'm suggesting we not interfere." For such a tiny thing, the woman looked as if she could hold her own against an advancing army.

"She's the one who's interfering, not me." The man ran his hands through his hair. "Besides," he added, "you know I'm the last one to want to get involved in these weird situations."

"Quentin," Mia said, "please just ask her."

"She can ask me herself," Amity said, jumping back into their conversation. "I can hear her; I guess she just can't hear me."

"Oh, of course." Quentin relayed the message to Mia.

Upon hearing that, she looked slightly less harassed.

"So, Quentin says you've met Mr. G and you've been in the Second Chance Room. We've, uh—we know of this place, enough to know he'd have given you a piece of paper with an assignment on it."

Amity rubbed the knot on her head and tried

to remember what had happened to her after her fall. Nothing about an assignment came to her, though. She shrugged.

"What did she say?" Mia sounded anxious to hear the answer.

"Nothing."

"Try harder to remember," Mia said. "Maybe a little girl on rollerskates appeared and handed you a slip of paper?"

"That does sound familiar. Anyway, I know I got some paper from somewhere because I sketched the old guy with the big nose and the cigar."

"What did you do with the sketch?" Quentin asked.

Amity looked in one pocket, then tried another. She did find a half tube of titanium white she thought she'd lost, but no sketch of the mystery man. "I must have thrown it away," she said.

"What did she say?"

"You think you threw it away?"

"Her assignment? Is she stupid?"

"Hey, let's not be mean," Quentin said. "Did you at least read it first, before you drew on it?"

Amity tried, really tried, to remember, but the harder she tried, the more the bump on her head ached.

"I can't stand it!" Suddenly, Mia turned and walked rapidly away, then swung back toward them. "Quentin, this is driving me crazy! Do you know what it's like, not being able to hear the entire conversation?"

He went to her and took her by the shoulders. Rubbing her upper arms tenderly, he said, "Mia, sweetheart. It's okay. We'll get through this." He bent and kissed her cheek and murmured, "You know how you always say there's a reason for the way things happen?"

She nodded, somewhat reluctantly, Amity thought.

"Well, maybe we're meant to help Amity and we'll learn something as a result."

"That's easy for you to say," Mia answered, but less heatedly.

Watching the two of them, Amity sighed. This long-drawn-out discussion might have attracted attention on the sidewalks of New Orleans, but apparently no one in New York gave a fig.

If they really *were* in New York.

Something Amity Jones hoped against hope wasn't true.

She gazed about her. When she'd first found herself in the park, she'd gone along with Quentin's plea for help with the dog, not so much for him or for the assistance he promised her, but because Amity never abandoned a lost animal, something Spike Jones and Fleezer and Marvel and her family of cats could attest to. But with the schnauzer safely delivered, Amity needed to get her bearings and strike out on her own.

Mia and Quentin seemed intent on one another just then. Amity took the opportunity to sidle away. At the curb, she waited for a break in the traffic. An opening appeared, snatched by a police car speeding up the block. Amity knew better than to step in front of a police car.

The car slowed as it reached her. A potbellied officer glanced out the window and waved a beefy hand, then called hello to the doorman, who waved back.

Amity drew back at the friendly behavior. Then she saw, bigger than big on the side of the car, the letters NYPD.

NYPD. Definitely not NOPD.

Not knowing whether he could see her or not, Amity fluttered her fingers at the cop, backing away from the curb at the same time.

Maybe she would stick with Mia and Quentin.

Just until she figured out what was going on.

"I think I need a few minutes alone," Mia announced. "Keep her company, decide what to do. I'm going to walk to the end of the block and back and count to ten."

"Or maybe a thousand and one," Mia said under her breath, as she left the shelter of the building's canopy and strode toward the end of the long block. She didn't care that her feet throbbed from the pounding they'd taken in the park. She needed time to think.

Not only did they now have Portia Goodhope to deal with, but it looked as if they'd added Ms. Invisible to their production entourage.

She couldn't disagree with Quentin that Amity was meant to be there, with them, at this very moment. But to take her along to California meant Mia had to cope. Despite her worries over her marriage, with them heading into principal photography in two days, the health of *Permutation* had to take priority.

Mia hadn't chosen to become a producer by happenstance. She had fallen in love with the movies at age ten. But unlike those who succumbed to the glamor of the footlights or the glory of the director's chair, she fell in love with the process of maneuvering craft and artisan and cash through the maze of production.

She and her twelve-year-old sister had been sent to spend the afternoon in the darkened cavern of the neighborhood art house. Someone on the block had died, in a manner Mia's mother and father hadn't wanted their female offspring to learn too much about. So she and Frannie had been given a dollar and deposited in front of the scratchy old screen where *Quo Vadis* had played, in all its blood-and-guts glory.

Frannie had slipped out when the Romans had started burning the Christians at the stake and throwing them to the lions . . . to get a candy bar, she said later, but Mia knew softhearted and devout Frannie hadn't been able to handle the scene.

For Mia, though, the experience proved a threshold. Instead of sympathizing with the Christians, she tried to understand how to assemble and orchestrate the crowd scenes and tried to calculate the cost of re-creating the Coliseum.

She'd grown up poor, and she valued money. Too much so, her father sometimes said, shaking his head when she negotiated for a nickel increase to her minimal allowance, an allowance her parents could scarcely afford. All around Mia, in her East Los Angeles neighborhood, lived people who survived on food stamps and handouts from the many churches. Mia's Irish mother and Sicilian father, though, never took a penny from the President, the governor, or the Pope.

Growing up without so much of what others took for granted, Mia most definitely knew the value of money.

The afternoon spent screening *Quo Vadis* remained a fixture in her memory. Years later, when she elbowed her way into UCLA on scholarship and began haunting the film courses and lectures, she focused naturally on the business aspects of the industry.

Mia, Quentin had been known to say, had been born a producer.

And now, on the sidewalks of New York City, Mia the producer fought a battle with Mia the believer, the secret side of herself that had played backup to the rest of her life in recent years.

Until Mr. G had entered their lives.

"Darn it," she said under her breath, turning and heading back to Quentin, "Mr. G must have sent her, so we have to take her with us."

For a brief moment, she considered whether the prayer she'd offered to Mr. G in the Chicago airport had had anything to do with this woman's arrival, then discarded the very idea. She'd prayed for the sanctity of her marriage, not to have it torn asunder by complicating blondes.

"Quentin," Mia said, reaching his side and gazing into the brown eyes of the man who'd claimed her heart the first time they'd met, and ignored her, "Quentin, we both know how much this film means, and how expensive a delay is." If they didn't make the completion date, they stood to lose points on the gross of the film.

"And?" Her husband leaned close, balancing on the balls of his feet, his eyes flashing.

Mia caught herself from reaching up to cradle the back of his neck and draw him near for a kiss. No matter how much they argued of late, she still found he made her swoon like a silly sixteen-year-old. She stashed her hands in the pockets of her jacket, then said, "I agree to take her to California, but I want your promise you won't let her cause us any trouble."

"Why is she my problem? I don't want to be able to see her. I don't want to be involved. But dammit, I seem to be." He kicked at the sidewalk. "But okay, we'll take her with us and figure it all out later."

Mia thought back to their own experience in the Second Chance Room of Mr. G's Purgatory. They'd had only a limited time to accomplish their intervention. "Remember the egg timer?"

Quentin nodded, looking fairly miserable. But then he brightened. "Let's just conjure up Mr. G and explain the situation." He flapped the front of his now bedraggled linen jacket. "And now, let's get back to California where the weatherman doesn't know the word *humidity*." Then, despite the seriousness of the situation, he winked. "She's invisible, so her ticket won't cost us a penny."

Mia smiled a bit, but her mind was far away, back in the chapel in the airport, to be exact. "Did you say conjure?"

"Light a candle, say a prayer? You know about those things better than I."

Mia worried her lip, deciding again that Amity's appearance was just too coincidental. "I'm not sure Mr. G works that way. He's never struck me as the traditional sort."

"Then let's try an unconventional conjuring. But not until we get back to California. Come on, let's get a cab, go to the hotel, pack, and get to the airport. You can ask her anything you want on the way." He smiled and looked over his shoulder, apparently searching for Amity.

"Is she gone?" Mia tried not to sound too hopeful.

"Amity?" Quentin looked up and down the sidewalk.

"Maybe it was all some sort of test," Mia suggested.

"She was right here only a second ago."

"Why don't we get a cab? If she's not back by the time one stops, then she was meant to disappear."

Quentin frowned. "I can't help but wonder where we would we be today if Ely Van Ness hadn't helped us when we were invisible and stranded in Arkansas."

"Oh, Quentin." Mia felt about two inches high. "You're right. I'm being a grouch."

"There she is!" Quentin pointed down the block. "What's she got?"

Mia stared. A small silky-furred object appeared to be floating toward them in mid-air. As it grew nearer, Mia could tell it was a rabbit's foot.

"Where did you get that?" Quentin asked.

"You'd better grab it before the doorman notices," Mia said, "because to mere mortals such as myself it looks as if that foot is wafting under its own power."

"Right!" Quentin took it from her. He listened for a few minutes, then said to Mia, "She's really upset that some cretin amputated an innocent animal. It seems she snatched this off someone walking down the street and the man's gone into the next building, shouting he's going to call the cops."

"Better get a cab," Mia said. "Pronto, unless you want to go to jail again."

"Me?" Then Quentin looked down at the rabbit's foot now in his hands. "Oh, great."

Just then a cab barreled up the busy street. Even before Quentin lifted his arm, the dented yellow car coughed to a halt.

The driver, an old man who looked as if he'd been driving cabs since the days of the Model T, glanced at them from under bushy white brows. "Going my way?" he asked from around the big cigar stuck between his teeth.

"The Sherry-Netherland."

Mia watched as Quentin dropped the rabbit's foot onto the sidewalk, then they hustled into the cab, Mia first. To her surprise, Quentin remained on the far side of the backseat, rather than scooting next to her, as he normally would. Then he crossed his legs and said, "Pardon me."

Mia looked at the empty space between Quentin and herself. "For what?"

Quentin pointed to the same space, obviously seeing something far different than the worn black vinyl of the cab seat. "Amity," he whispered.

"Oh."

"Of course not," Quentin said, apparently to some question of Amity's that Mia couldn't hear.

"This may drive me crazy," Mia said.

"Remember when you were invisible?" Quentin turned toward her but made no move to close the gap between their bodies.

Mia knew it was silly, but she resented those twelve or thirteen inches: not mere space, but a *woman* separated them. She furrowed her brow and wondered where Quentin planned on having Amity sleep.

The driver began whistling between his teeth in a way that sent Mia's already irritated nerves over the edge. She wished she could tell him to stop, but then, this was his cab. She wouldn't think much of someone entering her office in Burbank and asking her not to tap her nails on her desk.

Mia edged forward on the seat. "Ask her again what Mr. G said to her exactly. Ask her whether she's been sent back to win a second chance at life."

Quentin cocked his head toward the middle of the seat, holding a finger to his lips.

The cab jerked to a stop, tossing Mia forward in the seat.

Glaring at the space between her and her husband, Mia couldn't help but feel they were meant to put this puzzle ahead of *Permutation*. If they didn't, she hoped the universe could handle playing second fiddle to a film production.

When she couldn't take the absorbed expression on Quentin's face another second, she said, "So what did she say?"

"She could probably do a masterly portrait of the old coot." Quentin pursed his lips, then smiled. "But she can't recall anything else, especially about her assignment."

"Think harder," Mia said.

"She says it hurts her head to try to remember."

"Oh." Mia wouldn't want to cause anyone pain, but she sure wished the woman knew her own purpose. That would make their immediate future a lot less complicated. "Well, I still don't see how anyone could throw away a message from an old man who was probably raving about rules at the time she got it."

"She's an artist. You've got to make exceptions for them."

Mia drew back. "As if they're more special than us run-of-the-mill types?"

"Not more special, but different, yes."

Mia swiveled her head to stare out the window. She saw nothing past her own reflection in the glass. She sure wanted to know what she'd done to deserve having this "special artist" foisted on her in the honeymoon months of her marriage.

The cab halted in front of the hotel.

Quentin paid the driver. As Mia was about to slide out of the cab, the driver quit his annoying whistling and cranked his head around toward her. "Here's my card, if you need anything."

Her mind already turning toward business, thinking she'd best call Portia's agent and firm up the details before they left for the airport, Mia murmured a polite thank-you and tucked the flimsy card into the pocket of her linen jacket.

7 ~

Before his work on *Permutation*, Beetle Leonard had never been invited to a movie set.

Now that he'd scripted two critically acclaimed, if not financially flush, films, some people might find that a strange fact.

But the truism that the writer is the lowest rung on the splintery ladder that is Hollywood is nothing less than accurate. And a writer who suffered throes of discomfort when forced to maneuver a Hollywood party juggling canapes, cocktails, and chatter was especially low in the pecking order.

Today, waiting for the first day of the location work to begin, he shifted from foot to foot, thinking an expectant father pacing the floor of a hospital might feel something akin to what he felt about bringing *Permutation* to life.

A woman who had suffered five or six miscarriages prior to delivery would also pretty much mirror his feelings. No one in the Hollywood establishment had wanted to give *Permutation* a hearing, let alone green-light the project. His reputation, he'd been told, was too "literary." Too uptown. Not box-office enough. Making a commercial Jeffrey "Beetle" Leonard film would be like trying to sell James Joyce to a junior high crowd, one twenty-something exec had explained to him over a macrobiotic lunch bought and paid for by the last of Beetle's savings.

Tinges of pink lit the pre-dawn sky as Beetle swung his arms and looked around him, waiting for the others to start the bustle of production. Like a nervous groom, he'd arrived too early. Hiding a smile, he blew on his hands chilled by the air that crept up from the sea and down from the mountains to cool Santa Barbara. But like a groom, he was gripped by anticipation, eager, ready, and willing.

"Good morning," said a soft, sweet voice from beside his shoulder.

Beetle started and turned to see Mia Tortelli, the film's producer, and the woman he regarded as his guardian angel.

Without Mia, Beetle would've been back in Cairo, Illinois, by now, teaching Earth science and praying for a big break. An author might make a name writing critically acclaimed movies that played the art houses, but it was a damn sure hard way to make a living.

Teaching, his parents had explained to him more times than he liked to remember, was secure. Teaching, it had been drummed into his head, provided a steady source of income and an opportunity to help others.

You can reach out, his mother had said, glancing up from an endless mountain of her students'

English papers. You can share the marvels of science, his father, a math professor, would add, not even bothering to move his eyes from his computer screen.

Noting the lightening of the sky, Beetle smiled and turned to Mia Tortelli. Swallowing hard, he finally managed to croak out, "G-good morning."

She hugged her arms, warmed by a denim jacket, across her chest and nodded. "This must be a special day for you."

She understood. A producer, no less! Beetle gazed at her in admiration. He knew how very much in love she was with Quentin Grandy, and it was a good thing, because if she hadn't so obviously been a happy bride, he would've been oh-so-tempted to stupidly announce the schoolboy crush he'd developed on her.

And Beetle, having reached the ripe old age of thirty-two, had no business having a crush on anyone. What he needed, his parents were also fond of telling him, was a wife.

And as he well knew, Sheila Stokes continued to run the BookStop and wait for Beetle to come home to her.

Then his mother would frown (he could see it, even over the long-distance call), and he'd feel pressed to explain he wasn't ready to give up on his dream. And if she continued to nag, he'd promise to give Sheila a call. Then, after a sigh so deep it must have started in her kidneys, his mother would trail off and remind him to plan to come home for Christmas, if he couldn't make Thanksgiving.

And Beetle wouldn't phone Sheila.

He'd write instead—long letters full of rambling thoughts and ideas and half-assed philosophical opinions. Sheila liked to listen to him; Sheila liked to tell other people his ideas, though somehow they always came out as if she had thought them up. Way back in high school, that had amused him, but now he found himself wanting to insert truly stupid things in his letters and wonder if she'd know the difference.

Beetle realized all of a sudden that he'd been standing there like a clod, carrying on a dialogue in his head, when Mia Tortelli stood next to him, clearly expecting some return of conversation.

"Did you sleep well?" he blurted out.

"Yes, thank you," she said, looking at him with those big, dark eyes of hers, as if somehow she understood he'd been momentarily thrown and said the first thing that came to his mind.

And she just might understand, too. After all, she lived with and loved Quentin Grandy, the best director around, the director who'd given Beetle this big chance. If she could love a man as creative and unique as Quentin Grandy, perhaps she'd forgive a few lapses of conversational etiquette.

But she was the producer, and Beetle needed to think of his future.

How much happier he was, standing here in this paradise, with rugged mountains at his back and endless ocean down below, than back home, surrounded by cornfields and the occasional hill. How much happier he was, anxiously awaiting the first day of filming of his baby, his love, his creation *Permutation*, than he could ever be bringing the knowledge of hermaphroditic earthworms to twelve-year-olds.

It wasn't that he didn't like science; he'd always excelled. He'd only dropped out of his doctoral program at the University of Illinois because the voices in his head that whispered stories to him had been so strong that he just knew if he didn't listen to them and bring them to life, he'd end up hating himself.

So, deaf to the protests of his parents, he'd disappeared for a year and during that time poured forth the screenplays that had won him the acclaim and the words of promise.

And absolutely no money to speak of after the barest of living expenses and taxes.

So he'd lived on his VISA card and written the story so dear to his heart, the story of the possibility of change.

Permutation.

And one day, when he'd been about to give in to despair and destiny and return to Illinois, he'd gone into McDonald's on Wilshire and ordered the really cheap special, the All American Cheeseburger Meal, the one that came to only $1.95 with burger, fries, and an iced tea, no lemon, thank you.

He'd been turning from the counter when a woman had spoken to him.

"Don't I know you?" she'd said, picking up the napkins he'd dropped on the floor.

"Uh—" Beetle was pretty sure no one in Hollywood knew him from Adam. But being the damned optimist he secretly was, he hated to confess that fact. "*Barely There*? *Once Upon a Midnight Ride*?" He named his two films, holding his breath, feeling like a fool, but pleased he'd managed that much. Pleased, yet embarrassed. The dark-eyed woman with spiky brown hair could simply be someone who recognized him from the laundromat, and here he stood, rattling off his film titles as if he were Quentin Grandy.

Or she could just be a woman trying to pick him up, using a worn-out line. Beetle, despite his wild rash of red hair, unremarkable blue eyes, the freckles that sprouted no matter how much sunscreen he glopped on his face, and the funky way he had of never feeling as if he fit in, never had trouble attracting women.

"*Once Upon a Midnight Ride*," she said, tipping her head back to gaze at him.

Beetle held his breath. Maybe she really did recognize him from his work.

"You won the Most Original Short Film Prize at the LA Film Fest last year, didn't you?"

Beetle's heart stopped.

He nodded.

He dropped the sack containing his day's supply of calories on the floor.

Clucking softly, the woman bent, collected the

bag, and handed it to him. "Would you like to have lunch?"

He swallowed. "Now?"

She nodded. "Let me get my salad," she said, and stepped into line.

Trying to reconcile his recent run of bad luck with endless possibilities of good fortune, Beetle sighted a table and loaded it with napkins, salt and pepper, and catsup. He waited until the brown-haired woman returned before he opened his own to-go sack.

"I'm Mia Tortelli," she said, prying open the lid to her chef salad. "I produce for—"

"Quentin Grandy," he blurted out, to his embarrassment.

But she only smiled. "You know Quentin's work?"

"Oh, yes!" Beetle squirted catsup onto his scrap of a burger. "Who doesn't? He's amazing. There's never been anything like *DinoDaddy*. And *Quetzalcoatl's Overcoat* was pure genius." He lay the empty catsup packet on the table. "You," he said slowly and with reverence, "are a very lucky woman." Wow, he'd actually talked to a producer without stuttering. He dropped two catsup packets on the floor and kicked them away with a furtive foot.

"Oh, I know!" Mia smiled, in a way Beetle suddenly hoped some special woman would one day smile at him. "So tell me, what are you working on now?"

And so it had begun.

The magical time in his life when Beetle had met and was working with Mia Tortelli and Quentin Grandy. They'd only recently recovered from a death-defying accident on a sound stage, and rumors around town had it the two of them were sleeping together, rumors confirmed by the announcement of their impending wedding.

Only the day before he'd bumped into Mia Tortelli in McDonald's, Beetle had been envying the five hundred guests invited to the wedding, despairing that he'd ever be more than a starving artist lying on a lumpy couch in a West Hollywood walkup.

And then he'd gone out for his All American Cheeseburger an hour later than usual, and the rest, as they say, was history.

Beetle turned, thinking surely this time he'd think of something brilliant and clever and Hollywoodish to say to Mia, only to discover she'd slipped away. He saw her across the clearing, studying her clipboard and talking into her cell phone. It was just as well; without a keyboard, he never could think of what to say.

From the lowliest of gaffers to Hal Cormoran, the leading man, the entire cast and crew of *Permutation* knew the instant Portia Goodhope arrived on the set.

The sun had slipped into the Pacific, signaling an end of the first day's shooting only seconds before the famous contralto rang over the dusty hillside.

"Snakes!"

That one word froze Quentin's blood. He bolted, sentence dangling, from the cinematographer's side. Honing in on the beacon of Portia's hysterical and lusty screams, he raced in that direction. Those he passed stared, and he knew the business well enough to know everyone would be alert to any scene Portia Goodhope might create. And they'd watch how Quentin Grandy handled it.

Rounding a bend in the path to the parking lot, Quentin realized Amity kept pace with him. Early in the day, she'd planted herself by his side, apparently fascinated by the process of moviemaking. She'd proved an easygoing and insightful companion.

Another scream rent the air.

From just behind his shoulder, Amity said, "Do you suppose she screams for attention, or is this really snake country?"

Skidding to a stop in the clearing established as a parking area for the overflow of cars unable to fit in the normal lot of their operations base, a hole in the wall known appropriately as the Cubby Hole Lodge, Quentin didn't answer. Portia, her maid, the limo driver, and three production assistants stood in a semicircle on the far side of the limo, all gawking toward the open passenger door.

If there was a snake, no one made a move to drive it away.

Spotting Quentin, Portia sobbed and cried out,

"Thank goodness! Quentin, come and save my baby for me!"

Suppressing a frown, Quentin stepped forward. Having seen no sign of the actress's schnauzer, he'd allowed himself to hope, if only for a second, that she'd left the mutt behind.

A piteous whine from within the limo killed that thought.

He rounded the car. The group edged back slightly. Just then, with his peripheral vision, he caught sight of the snake. It lay, most of its length coiled, its head darting in and out of the limousine's open passenger door, as if deciding whether to get in for a ride.

"Big snake," he muttered under his breath. Then, louder, he said to Portia, "Don't worry, we'll have Mr. Pish out safely."

Looking at the thick reddish-brown body of the snake, marbled with white ovals, Quentin wondered just how he planned to do that, when suddenly he realized how stupid they all were, standing there. The best way to get the dog out was to walk to the opposite side of the car.

He shook his head and moved in that direction.

Amity put a hand on his arm. Her touch caused a strange sensation, as he saw her hand on his skin and knew she'd touched him, only it wasn't the feel of flesh on flesh.

"Want to impress Miss Sixty-going-on-sixteen?"

The answer to that question took no thought at all. Quentin nodded.

"Follow me," she said, and walked straight at the foot-long reptile. She grasped it by the back of its head and slowly eased it, a few slithering inches at a time, away from the spellbound watchers. As she passed in front of Portia, she lifted the snake's head off the ground an inch or so, then darted it toward the actress.

Portia, quite predictably, screamed.

Quentin grinned despite himself, then leapt to action, bounding to the car to pull Mr. Pish from danger.

The ungrateful schnauzer nipped at his wrist and dug his back claws into Quentin's belly, but Quentin held on until Portia rushed up and held out her arms for the dog.

Sure the damn dog had drawn blood, Quentin hid his wrist and accepted the kisses of gratitude Portia bestowed on him.

"Whatever would I do without you?" Portia settled Mr. Pish onto the ground by her feet and tottering on her spike heels beamed up at him.

Brushing dog hairs from his clothing once again, Quentin mustered his most gracious smile for Portia and wondered whether he shouldn't have listened to Mia.

"So," Portia said, placing her hand in his and fixing him with her world-famous green eyes, "when do we start rehearsals?"

Quentin swallowed his shocked retort in a fit of coughing. Surely Portia's agent had explained she was coming into the production at a late date. The read-throughs had been completed before Francine May's heart attack. Portia would have to take her lead from briefings he'd do with her and the other actors prior to each scene. Instead of answering directly, he said, "Did you read the script on the plane?"

Portia tapped him on the hand as if he were the naughty pet and delivered a wiggle of her finely painted-on brows. "You should know that reading in the poor light of an airplane is very bad for one's eyes. And what's bad for one's eyes is very, very bad for one's complexion!" She nuzzled closer. "Besides, I was hoping you'd have dinner with me tonight and explain your vision of the character to me."

Quentin thought of the time he'd intended to spend going over the next day's shooting schedule, of the time he needed to review the rushes of today's filming. But he needed to keep her happy; he sure hoped Mia understood. "We could arrange that. Perhaps by eight we—"

"We?" Portia squeezed his hand, but her touch was gentle compared to the steel of her voice. "I prefer just the two of us." She fluttered her eyelashes, but the soft act didn't fool Quentin one bit.

She'd issued a command, pure and simple. Quentin found himself nodding. Mr. Pish, probably sensing his weakness, took that moment to launch an attack on Quentin's ankle.

Quentin muffled a curse and tried to shake the dog off.

Portia, obviously none too pleased, said in an accusing tone, "I thought Mr. Pish liked you."

"Oh, he does," Quentin said, baring his own teeth in what he hoped would pass for a grin.

Thankfully, Amity spotted the snarling schnauzer. To her credit, she raced to his side. Bending down, she stroked the dog's muzzle, and before Quentin could say Alfred Hitchcock, the snarls changed to yelps of canine joy.

A sheepish look on his face, Quentin knelt to let the dog lick his hand, now carefully wrapped between Amity's fingers. Smiling up at Portia, he said, "He remembers me now."

Looking every bit the conquering queen, the actress smiled. Rising slowly and brushing dust from his jeans, Quentin wondered whether he'd sunk to an all-time low in his career or whether the days ahead would bring him even lower.

From her vantage point near the edge of the small crowd that had gathered, Mia sighed and hugged her clipboard to her chest. Even though she couldn't see Amity, she knew, in a way any woman would, that the beautiful, sensitive, artistic, insightful, animal-loving blonde hovered near Quentin.

Too, too near.

8 ⌒

"I hope you don't expect me to go to dinner with you and this manslayer." Amity pulled her hand from Quentin's, grateful the maid had been ordered to whisk Mr. Pish off to the sidelines.

"Dinner?" Quentin managed, still sandwiched between the invisible Amity and the all-too-present Portia Goodhope.

"Darling, I thought you'd never ask." Portia giggled in a throaty way.

"Yes," Amity said, patting the pockets of her lavender smock. She came up with a pencil stub and went back to her patting routine.

For a second, Quentin held his breath, wondering if she'd retrieve the paper that held the answer to the mystery of her Intervention target.

She pulled out a pink plastic fish, an empty tube of paint, and a gaudy string of purple, green, and gold beads—but no paper. With a frown, she stepped away, apparently in search of sketching materials. She seemed to have forgotten Quentin, Portia and everything else. The artist at work. Quentin gazed after her, admiring the intensity of her concentration. Mia was the same way when she worked on a problem: singleminded and undistractible.

Two hands swiveled his chin back toward Portia. "Yoo-hoo, over here, darling." She smiled, but the look proved more feral than tender.

Quentin found a smile for his new star. Knowing when he'd lost a round, he said, "Pick you up at eight?"

Portia clamped a hand over his wrist, then cocked it to check his watch. Quentin noted she had a perfectly good Piaget on her own skinny arm.

She let go and said, "I'll just take a peep at my trailer, then return to the hotel. I always like to freshen up before a special night out."

Ignoring Portia's wink and thinking to hand the actress off, Quentin waved one of the gawking production assistants over. The young woman had grown up in the movie business, but she stared at Portia like any first-time visitor to Hollywood. The legitimate theater still held reign over the upstart movie world, Quentin noted with wry amusement.

But that hunch had been one of the reasons he'd been driven to cast Portia Goodhope. The world would come to see her, and box-office history would be made yet again.

Glancing down at Portia, he caught her gazing back at him, a hungry look in her famous emerald eyes. Well, he'd gotten his wish; he just hoped he hadn't made a deal with the devil in order to bring this particular movie first into being.

"Shawna," he said to the production assistant, "show Miss Goodhope to Trailer A."

"Like, I am honored." The youngster practically bowed as she issued her giggly greeting. "My sister is working on Broadway—well, off-off, actually—and, like, she says you are the top dog!"

Portia raised her painted-on brows till they almost reached her widow's peak. "Charmed." She didn't offer her hand, and rather than turning to leave with the eager girl, stood her ground.

Waiting for him to show her the trailer, no doubt. Quentin wanted to finish his discussion with Jack, the cinematographer, before he had to dress for dinner. The sunrise that morning had been a masterpiece of crimson and gold, and should nature cooperate by supplying an encore while they were camped on this mountainside above the sea, Quentin wanted to incorporate that in one of the next several mornings' scenes.

The symbolism of a golden new day worked well with the premise of *Permutation*. And along with refining the images of the film, Quentin wanted some time to ponder Amity's appearance and the mystery of who her Intervention target was. He had a hunch Mr. G had sent the artist to Mia and him for a reason, and it only made sense that her target was someone connected with *Permutation*. A cast and crew list could perhaps lend a clue toward solving the puzzle.

"Miss Goodhope, welcome." Mia had materialized so quietly Quentin hadn't even seen her approach. He smiled at her; she returned his smile, but to his dismay, it didn't quite reach her eyes.

Of course. She must have heard him agreeing to have dinner with Portia, but he'd make it up to her. He warmed just thinking of the magic hours of the night when the world left them alone and they found harmony in one another's arms.

Funny, but sex had always been sex for him, no more, no less. Good, great, sometimes not so perfect, depending on the woman. But with Mia, he found himself thinking in terms he might once have pooh-poohed as silly and romantic. He'd never known the peace that love and sex and spiritual completeness could bring until he'd fallen in love with Mia.

And he'd never known the emptiness he felt when all was not right between them.

"I want to make sure we have everything exactly the way you like it," Mia was saying, when Quentin jerked himself out of his reverie. "Thank you, Shawna, but I'll escort Miss Goodhope."

"Sure thing. Oh, would it be okay if I, like, got your autograph?" As she asked, the production assistant produced a small notebook and pen.

A Mont Blanc, Quentin couldn't help but note. Well, no wonder. The girl's father had at least three network commitments running at a time, and one or two usually ended up at the top of the Nielsen heap.

The question might have annoyed other members of the cast, but Portia warmed immediately. Placing a hand against the base of her swanlike neck, she cooed, "My autograph? Why, how flattering." She fluttered her lashes. With a gracious hand, very much the lady of the manor, Portia accepted the pen and scrawled her signature across the girl's notebook.

"What a lovely writing instrument," she said, recapping the fountain pen.

"Well, gosh, if you like it, it's yours." Shawna's face glowed. "I'd be honored."

Portia fingered the pen. "What a sweet young woman. What's your name?"

"Shawna Forrester."

Quentin spotted the look of interest in Portia's eyes and glanced over to check Mia's reaction. He caught her smile as they exchanged looks. Portia didn't miss a beat; he wouldn't be surprised to find her adding television to her repertoire within the year.

"You're not related to that naughty Will Forrester, are you?"

"He's my dad." Shawna looked around. "But I don't tell a lot of people. I'm, like, trying to make it in this business on my own."

"Oh, of course. I understand." Portia slipped the Mont Blanc into her purse. "Feel free to visit with me anytime. Perhaps you and your sister might like to come see me after I return to New York."

"Gosh! Wait till I tell her."

Mia made a slight rustling motion with the papers on her clipboard. "Perhaps we'd better check that trailer before it gets dark."

Portia looked down her nose at Mia. Quentin

bristled and opened his mouth to insist Mia join them for dinner, but before he could speak, Portia said, "Well, I do want to make sure I have everything I need for tomorrow."

Mia pointed to the path that led toward the lodge they were using as production offices. Shawna retired to the background, autograph clutched in both hands.

Apparently resigned to having Mia as escort, Portia gave Quentin a flirty wave of her hand and moved off with Mia, her maid and dog tagging behind.

To Quentin's dismay, he heard Mia say in a most un-Mia-like gushy voice, "If there's anything you want, anything at all, you just let us know. I've had the fridge stocked with caviar."

"Beluga?"

"Is there any other?" Mia said.

Quentin had to hand it to Mia. In the past two days she'd no doubt assigned someone to investigate Portia's tastes. And beluga! Of course Portia would go for the top-of-the-line stuff, something his frugal darling would never think of even sampling herself.

The little minx. Was she trying to help win Portia to the cause, or simply making him pay for casting the aging princess?

By the end of the first day of filming, Amity had pretty much figured out the moviemaking process. Each of the many people milling about like parade goers waiting for Zulu on Mardi Gras morning had a specific task. Actors, camera people, cinematographer, assistant director, gaffer, makeup, wardrobe—all played their assigned roles.

They might work for five minutes, then stand around drinking coffee or sipping Evian for the next fifty, but work they did.

The way they shot the same scene over and over again from different angles and with different cameras almost drove Amity nuts. She kept thinking what she'd feel like if she had to paint the same canvas three times. As spontaneous as she was, that would be the end of her. She could never, ever paint the same thing identically even twice.

Why, tourists who purchased the paintings she did in Jackson Square often commented that they preferred the unique look of her work to so many of the other paintings that looked as if they'd been turned out at a postcard factory.

Amity had figured out everyone's job except for one guy, a tall, broad-shouldered redhead dressed in black turtleneck, jeans, and boots, his face half-hidden by dark glasses. Again and again she returned to study him, noting a lot of the other women doing the same thing. The man seemed oblivious, cool and aloof, whatever thoughts he might be experiencing hidden from the world behind those dark glasses.

Given a cigar and a beret, the man would have fit in at any number of New Orleans coffeehouses. Amity wrinkled her nose at the thought. She loved her artsy friends, but most of them, she hated to admit, would never amount to anything. They dabbled, they played in an odd production now and then, they claimed to be writing novels as they bussed tables and emptied ashtrays in half the bars in the French Quarter.

But this man had to be some sort of VIP. He'd been given a chair beside Quentin. Perhaps he represented the studio. Or perhaps he was a mobster, a capo or lieutenant sent to oversee production from a studio that had borrowed from the wrong sort of financiers.

Amity got very excited about that idea, imagining the great number of innocent victims the mysterious man had buried in concrete. New Orleans had its own brand of Mafia types, and she'd grown up hearing whispered stories of such doings. But flights of fancy aside, this red-haired man didn't look as if he had one drop of Sicilian blood in him.

And Quentin seemed like a pretty down-to-earth guy, not someone who'd be taking money from the mob. The only fault she had found with him had been his chasing the dog, something she'd finally decided had been the result of miscommunication between him and the hapless schnauzer.

Just at that moment Quentin turned to her mystery man. She didn't catch the comment, but whatever he said sent the guy into a tizzy. He blushed, and his voice strangled in his throat. Just as Amity was about to pound him on the back, as she would a dog choking on a bone, he uttered, "Thank you."

Jeez! Amity drew back, her speculations shot to the breezes. This guy would probably turn out to be the studio head's idiot son. To Amity, for whom words and images flowed as naturally and unceasingly as the waters of the Mississippi, to have such trouble with the simple act of speech was incomprehensible.

She sighed, preferring the creations of her fancy to the reality, something that had gotten her into trouble more times than she could count. Oh, well, if she closed her mind to the man's stumbling attempts at speech, she could still get quite a good sketch of him, one she could work into some New Orleans–themed watercolors she'd been commissioned to paint as soon as she finished the chapel mural.

She hadn't drawn a thing all day and her fingers itched to touch a pen, stroke a pencil, hold even a stub of chalk or charcoal. She especially wished she'd fallen into this strange adventure with one of her small sketchbooks tucked into a pocket of her smock, but they must have tumbled from her pockets when the scaffolding had given way.

Amity liked to make her small sketchbooks out of rag paper. The process of folding and tearing the paper and arranging the pages, then prepping some with watercolor washes, pleased her and readied her to do what she called "preparing to see."

But all day long, every time she reached for a pen or pencil, Quentin managed to distract her with a question or an explanation of what was about to take place. For some reason, he didn't seem to want her to draw anything.

So Amity kept busy watching and listening, and it wasn't until after Portia Goodhope's dramatic arrival near the end of the day and the silly business with the snake that she thought of the redheaded man again.

And then only by accident.

She wandered into the rustic mountain lodge that bordered the clearing. Most of the building had been taken over as production offices, but the small dining room remained open to the occasional local who wandered in for a beer and a burger.

Amity still found it next to impossible to believe no one other than Quentin Grandy could see or hear her. She'd been so caught up in learning about the filming process that she'd neglected to experiment, something she'd promised herself to do to test Quentin's theory.

A theory which anyone would think ridiculous.

Though Amity had to admit she'd gotten goosebumps back in New York when she'd agreed to go to California with them, given one condition.

She had to call home and make sure someone cared for her animals. Quentin had placed the call for her, using his phone card, then when she insisted, handed her the phone, murmuring, "Don't be surprised if she can't hear you."

Breeze, her pal and next door neighbor, came on the line. Amity started to speak, and the woman, after repeating "Hello, who's there?" several times, hung up on her.

With a look that said "I warned you," Quentin redialed and upon reaching Breeze, relayed that Amity might not be home for a while and asked would she check on her pets. Breeze, always a brick, had agreed immediately.

Feeling weird just remembering that conversation, Amity pushed open the door of the Cubby Hole, its name scrawled on the weathered sign. With no one to talk to, she was lonely. At home she always had her family of animals. Spike Jones, especially, loved it when she talked nonstop to him. Fleezer thumped his tail, and Kitty Cassatt usually purred in agreement, as long as Amity kept up a rhythmic scratching of her ears. With Quentin gone off to dinner with Portia, she had only herself.

Unless . . . poised on the balls of her feet, she surveyed the almost empty room. Perhaps that call to Breeze had been some kind of fluke, a bad connection, or some such. Perhaps Quentin had been pulling her leg and getting people to pretend not to be able to see or hear her. Perhaps some local would wander in and the jig would be up.

A foursome she recognized as crew members sat at a nearby table, sipping Anchor Steam and chowing down on guacamole and chips. Amity made a face. How people could actually like avocado was beyond her. Give her a good crawfish dip any day, with a healthy-sized bottle of Tabasco on the side. She licked her lips, realizing she hadn't eaten all day. Or the night before.

She didn't bother with the crew. Quentin no doubt would have let them all in on his odd joke. Instead, she drifted over to the bar, a tipped over tree trunk with coats of varnish smoothing over any stray splinters.

"I'd like a Hurricane," she said. In New Orleans, mostly tourists drank the sweet concoctions of rum and fruit juice, but Amity, not knowing much about drinks, other than the jug bottles of wine her friends tended to bring over for parties, pulled the name out of her memory hat.

The man behind the bar reached for the VCR remote control. Chuck Roberts and the news of the day vanished, replaced by two brunettes and a blonde jiggling across a beach, waves kicking at their skinny heels.

Amity cleared her throat. "Make that a Bud," she said in a loud voice.

Charlie's Angels gave way to M*A*S*H. Jeez, didn't people make original shows anymore? Disappointed and feeling even more lonely, Amity turned away from the bar. The man wasn't just ignoring her.

Or was he?

Determined to answer the weird question once and for all, Amity swung back to the bar. With an agile leap, she landed atop the bar.

Click.

Without even glancing in her direction, the man

had switched to Vegas and settled back, his arms crossed, working a toothpick in his bottom teeth.

Amity waved her arms and wiggled her bottom.

To no avail.

She screamed, an outpouring of her lungs worthy of any actress.

The crew members chatted on; the man behind the bar switched the toothpick to the other side of his mouth.

Ever so slowly, Amity climbed down from the bar and backed away. She bumped into the hard metal edge of something and turned around to find a jukebox.

Music, she thought, checking the song titles, would at least keep her company.

But as soon as Quentin got back, she'd track him down and ask him just what in the heck was going on. She'd played along, traveled with him and his reserved bride to the other side of the country. But now, rubbing the gooseflesh on her upper arms, she wanted nothing but to go home.

Back to New Orleans. Back to safety.

The jukebox had selections ranging from Hank Williams to Iggy Pop. Amity felt in her pockets, but as usual, she came up short on change. Now that she considered the question of money, she realized she had zero funds. She was worse off than in the first days when she'd struck out on her own from the foundling home. Then, at least, she'd been able to live off her art.

And her agile fingers.

Out of long habit, Amity glanced around to see who might be paying attention. Then she laughed dryly. If no one could see her, no one would notice her pilfering the cash drawer.

The guy behind the bar continued to work his dental miracle, every so often checking the toothpick for results. Yuck! At least she'd learned a few manners from the sisters. Amity crossed the room and walked behind the bar.

As she rounded the corner of the massive tree trunk, the door creaked open and the redheaded guy strolled in—still wearing, she noticed, those dark glasses, despite the dim light of the Cubby Hole.

She hesitated. If no one else could see her, why would he be able to? She wavered, but decided against taking a chance. In her earlier, wilder days, she'd spent one night in jail and had no intention of a repeat performance.

Redhead seated himself at the table farthest from the bar. He lifted something onto the table, and out of curiosity, Amity forgot about the money and walked to his table.

A laptop.

Surely he'd take those darn glasses off now; then she could tell whether he was watching her. When he began to type without doing so, Amity couldn't stand it. She leaned across the table and pushed the glasses back on his head.

And found herself staring at eyes the blue of ultramarine, eyes that stared past her face and into her very soul.

She fell back a step, certain this man could see her.

"Excuse me," she said. "I don't know what came over me." No wonder he wore those glasses. With eyes that gorgeous, and framed with impossibly thick and silky lashes, every woman who crossed his path would be after him. Why, as long as the man kept his mouth shut, he could be Adonis.

The man blinked and looked at his screen, then across the room. He left the glasses on top of his head and continued to type.

She waved her hands in front of his face, back and forth between those incredible eyes and his hands that stroked the keys.

He continued to type.

Amity sighed, feeling lonelier than ever.

Each movement of her foot felt weighted with lead as she returned to the bar, approached the cash register, and slid it open just enough to slip her hand in. She wouldn't take much, as she didn't want to get anyone in hot water for being accused of dipping into the till. Tomorrow, she'd ask Quentin to pay her for her time and trouble.

She worked meticulously and quietly, easing the drawer open. Even if she was invisible, the movements of the cash register wouldn't be. Fortunately, the guy behind the bar at that moment stepped into the kitchen. Amity had palmed enough for four songs and a burger when she heard a noise behind her. The next thing she knew, a meaty hand slammed the drawer shut.

"Oh, no you don't, buster." Toothpick abandoned, the guy behind the bar glared at a shocked-looking Redhead, who also stood behind the bar, right at the cash register.

Amity, suspended between them, tried to figure out what was going on.

"You—you—d-don't think—"

The keeper of the till crossed his arms over his burly chest. "That's exactly what I think. I turn my back for a second and you try to slip over and help yourself. With all the money you movie types make, you gotta try and take it from us working stiffs." He shook his head and ground a fist against the palm of his other hand.

"B-but someone opened your d-drawer."

Amity hung her head, guilty as charged. And the poor guy was taking the rap for her. She believed in confessing her own sins. She raised a hand and pointed to herself, but the two men continued to argue.

Obviously, the man had glanced up from his laptop long enough to see the cash register drawer slide open. He'd come to investigate and been charged with the crime.

The door creaked open.

Amity turned to see Quentin's wife standing there, studying the scene behind the bar. Of course, all she could see were two men shouting at each other.

"Beetle?" Mia stepped quickly to the bar.

Beetle? Amity looked toward both men.

"S-sorry, just a mis-misunderstanding."

"That's a fancy way to call yourself a thief!" The guy behind the bar reached for the phone. "Tell that to the sheriff."

Mia reached out a hand and placed it on the man's fleshy arm. "I'm sure we can work this out among ourselves, Cubby." She smiled at him, yet her voice remained firm and businesslike. Amity had to admire her style, the way her low voice commanded respect without demanding it.

Of course, as producer, Mia ran this show, and Amity had a feeling Mr. Cubby Hole must be getting paid pretty darn well for the use of his lodge and grounds.

Cubby found another toothpick and let one arm drop to his side. "Miss Tortelli, I run an honest business here, and I'm not in the habit of twerpy guests helping themselves to my hard-earned cash."

"Who's he calling a tw-twerp?" Beetle, looking ready to take on the lug, ground his hands into fists.

"Beetle," Mia said, in a voice that sounded as if she'd rather be anywhere but the Cubby Hole and would do what it took to put an end to the scene, "we have a long day tomorrow. Why don't we go grab a bite down the road? My treat."

Beetle launched another glare at his adversary. "Only trying to . . . help." Beetle headed for his laptop, Cubby watching him every step of the way.

Amity noticed Mia pull several bills out of her wallet and lay them face-up on the bar.

Cubby chewed hard on his toothpick, then pulled it out. "Maybe I can see my way straight to overlooking this little hubbub, but I don't want to see his mug in here again."

"Mr. Leonard is part of this production, and as long as we're here, he'll be here."

The beefy guy stared at her, then nodded, none too graciously.

Mia added in a sweeter voice, "Oh, and I'll need a receipt for this, but I'll pick it up later."

Amity had to hand it to the woman, she knew how to handle a tough guy.

Beetle paused by the door and swung a searching look around the dining room, concentrating on the area behind the bar. Beetle's vivid blue gaze pinned her to the spot on the creaky floorboards. She knew that was a ridiculous feeling on her part, since he couldn't see her. Yet she guiltily shifted the money in her palm, now damp, to a pocket in her smock.

He stood there, his hand on the door, for what seemed the longest time, until Amity found herself wishing he could see her, if only long enough for her to apologize.

9 ~

The door of the Cubby Hole swung open, smacking Beetle's left shoulder. Mia stepped back in surprise, noting he scarcely flinched at the blow. They both turned toward the door, but no one came their way.

Beetle shrugged it off, while Mia heard herself saying, "If you really don't want to take much time for dinner, you're welcome to share a cup of soup with me."

Beetle shifted the laptop to his other hand. A smile crept onto his face. "Th-thanks," he said.

Mia didn't offer to feed Beetle out of selflessness, nor did she do it because Quentin was off with Portia. She did it because she sensed Amity's presence. If the invisible artist was interested in Beetle, Mia would keep him close.

Doors didn't open and close under their own power. Now that she thought about it, she'd lay odds Amity had been the one with her fingers in the cash drawer. Walking toward her cabin with Beetle in step beside her, Mia wished more than ever to be able to see the woman Quentin described. If only she had that power, perhaps she'd gain some clue to her presence.

At least Beetle didn't chit-chat. Grateful for that, Mia unlocked the cabin door. Still, a moment of wishing Quentin were there and Beetle tucked in his own cabin garnered a sigh from her.

"Something wrong?" Beetle asked, as he followed her into the cabin.

"Hard day, I guess."

He nodded and set his computer on the crowded floor.

Looking at the chaos, Mia wondered how she could have asked anyone, even a bachelor, inside. "Don't mind the mess," she mumbled, scooping an open suitcase off the orange velour chair before crossing into the tiny kitchen area. Always one to plan for emergencies, she'd stashed some instant soup in their gear.

"You don't have to feed me," Beetle said. Concern showed in his eyes. "You're being very kind and I'm being a bother."

Mia could hear her mother's voice echoing in her head. *Sit. Eat. It's good for you.* She laughed. "You're no bother at all. I enjoy your company. Quentin does, too, you know." He certainly didn't invite every screenwriter to sit nearby during filming.

Beetle colored at the compliment. Rather than taking the chair she'd cleared, he followed her to the bartop separating the kitchenette from the sitting area. "At least let me help."

Mia started to answer, then stopped when she

heard the door of the cabin squeak. Again, they both turned to the sound, but saw no one.

It had to be Amity.

Following them.

"I'll check the latch," Beetle said, already rising and covering the few steps toward the door. He jiggled the handle, then said, "Must have been the wind."

"Right." She could hear herself saying: *It's not the wind at all. It's Amity, the invisible woman who's adopted Quentin and me and who's driving me nuts.* Mia shook her head. "Must be the wind." She held two paper cups out. "Split pea or lentil?"

"Either one's fine with me." Beetle leaned an elbow on the counter but kept his body half-turned toward the door. He made a handsome picture, with the light casting a burnished halo around his hair, and Mia drew comfort having him between her and the door.

It was funny, Mia thought, as she found a pot in the cupboard and filled it with water, here she was, fixing dinner for another man while Quentin wined and dined Portia Goodhope. Life seemed topsy-turvy, and she wanted it right side up again.

A tiny sigh escaped her.

A sigh Beetle picked up on at once.

"If I'm imposing, just kick me out." He fixed her squarely with those marvelous eyes of his.

"Don't be silly, Beetle. Soup is no trouble at all."

"And you have to eat something anyway, right?"

She laughed. "Right."

"But not here, cooped in your cabin. You could be anywhere, driven in a chauffeured limousine."

"That's not my style, though."

"Because you're not used to it, or because you're afraid you might get used to it?"

"What a funny question."

"Is it?"

Again his eyes pierced hers. This man had a way of seeing too much. Too bad he seemed so down-to-earth. Mia would like to be able to put him first on her list of suspects for Mr. G's purpose in sending Amity their way. What better supernatural match than an artist sent to save a troubled screenwriter tormented by his ability to peer into the souls of others?

But everything she knew about Beetle showed him to be a fairly stable guy with his head screwed on straight.

Realizing she'd strayed mentally from their conversation, she finally said, "I'm not quite accustomed to the wealth and privilege this business takes for granted."

Beetle smiled. "Otherwise, I would never have met you in McDonald's."

"I guess not." Mia lifted the pot of boiling water and filled the two cups. Then, feeling rather silly, she found a third soup and poured water into it, too. Beetle would think she was making seconds. And if Amity was hungry, she would help herself.

"So, you're life is fairly stable, isn't it?" Mia might as well take the opportunity to check for

hidden land mines in his personal life. As much
as she hated to admit it, she wanted to solve the
mystery of Amity's presence before Quentin did.

Beetle accepted the spoon she handed him and
stirred his soup as he let it steep. "Stable?"

"You're doing a major picture, you've won crit-
ical awards, your star's on the rise."

He shook his head. "All that can evaporate in
one sunny afternoon."

"So no big head, huh?"

"You're only as good as your last film. Next
year could find me back in Cairo, teaching."

Mia thought of the cash drawer. Had he—and
not Amity—filched the money? "It's tough saving
up for the hard times, isn't it?"

He looked a little puzzled. Instead of answering, he tasted his soup. "Good. Thanks. Quentin's
missing a good dinner and great company."

"Why, thank you, Beetle," Mia said, flattered.
Funny how she'd never noticed other guys for
years. She'd been so focused on getting Quentin
to notice her, it was as if she'd been blind. Even
though she had no interest in any man other than
her husband, she'd be lying if she denied it felt
good to be the subject of male attention. Especially
from a guy as attractive as Beetle Leonard.

From her post near the door, Amity watched
Mia and Beetle sip their supper, wishing she could
materialize and give Mia a run for her money at
Beetle's attention.

True, it was now evident to Amity that Beetle

was a writer, a calling as suspect as musician or artist when it came to flakiness.

But to learn that he could teach, could back up his life with a serious, steady sort of job, well, that made Amity sit up and take notice. That, and the way he gazed at a woman with those dark blue eyes of his, letting her know she was the only female on the face of the earth.

Given what she'd seen and heard, it seemed expedient to Amity to call a halt to the time Mia and Beetle spent together. Edging toward the counter where Beetle lounged, Amity waited until he'd dipped his spoon into the half-empty cup, then reached and tipped it over.

As the thick green soup oozed onto the counter, Beetle stammered an apology. Mia grabbed a cloth.

Within minutes, Beetle had said goodnight and backed out of the cabin.

He had to return only twice, first, to retrieve his laptop; the second time, to thank Mia for supper and to apologize for making a mess.

Both times, Amity kept an eye on him.

"I hope you don't think," Mia said later that night, as she turned on her side to fit herself in her favorite sleeping position, spoon-fashion against Quentin's back, "I'm upset that you had dinner with Portia Goodhope."

He laughed somewhat nervously, a sound that upset Mia more than any words of denial could have. "It was business."

"Exactly." She stroked the curve of his hip. She knew exactly how to please him, how to drive him to distraction. Lying in bed beside him, that was pretty much all she could think about.

Almost.

"I understand business. Was she beastly?" She continued to stroke his warm flesh as she asked the question, continuing also not to tell him what really bothered her that warm August night. She also neglected, for what reason she couldn't name, to tell him she'd fed Beetle dinner in their cabin.

Quentin laughed and reached to pat her thigh. "Absolutely." He shuddered. "God, I hope I age gracefully and don't throw myself at sweet young things who could be my granddaughters."

"Well, if you do," Mia pinched his firm and sexy butt to emphasize her words, "your life won't be worth much."

He turned to face her, held her in his shielding arms. Softly, he said, "I have a feeling I'm already skating on the edge. If it's not Portia, what *is* bothering you, Mia?"

She blinked. She refused to acknowledge the dampness at the corner of her eyes, refused to give in to the weakness that made her love this man with all her heart. Hating herself for her own insecurities, she said, "Where do you suppose Amity is tonight?"

Quentin tipped her chin up. In the light that shone in their cabin window from the main lodge, she saw the caring in his expression. And she suddenly felt very, very silly, lying there worrying over an invisible woman when Quentin lay beside her.

He feathered a stroke over her forehead. "So that's what this is about?"

Mia gave a slight laugh and shifted on the lumpy bed. "Let's forget it, Quentin. Rack it up to the strain of finally getting this film under way." She kissed him, then said, "I'm absolutely, positively not jealous of a woman I can't even see."

"Hmmm." He kissed her again, a nibble on her lips that warned her he didn't believe her. Then, as he deepened the kiss and her body heated to his touch, Mia forgot about everything else but loving the man who held her in his arms.

In the cabin across the way, Beetle Leonard hunched over the scarred dresser, his fingers poised over the keys of his laptop.

Poised, but unmoving.

He stared at the knuckles of his hands, reliving the scene in the Cubby Hole. When he should be finishing a rewrite Quentin wanted for tomorrow, he sat there, unable to believe that he hadn't seen what he'd seen.

As a man of science, Beetle had been schooled in a concrete world. Unproved hypotheses were to be quickly discarded. Molecules, atoms, elements, quarks—all these behaved in predictable fashion. Or so the stoic lecturers in the halls of the University of Illinois would have all the poker-faced PhD candidates believe.

Yet something or someone had slid that cash

register drawer open and extracted four quarters and a five-dollar bill. Beetle had just reached the side of the register when he'd seen with his own eyes the money, for all practical purposes, walk out of the drawer.

He'd suspected a sleight-of-hand by someone hidden behind the bar. But before the burly keeper had nabbed him, Beetle had examined and found that theory lacking.

When the facts failed, Beetle tended to rely on his imagination. He might have maintained a summa cum laude grade-point average in his science studies, but it was scriptwriting that owned his heart and soul.

Considering he'd scripted *Permutation*, a story in which Ma Belle, a good fairy, inadvertently changes bodies with recidivist robber Moe the Biker, he was pretty much at peace with concepts that most people would label completely unacceptable.

He'd thought, more than once, growing up in his stable middle class home in stolid midwestern U. S. of A., that he'd probably been an orphan child left under a pumpkin leaf. Surely his phlegmatic parents had been given the wrong baby in the hospital nursery.

But his mother had assured him, before finally threatening to swat him on the behind for fabricating tales, that he was the direct issue of both Mr. and Mrs. Arnold Leonard, destined to teach science, destined to bring order and structure into the lives of otherwise unruly children.

Beetle, learning to keep his opinions to himself, thought otherwise.

It was about that time, at age twelve or so, that he found himself stuttering when called on unexpectedly in class or asked to recite the story of the Flood in Sunday School.

This tendency to stutter at moments of crisis or self-contradiction continued to plague him. Urged to pursue a teaching career, he did so reluctantly, knowing deep in his heart the tendency to trip over his tongue would provide fuel for laughter from students and serve only as a source of humiliation.

A wiser man would have remained hidden in a laboratory, but Beetle preferred people to test tubes. They fed his imagination so much more tastily.

It was his imagination he now fueled as he sat before the dresser in the rustic cabin. Thrilled to be on location with a major studio production, Beetle didn't question his scabby surroundings. He'd heard grumblings from other cast and crew members about the lack of refinement to be found at the Cubby Hole Lodge, but he paid it no attention.

He watched them all, safe behind his dark glasses, as he now sat and stared at his screen. Only, of course, he'd removed the glasses.

Quentin had asked him to reconsider the scene where Ma Belle first found herself transformed to the leader of the biker gang. He'd made the request in a respectful and tactful way . . . for a director, anyway. No beating around the bush, either, like that of the pseudofriendly director Beetle had worked with on his last small film.

Just a straightforward "I've thought and thought about this, Beetle, but I can't quite see Ma Belle accepting the change quite so easily. She may be a fairy godmother, but she's still human."

That statement, simply put, had set Beetle's mind to spinning. She might be a fairy godmother, but she was still human. Now, hunched over his keyboard, he started to grin. His fingers picked up momentum as he considered what he'd done wrong. Only a nuance, but Quentin had put his finger on it: people resisted change. People fought against the new and different. People didn't say, oh, so that's the way it is from now on, is it? Okay, pass the remote control, please, and the potato chips.

As he thought of exactly the right dialogue he needed to rescript the scene, Beetle gave a shout out loud. Nothing made him happier than when a scene worked right.

From her perch outside Beetle's open window, Amity jumped back. Goodness, he'd startled her! She'd been enjoying the sight of Beetle's bare back. Right after she'd crept up to the window, trying to think of a way to make amends for causing him to be called a thief, he'd stripped off the black turtleneck and bent over a computer set up on the mirrored dresser.

If Amity had thought him a likely subject for an artist's admiration before, it was all she could do to keep from slipping through the window to run her fingers over the well-formed muscles of his upper back, to trace the path of his backbone, vertebra by vertebra, to where denim swallowed up his golden flesh. She fixed her gaze on the spot where his jeans gapped at the very center of his back. She imagined tracing the path farther, could feel the heat rising from his flesh even in her mind.

For a second, Amity experienced a slight buzzing in her head, a fleeting moment of total disorientation. Was she studying him as an artist, or as a woman eyes a man? Thankfully, his shout rattled her out of her reverie.

Keeping her mind to her professional interests, she raised her gaze from his hips to the reflection of his face in the mirror against the wall. He'd settled into his work, typing rhythmically on the keyboard.

As an artist, she appreciated the composition of the scene. The angle of the aging dresser, the glare of the lamp, from which he'd removed the yellowed shade, the complementing shadow falling over the mirrored image of his face. All these parts presented themselves for what Amity saw as a study of creativity in motion.

She'd use swift strokes and bright colors. The whir of activity in Beetle's mind showed in the concentrated gaze of his fabulous blue eyes, and even more in the way a slight smile played across his lips.

Amity recognized that smile.

She smiled exactly the same way when a canvas came to life under her brush strokes. She often laughed to herself as the vision in her head appeared before her, whether on a ceiling, a canvas, or sometimes, on the back of a menu.

She smiled now, willing to bet this man had scribbled his own share of words on menus and napkins.

Beetle's hands ceased to move. He stared straight into the mirror. She met his gaze, marveling at the depth of his eyes, at the way they seemed to see through the mirror and beyond. Wistfully she lifted a hand and waved.

Beetle narrowed his eyes, shook his head, then pushed his chair back from the dresser.

Her shoulders slumped. It would have been nice to have a friend. And if Beetle could have seen her, she could have apologized for the trouble with the lifted money and for the impulse that had led her to spill his soup.

Oh, well. Amity wasn't one to worry much over what couldn't be. She watched as Beetle kicked off his shoes and noted he wore no socks, then her mouth formed an appreciative "O" as he unfastened his jeans.

He had his back to her, and darn, he'd moved out of range of the mirror. Still, Amity admired the finely honed buttocks, the thighs, solid and dusted with gold-tipped hairs, the muscled calves. He stretched his arms over his head and a flow of energy rippled from head to toe.

Amity shivered. She valued beauty. Part of her

wished he'd turn around, part of her hoped he didn't. What good was it to be able to look but not touch?

He stepped into what had to be the bathroom and in a moment Amity heard the shower gush on. Seizing her opportunity, Amity hopped through the window.

As she lowered her feet to the floor, she heard a ripping noise. Her smock had caught on the splintery edge of the sill, the hem wedged against the half-exposed head of a nail. She tugged, leaving behind a purple scrap, then walked over to the computer.

She wanted to see what he'd been writing. He'd seemed so happy, writing away, but right there at the end, when he'd stared into the mirror, Amity had gotten the sense not all had gone the way he'd wanted it to.

Leaning over, she read what showed on the screen. Before she'd read half the page, she made a face. No wonder he'd stopped. It appeared to be a love scene, the first time between a man and a woman. The problem was, he had the woman talking and acting exactly like the man.

Amity might have sworn off men, in despair of ever finding Mr. Right, but she knew she'd never acted that way, not even in the stupidest of mistakes she'd made with men. What woman really said, "Do me now"?

She shook her head. A man, yeah—a man would say that. Amity had known plenty of them for whom that line would be genuine. But a woman wanted kissing and stroking and sweet words whispered in her ear.

Maybe this was a way she could help him out, pay him back for causing him trouble.

Amity knew a little bit about computers from letting Tuggle Breaux sleep on her couch. Tuggle was a French Quarter regular who by day fashioned balloon animals for tourists and claimed to be writing the great American novel at night. He had a laptop computer which Amity had let him set up in her dining area.

Amity wrinkled her brow, trying to remember what he'd told her before she'd kicked him out for violating her no-smoking rule. He'd once claimed that the best thing a novelist could know was this special command. Whenever his stuff wasn't working, Tuggle had said, there was something he did to his keyboard and then he'd start over again.

Amity tapped a finger against her forehead. If she had a brush to hold in her hand, her memory always worked better. Deep in thought, she reached for one of Beetle's pens and used that to tap against the side of her head.

Meanwhile, she checked for the continued roar of the shower and thought about what the woman in the scene should say.

Then the command returned to her mind and she smiled.

Control-Alt-Delete. Tuggle had even made up a little rhyme which came to her now. When all that

I've written I find quite effete, I simply key in Control-Alt-Delete.

Amity leaned over the keyboard and found the right keys. Humming Tuggle's silly little rhyme, she hit the three keys simultaneously.

The screen went blank.

The bathroom door opened.

Amity gasped. Now she wouldn't have time to fix it for him!

She backed toward the window. Even though she was invisible, she somehow didn't want to be there when Beetle looked at the screen. It was just beginning to occur to Amity, as she clutched her tummy and wondered when she'd ever learn not to interfere, that Beetle might think "Do me now" were the most clever words he'd ever written.

And now they were gone from the screen.

Because of her.

She vaulted through the window.

A bellow rent the air. She turned to see Beetle's fists raised above his head.

"Oh, dear," Amity whispered, "I was only trying to help."

"Crashed!" Beetle stared at the screen of his laptop, unable to believe his eyes. "You miserable, moth-eaten mother of an excuse for a computer!" He kicked the chair and it fell to the floor, the bottom part of one leg giving up the ghost and rolling under the bed.

"Just when I'd done what I needed to." He slumped onto the bed, kicking himself. He'd fixed the scene Quentin had asked him about and gone on to consider what was wrong with his love scene when he'd stopped to take a shower.

He did some of his best thinking under a hot stream of water. The flow of the water over his scalp and down his body helped free the current of ideas. But only an idiot would have walked away from his computer after a successful rewrite before saving the changes to disk.

Which is exactly what Beetle had done.

"You idiot." Flopping back on the bed, still wearing only the towel he'd wrapped himself in after he stepped out of the shower, eager to fix the love scene, he stared at the water-stained ceiling.

And cursed himself for the fool he undoubtedly was.

The power in this misbegotten hideaway or cubby hole or whatever the heck they called it must have faltered. It would have taken only a moment to ruin his effort. Any interruption of power could have caused the machine to fail. He hadn't been running off the battery, hadn't seen the need to waste his reserve.

"You idiot," he said again.

Now he'd have to reconstruct his rewrite of the scene Quentin had discussed with him. And the brilliant inspiration he'd had in the shower regarding the love scene had completely fled his mind.

"What a night," Beetle muttered, rising from the bed. "First you get accused of thievery, then you lose your rewrite. Hate to think what'll happen next."

Then he laughed at himself. Two mishaps did not a disaster make. Puckering his lips, he managed to produce a few bars of a tune. Things could be worse; he could be preparing lesson plans for three sections of eighth-grade Earth science.

With a shake of his head, he repaired the chair he'd knocked over, then sat back down at the computer.

Amity's eyes widened at the sight of Beetle returning to work so quickly. Why, if someone had dumped her canvas and paints, she'd give herself at least an hour of temper tantrum time. She couldn't help but admire a guy like that. And now she owed him double the apology.

His red hair, damp from the shower, stood in clumps. A few drops of moisture sparkled on his back where he hadn't dried off completely. The towel around his waist inched lower as the movement of his hands over the keys gathered momentum.

Amity moistened her lips with her tongue. She thought of slipping back through the window. She'd only watch him work, admire his concentration.

Then the echo of his bellow of rage sounded in her mind. Maybe she'd better not. Perhaps she should leave bad enough alone for the evening.

Well, the least she could do was get the guy a soda. Fishing in a pocket of her smock, she found the quarters from the cash drawer and the five-dollar bill. Despite the fact that she remained invisible to everyone but Quentin, she did seem to be able to interact with objects.

As she fingered the bill, Amity realized how silly it had been for her to take cash for a burger she couldn't order when she was invisible. She could just as easily have waltzed into the kitchen and taken one for free.

If she'd done that, poor Beetle never would have gotten into trouble.

Yes, the least she could do was get him a Coke.

By the time she located the machine, fed in her quarters, grabbed the cold drink, and scurried back to Beetle's cabin, he didn't look quite so cheerful anymore.

He gnawed on a pen clamped between his teeth as if he wished he could grind it in two. He mumbled and muttered, a fierce frown on his face.

Amity winced. She couldn't help but recall the time she'd volunteered to return to the foundling home to help the sisters with the annual arts and crafts show.

She'd taken Spike Jones with her. She and the fifth graders had just laid out all two hundred pieces of red and green felt and applied the first layer of glue for the stockings they were putting together for the home's Christmas bazaar when one of the girls had pulled Spike's tail.

He'd barked, dashing about in a mad circle. Spike, being blind, had no idea of the havoc he caused as he ran across, then rolled in, their sea of red and green felt.

Amity giggled now, remembering the look of

horror on Sister Ignatius's face when she happened into the room as Amity was trying her best to gently remove the squares stuck to Spike's fur.

Sister had suggested in a trembling voice that Amity would never grow up and it would be best if she forgot all about helping with the bazaar.

Sadly, in disgrace once again, Amity and Spike Jones had removed themselves.

With a sigh, Amity pictured Spike Jones as she'd last seen him, barking at the thunder and charging the scaffolding.

She set the soda on the window ledge and knelt on the ground beneath Beetle's window.

Reliving the terrifying fall, she whispered, "What if I'm dead? What if the sisters were all wrong and I'm dead but I haven't gone straight to hell? What if I've been reincarnated?"

Then she shook her head. It made no sense at all to reincarnate someone and make them invisible. Besides, wouldn't she be someone—or something—else? Amity patted her pockets to reassure herself she was still Amity Jones. Who else would be carrying Spike's favorite dog biscuits?

The bushes nearby stirred in the evening breeze, the motion and sound bringing with them a sense of comfort to Amity. With trees and flowers as beautiful as the ones on this mountainside, she surely hadn't landed in anyone's concept of Hell. Or even Purgatory or Limbo or any of those chambers of torture.

No, she had her feet squarely on planet Earth. Trouble was, no one could see her size nines.

Except Quentin, of course.

Unable to fathom why that might be, Amity decided she'd best finish her task of helping Beetle. She rose and reached for the cola she'd left on the windowsill.

Only to find it gone. Eyes wide, she peered through the window once more. Beetle, looking more relaxed now, took a swig from the can, then placed it back on the dresser. The glare had left his face and he'd ceased to clench his teeth. So maybe she'd helped in some little way.

Amity only hoped, as she gave a wave goodnight and went in search of a place to bed down, Beetle didn't try too hard to figure out where the drink had come from.

10 ⌐

The sky hadn't lightened to much more than a pearly gray when Quentin first cracked open one eye. He hated getting up in the morning almost as much as he hated admitting he was wrong.

But this morning, he had a premonition he might be called upon to perform both tasks.

At the very least, he had to get up.

He also thought he probably ought to go on and admit, after last night's torturous dinner with Portia Goodhope, that he'd been wrong to insist on casting her.

But Quentin, stubborn to the end, had to see her in front of the camera. If she came to life the way he thought she would, he'd have to grin and bear the way she positively ogled him. Ogled, hell, she'd manhandled him last night.

In between trying to get into his pants, though, Portia had given Quentin two strong reasons to keep her and keep her happy. First were the occasional comments she uttered almost as an aside, showing she did understand her character, that of a man trapped in a woman's body.

And second, Quentin couldn't find a better candidate on the set of *Permutation* for miraculous intervention. Portia Goodhope, despite her successes, was pretty much a mess.

Quentin could taste his victory. He hoped to solve Amity's target and send her on her way. That, more than anything he could say to Mia, would prove to her she was secure in his love.

As much as he hated waking up, Quentin forced one eye open a tad more and reached to cradle Mia in his arms.

Snuggling up to Mia made waking up almost bearable.

But to his surprise, rather than finding his wife's sleep-warmed flesh, he met only a lump of rough cotton where the sheets had been drawn up to her pillow.

He and Mia always woke up together. Mia out of bed meant only one thing to Quentin: something else had gone wrong with *Permutation*.

With a groan, he thrust off the covers, both eyes wide open. He grabbed his bathrobe, then stumbled the three steps toward the sitting room of their cabin, the largest the Cubby Hole boasted.

Quentin stubbed his toe on the edge of a suitcase and swore. They could have stayed at one of the tony hotels down the road in Montecito, but Mia didn't see the point of the extra expense. That was Mia, saving money on an eighty-million-dollar budget. As for Quentin, he preferred being right on top of his location, rather than secluded in luxury that contrasted too extremely with the rough-and-tumble setting of the biker gang's camp.

Even now, Quentin thought, as he finally managed to poke both arms into the sleeves of his robe, Mia had probably gone off to take care of whatever problem had arisen. It would be just like her to let him sleep. He smiled, touched by her consideration. All the same, if *Permutation* were facing another crisis, no matter how minor, he wanted to be there.

No lights shone in the sitting area. The corner of a room that passed as a kitchen stood dark, as well. He frowned. Intent on finding out where Mia had gone, Quentin just missed the packing box from a laser printer, saving himself another wound to his toe by a millimeter.

What a mess. Stacks of scripts, computer equipment, luggage—all pretty much had been left where they'd landed. Quentin ranked right up there with most guys he knew when it came to housekeeping. Mia usually insisted on order in her working conditions, leaving their home the domain of the housekeeper. Here she had carved out one corner of the sitting room where her laptop and active paperwork sat in a neat stack. Elsewhere, chaos reigned.

Quentin stepped around the ugliest orange velour chair he'd ever seen and reached for the doorknob. He'd begun to turn it when it finally registered with him that Mia wasn't out solving a production crisis.

It looked a heck of a lot more like she was contemplating a personal problem.

She knelt, half-hidden by that shocking armchair, working her hands methodically through the contents of a suitcase. Her face scrunched in concentration, Mia didn't even glance his way.

He cleared his throat loudly enough to get her attention.

Then she looked up, her face every inch the sight of a deer caught in the headlights of a car. "I thought you were still asleep," she said, pulling the lid to the suitcase shut and standing up, a scrap of a garment clutched to her chest.

Quentin couldn't make out what she held in her hands. He gestured toward the suitcase, letting his expression ask his question.

Mia laughed in a silly way that didn't sound at all like his Mia. "I realized I don't have a thing to wear."

The chill in the floorboards had crept into his feet. Thinking of his warm bed, where the two of them ought to be, Quentin couldn't help the snort of disgust that issued from him.

Mia hugged her arms to her chest, a hurt expression on her face.

He should've swallowed the snort. Reaching a hand toward Mia, he said gently, "Come on back to bed and tell me about it there."

She hesitated. Not quite looking him in the eye, she said, "In a moment."

Wounded by her refusal, Quentin pivoted. Well, he'd go back to bed. As he swung around, his toe made contact with the metal hinges on a box of odds and ends.

"Dammit!" Stomping now, Quentin headed back to the lumpy bed. What had happened to his sensible, logical, predictable wife? Never once had he heard her worry over what to wear. She didn't even like shopping.

One of the reasons he enjoyed buying gifts for her was her tendency not to indulge herself. That had been half the joy in selecting the outrageously expensive sapphire and diamond necklace he'd bought her the other day at Tiffany's.

The necklace that still lay in its blue box, locked in his briefcase.

He hadn't given it to her that night in New York. Once she'd started that riveting striptease, all coherent thought had fled his mind.

Then, as soon as they'd gotten back to LA, he'd headed straight to Santa Barbara with Amity in tow, much to Mia's chagrin. But Mia had to stay over a day to tend to a production meeting with one of the studio's money watchdogs.

Screw Portia. Tonight he'd take his own wife to dinner. Over candlelight he'd give her the necklace. Then she'd realize nothing, but nothing, had gone wrong in their marriage, and maybe she'd quit worrying so much.

"Oh, dear," Mia murmured, still clutching the sheer black silk baby doll nightie she'd retrieved from the depths of her luggage. "So much for good intentions." She and Quentin slept naked, bodies entwined most of the night. The frilly, sexy, see-through sorts of lingerie she'd received as bridal shower gifts she rarely had a chance to wear.

But with the presence of this woman, someone she couldn't see and therefore felt incapable of competing with, Mia felt the need to fight the feminine with the ultrafeminine. Not normally an insecure person, she pondered being caught between Portia Goodhope, who treated her as if she were invisible, and Amity, who was invisible. No wonder her self-confidence needed bolstering.

Quentin so hated getting up early, she hadn't thought he'd awaken. With the shooting schedule they had to stick to for the next week, every day would find the alarm ringing way, way before Quentin wanted.

So she'd eased out of bed, thinking to don the nightie and slip back in without disturbing him. She'd been imagining the delight on his face when he saw what a picture she made.

But now, standing in the midst of the messy room in the wake of Quentin's irritated departure, the scrap of silk wadded in her hand only mocked her.

"Mia?"

"Be right there."

She stared at the silk, then bent and tucked it back into the suitcase. Somehow, the moment wasn't right. Perhaps tonight, or tomorrow, she'd try it again. As she rose, then moved toward the bedroom, Mia almost managed to laugh at her worries and fears. Quentin loved her, Quentin adored her, Quentin wanted her.

Then why did she feel so anxious?

Amity heard the high-pitched meowing of the cat even before she became fully awake. The insistent cries clamored for attention, repeating without stopping for breath. *Meow! Meow! Meow!*

The poor thing had to be starving—either that, or very spoiled, but in the years Amity had spent rescuing animals, she'd found to her sorrow that the abandoned far outnumbered the pampered.

She'd slept on a couch in the lobby of the Cubby Hole Lodge. As beds went, she'd spent time on worse. Glancing around for the source of the demanding mewing, she stretched, rose, folded the throw, and returned it to the back of the couch. Then she opened the front door. The volume increased, almost drowning out the jingle of the cluster of bells hanging from the lodge door.

Fortunately, no one appeared to see who had entered or exited. Amity stepped onto the porch of the lodge, intent on helping the crying kitty.

She spotted it, a short-hair with fur a velvety blend of cocoa, caramel, and off-white. The cat sat on the grass near the base of the lodge steps, continuing to speak its mind.

"Hello," Amity said.

The cat ducked its head, backed away a few feet. As soon as it had repositioned itself, the crying began again.

"You see me, don't you?" Retrieving one of

Spike's remaining dog biscuits from her smock, Amity broke off a piece and chipped at it with her nails till she had produced a reasonable-sized snack.

She settled onto the top step and held out her hand, offering the biscuit crunch to the cat. The cat retreated another foot, then crouched, eyeing her as if undecided on whether to accept her presence and gift of food.

As the cat began to inch forward, the door behind Amity flew open. The burly keeper of the toothpick and the barroom of the Cubby Hole stuck his head out and yelled, "Scram, you damn noisy cat! We don't feed strays here!"

The cat bolted to the bushes.

Amity whipped around. "You jerk," she cried, then remembered he probably couldn't hear her.

People who were mean to animals deserved to be punished. If she could speak to him, she'd sure give him a piece of her mind.

The cat cowered by an oleander bush, its head drawn back against its body, its eyes wide with fright, obviously expecting the worst.

The man remained in the doorway. Fishing a cigarette and lighter from his shirt pocket, he started to light up.

Hah! So what if she couldn't give him a lecture? Amity bolted toward him, snatched the lighter from his hand, and began flicking it while dancing it in a figure eight in front of the man's now bug-eyed face.

He dropped his cigarette, still unlit, and backed

away, hands held up as if to fend off an attacker.

Amity opened the door and chased him a few feet, laughing herself silly as he turned and ran, blubbering and yelling.

Then she pocketed the lighter and went back outside. It served the bully right. She hoped he peed in his pants.

"Guess you showed him."

Amity jumped. An old man in white overalls sat on the top step. Despite the summer day, he wore a cap with ear flaps. Bits of red fabric stuck out from the straps and ankles of his overalls. An unlit cigar hung from between his teeth. Large sunglasses, still with a tag hanging from the frames, covered most of his face.

"Who are you?" she asked, checking to make sure the cat hadn't run off too far.

"I could ask you the same question, ya know." He spoke without removing the cigar.

At least he could see her. That was a pleasant change, even though this old guy seemed pretty crotchety.

"That's what happens when you get old."

"Excuse me?"

"Old people tend to get crotchety."

"I didn't say—" Amity stared hard at the man. "Haven't I met you somewhere before?"

The man cocked a finger toward the grass beside the steps. "Your friend's coming back."

"Good. Don't scare her away. I know she's hungry."

"You always this nice to strays?"

Rather than answering, Amity trod softly down the steps, approaching the cat once more.

"Hungry?" Amity fingered the dog biscuit crumbs. "I know it's for dogs, and you're most definitely a cat, but it's all I've got at the moment."

The cat sniffed the air, then crept forward, legs crouched, obviously ready to flee again if necessary.

"I don't know what kind of people you've been hanging out with," Amity said in a low, matter-of-fact voice, "but I won't hurt you."

The cat cocked its head, then, with a less defensive posture, crept toward her hand.

Amity turned toward the old man. "All any stray wants is a little food and a lot of love. Or sometimes the reverse."

He grunted and bit off the end of his cigar. "And that's what you do with your life? A one-woman animal rescue squad?"

Amity shrugged. "Lots of people do a whole lot worse."

The old man nodded. "So they do." Then he laughed, a harsh cackle that caused the cat to jump back. "But that doesn't mean you can't do more than that!"

"Hey, who are you, anyway?" Amity wanted to yell at the man, but she forced herself to speak in a low voice so as not to scare the cat. "I'm here minding my own business and you're trying to boss me around."

"Maybe that's my job." He laughed again.

Amity narrowed her eyes. The old man looked familiar, but she couldn't place him. She looked at the cat, then back to the steps. "What more can I do?" The words fell off her tongue, but the old guy had gone.

Disappeared.

How very odd.

Wondering just how badly she'd hit her head in the fall from the scaffolding, Amity turned to coax the cat back to her side.

"That's amazing." About ten feet away, Quentin, walking with Mia, slowed to watch Amity coax a cat to her side.

"What is?"

Mia still sounded a little out of sorts. Despite the fact that she'd come back to bed and driven him over the edge in a frenzy of lovemaking, Quentin knew Mia was still troubled.

"Amity." Quentin jerked his head toward the grass beside the front steps of the lodge. "See that cat?"

Mia nodded.

"What a great picture! Amity is kneeling in the grass, wooing the cat with food. The ASPCA could use that for a poster."

Mia looked where he pointed, in time to see the cat edge forward, then begin to nibble at what appeared to Mia to be thin air.

Great, now the artist wasn't simply beautiful and talented, she was a poster child, too. Whatever he was up to, Mr. G wasn't playing fair. Mia sighed, and her spirits fell a little further.

No matter how hard she stared, Mia couldn't see the woman.

Instead, she created her own image. She pictured a willowy woman, at least five inches taller and five times more graceful than Mia could ever hope to be. She saw her lean toward the feline, the front of her blouse dipping to her waistline, revealing cleavage to die for.

One glance at Quentin's admiring expression confirmed her image more convincingly than a Polaroid. And to make matters worse, the woman wasn't only beautiful. No, that wasn't enough; she had to be a paragon of virtue, to boot. Dogs loved her, and apparently cats did, too.

Mia drew down the corners of her lips. "Very nice," she said, hating the prissiness in her voice even as she spoke the words. What she'd intended to sound brisk and businesslike came out snitty. "I'd better run," she added. "I've got tons of paperwork, and I'm expecting Randall this afternoon."

Quentin nodded, his attention still clearly fixed on the sight of his invisible Maid Marian of the animal kingdom. Normally Quentin would at least have reacted to Randall's name. He'd taken a strong and immediate dislike to the accountant the day Mia'd hired him, a reaction Mia did not understand.

Randall might be the dullest man she'd ever met, but Mia had yet to meet anyone who could equal his skill with figures.

"She'd be a natural as an animal trainer," Quentin murmured.

"See you later," Mia said, and strode toward the lodge, heading for the temporary on-site production office. In order to get there, she had to pass Amity.

As she approached the porch, the cat hissed and backed off a few feet. Even though she had nothing against cats in general, Mia made a face at this one and climbed the steps, treading on the outer rim of the stairs, on the edge near the railing.

Out of curiosity, she swept her hand in a broad arc, but she met nothing solid. Still, Mia had a weird sensation she was stepping on, over, or through the invisible woman.

Prickles ran over the skin on the back of her neck. She took the last step at a run and hurried inside. Even though she'd touched no one, she couldn't shake the feeling that Amity watched her.

And judged her.

How very weird. When Mia had been invisible before, both during their Purgatory adventure and on the day of their wedding, when she'd wished herself invisible, she hadn't appreciated how very odd it must have been for Quentin to be there beside her and unable to see or grasp her.

But he'd been able to hear her and to know when she was near.

If only she could hear Amity, she'd be able to size her up better, learn more about what they were dealing with. Neither she nor Quentin could afford to forget Amity had to have stumbled into their lives for a reason.

Mia paused inside the doorway and looked back outside. The cat had returned to the stairs and now sat licking its paw, then rubbing it over its face. The cat was kind of sweet. Mia had never had a cat or a dog, and now, watching the animal tidily groom itself, she wondered if she hadn't missed out somehow.

She'd started to turn away when she saw Quentin follow her path, then stop when he got to the steps. He sat down and the cat made no move to bolt.

Feeling like the last girl chosen for the dodgeball team, Mia squared her shoulders and headed for the production office.

Half an hour later, staring at a stack of computer printouts, the numbers wavering and blurring in front of her eyes, Mia let her mind light on Randall's scheduled meeting with her.

Normally she'd conduct her business with the accountant in the production office.

But today, she just might invite him to the set.

Randall, Mia decided, as she snapped the papers and prepared to read the budget sheets once more, planning this time to actually focus on the numbers dancing before her eyes, could earn his exorbitant fees in more ways than one today.

11 ⟿

"You expect *me* to wear these rags? We'll just see
what Quentin has to say!"

From forty feet away, Quentin heard his name
roll off Portia's tongue. A woman who had spent
her life in the theater knew how to project her
voice. Fighting the urge to clap his hands over his
ears, Quentin wondered what could possibly be
the problem now.

Dragging himself from a discussion with the
first assistant director, he turned and steeled himself for Portia's onslaught, a smile worthy of a
dental poster child planted on his face.

She barreled toward him as fast as a fifty-nine-
year-old woman in spike heels could barrel. "Oh,
Quentin," she said, with a flutter of her hands,
"just look what they've concocted! And they call
this a costume worthy of Portia Goodhope!" She
posed, one hand on a skinny hip, her head thrown
back.

Quentin studied the effect. Portia's role as Ma
Belle called for her to swap bodies with Moe the
Biker. That meant she dressed as a fairy god-
mother, but acted, spoke, and thought like the

rough-and-tumble gang member would.

Wardrobe had garbed her in a black silk shirt-waist that resembled a hotel maid's uniform, complete with a white bibbed apron and silver shoes with four-inch heels. Her rich chestnut hair had been covered with a purple-tinged white wig that turned her into everybody's grandma. As she strode toward him and the gaping crew, she wielded a silver-tipped wand, a wand she now had planted in the soil.

"Look at me," she repeated, and Quentin obeyed the command without his usual desire to object to her imperious way. Something was definitely off, but he couldn't put his finger on it.

From behind his shoulder, Amity said, "The uniform's all wrong."

"What do you mean?" Quentin asked aloud, without realizing Portia would think he spoke to her.

"What do I mean?" Portia's voice shrilled, the famous contralto quickly reaching high C. "If you have to ask, I don't think I should be working with your production, Mister Quentin Grandy!"

"Portia, please." He smiled at her, surprised to see the almost pathetically desperate look in her eyes. Portia Goodhope, insecure? Somehow that thought compelled him to treat her more gently. "I'm speaking rhetorically."

"Oh," she said, fluttering her lashes.

Under his breath, so only Amity could hear him, Quentin said, "What are you thinking?"

"No one, but no one, will buy a fairy godmother in a maid's uniform. Come on; you may be doing social satire, but you've got to flow in sync with the universal imagination. Fairy godmothers are beautiful, graceful, and alluring without being overtly sexual." Amity had cocked her head to one side and she waved a hand about as she spoke.

"Can you sketch that for me?"

"Is the Pope Polish?"

Quentin laughed.

"I don't find it funny," Portia said.

He kissed Portia on the cheek. "My dear, I know exactly what you mean. Why don't we just stroll over and have a nice cup of tea while Wardrobe does something much, much more appropriate?"

"Well!" Portia's shoulders relaxed by at least two inches. She collected the silver-tipped wand from the ground where she'd imbedded it. "I knew you were simply the best," she said with a purr, linking her hand into his arm.

At that moment, an older woman with wild red hair jogged into sight, then slowed her steps, hanging back a bit. Quentin knew the wardrobe woman wouldn't have shown up on Portia's heels unless she wanted to add her two cents' worth. And with Queenie Gillmore, that could be worth a lot.

"What is it, Queenie?" He smiled at the woman who'd joined his wardrobe team immediately following his wedding, on which day he'd been such a supreme idiot he'd gotten cold feet and almost not made it to his own ceremony. But thanks to Mr. G and the assignment he'd given Quentin and Mia, they'd met Queenie and her granddaughter Susannah, along with billionaire A. G. Winston and Jemi Dailey, now Jemi Winston, and they'd saved their own future.

Queenie had proved to be a whiz at wardrobe. A garment she couldn't create didn't exist. So Quentin bent an ear when she approached him.

"I know it's none of my business, Dutch," she said with a wink, using the nickname from his Arkansas adventure, "but I really don't think that uniform works out quite right on Miss Portia."

"Queenie," Quentin said with a return wink, "you're a genius. And in about"—he glanced toward Amity, body bent over a sheaf of papers and scribbling furiously—"oh, ten minutes or so, I'll have a sketch that I think will better serve our purposes. Got that sewing machine warmed up?"

"You betcha." Queenie smiled, and looking quite satisfied, headed toward the canteen, where she poured a cup of coffee and scrunched down on a bench with a satisfied sigh.

Quentin watched her, pleased to see her looking so well. Queenie and Jack Daniels had had quite a working relationship, but the first thing Queenie had done after relocating to LA with her granddaughter was to check into a rehab center. She'd come clean, and Quentin had been thankful ever since—to Mia and Mr. G and all the mysterious powers of life—that their paths had crossed.

The thought of Mr. G caused Quentin to smile.

Fortunately, Portia seemed to think the smile was meant for her. She gushed on about how she knew he'd understand, while Quentin let his mind return to a question that had been nagging at him.

Both times Mr. G had crossed his and Mia's paths, the old codger had been quite specific—overbearingly bossy, actually—about assigning them a person in whose life they had to intervene.

Amity stumbling across them in Central Park just didn't make sense. Mia liked to say things always happen for a reason, but for the life of him Quentin couldn't figure out how they were supposed to be involved in Amity's assignment.

An assignment Amity couldn't even name!

"A penny for your thoughts," Mia whispered quietly, stopping close by his side. Then she added, "Good morning, Miss Goodhope."

The actress inclined her chin, managing even in her unflattering garb the impression of royalty acknowledging a peasant. In a dignified voice, she said, "Quentin, darling, I'll be in my trailer. And I'd like to see the preliminary versions of the new and improved costume." She batted her lashes. "That is, if you don't mind."

"No problem. Thanks for being such a good sport."

She gave a tiny shrug. "I am a professional." She strolled off.

Quentin shook his head and reached for Mia's hands. Clasping them gently, pleased she hadn't remained holed up in the production office, he said, "I was thinking about Mr. G, and how strange it is to simply accept him."

"You mean rather than waste all your energy denying such a being could exist?"

She didn't pull her hands away, but Quentin didn't get the feeling she really wanted to be touched at the moment. Slowly he let go. He saw Amity stand up and wave her sketches. "Yep. Remind you of anyone?"

Mia stiffened. "Are you making some kind of point?"

"Maybe. Maybe not."

"If you're referring to Amity, I can assure you I believe she's here with us."

Mia's lips set in a pout and Quentin could've kicked himself. He hadn't meant to make Mia uncomfortable.

"Too much so, if you want my opinion," Mia added.

Amity had started toward them. Great! Just what he needed right now. But they had a cast and crew standing around waiting.

"I do want your opinion," Quentin said, "but not on that topic. Portia's wardrobe is all wrong. Do we shuffle the shooting schedule, or wait while we solve the problem?" Since Portia's character wore the fairy godmother outfit in at least two-thirds of her scenes, they needed to settle the issue, and fast.

Mia tapped her foot. Her eyes looked even darker than usual. "I don't like to say I told you so, Quentin, but I distinctly remember telling you two weeks ago that Francine May or any actress would look ridiculous in that maid's uniform."

"And what did I say?" With a sinking feeling, Quentin remembered his comment. He only hoped Mia had forgotten.

"If we scrapped Francine and went with Portia, the costume would work just fine." Mia's foot worked doubletime as she added, "And I quote, 'Portia Goodhope can carry off any costume.' "

"That's a pretty good memory you have there, my sweet."

"That's one of the things that makes me such a good producer," she said in a saccharine voice. "But perhaps you'd rather turn that job over to your new wonder woman?"

"Mia, you know I couldn't work without you. We're a team, indivisible."

Mia dipped her chin. The spiky top of her hair waved as she shook her head. "We're not working like a team. We're like two mules pulling in opposite directions. You didn't listen to me when I brought up the costume problem because all you could think of was how you wanted Portia." She lifted her head and fixed him with her gaze. Her chin trembled. "In the old days we would have fixed the problem together. You and me—then we *were* a team."

He reached for her hand. "I love you, Mia."

She pulled away. "I love you, too, Quentin, but I don't think that's got anything to do with this situation."

"Quentin, I think I've got it!" Amity bounced

up, beaming, and thrust several sketches at him.

Talk about timing. Quentin took the sketches from Amity. He jerked his head, hoping she'd take the hint and vamoose.

Mia reached over and fingered the sketches.

Quentin realized that to Mia, the sketches would have seemed to have appeared out of thin air. He waited, hoping she could ignore that and concentrate on the images.

She studied them a moment, then dropped her hand as if the contact scorched and cried, "I can see these, so why can't I see her?"

"Oops," Amity said.

"You're the one who always says things happen for a reason. Just try not to let her bother you."

"It's driving me nuts."

"And that's driving me nuts."

"Well, that's just too bad." Mia was glaring at him, but she looked more hurt than angry.

"Try to have a little faith, Mia. Both in me and in Mr. G."

"Oh, that's good, Quentin. *You're* the one who refused to believe we were in Purgatory after that crazy accident. *You're* the one who kept trying to find rational explanations for every phenomenon."

"Maybe I learned my lesson. Besides, you agreed that we had to keep an eye on Amity and try to figure out her target."

"That's easy for you to say. You can see her!" Mia's voice rose.

"May I say something?" Amity broke in.

"Go away," Quentin said with a growl and bent to pick up the sketches.

Mia's mouth formed an "O" of shock.

"It could be important."

"Not you." Quentin said, ignoring Amity for the moment and addressing Mia, "Her."

"I just thought you might like to know everyone is staring at you two."

Quentin swung around. Sure enough, he and Mia were performing for an avidly interested crew. The only two not keeping an eye on them were Hal Cormoran, aka Moe the Biker, and the hairstylist he'd been hitting on since he'd arrived.

Even Queenie, nursing her coffee, had an eagle eye fixed on them.

"Oh, great," he muttered.

Mia had turned to look, too. "How unprofessional," she said, "airing our laundry in public. Though," she added, drawing herself up to her full five feet four and a half, "if you and the cinematographer decided to argue, no one would look twice."

"I don't sleep with him," Quentin quipped.

"The last thing I want to be is fodder for the tabloids."

Quentin extended a hand. "Truce?"

She brushed his fingers and nodded, but the expression on her face left him unconvinced he'd won her over.

"I guess we'll finish this discussion later," he said.

"After you decide on Portia's costume?" Her voice carried an edge of challenge.

He looked down at the sketches. He'd forgotten he held them. Now he offered them to Mia again.

She glanced at her watch, then shook her head. "I've got to run. Randall's due in. I'm sure whatever you and Amity decide will be just fine." She turned on her heel.

Quentin let her go, watching after her as she strode down the path leading to the lodge. Something had to be done, and quickly. He couldn't stand to see hurt in Mia's eyes.

And he hadn't been kidding when he'd told her she was driving him nuts. It wasn't as if he was flirting with Amity. Jesus, Mia had to know she was the only woman in the world for him!

But as long as she felt threatened by the woman she couldn't see, until Amity figured out her mission and went on her merry way to fulfill it, Quentin knew there'd be trouble in paradise.

"Gee, maybe I should make myself scarce."

Quentin looked from Amity to the papers in his hand, then back to her. Shoulders slumped, twisting a long strand of free-flowing blond hair with a nervous finger, she looked almost as uncomfortable as Mia had looked hurt and angry. "What do you mean?" Quentin asked.

"Clear out of your life. Go back to New Orleans where I belong."

Had he been that stubbornly resistant to the facts of the situation when he and Mia had found themselves hovering between life and death? Not bothering to hide his impatience, he said, "You still don't get it, do you?"

"No need to yell at me. I'm not your wife." She sniffed.

"You're dead! Can't you get that through your head?" He slapped the papers against his thigh, and added to emphasize his point, "D-E-A-D."

Amity backed away, eyes wide, one hand over her mouth. "You're crazy. I mean, I understand something weird is going on, but there's no way I'm dead." She pinched her wrist. "See, it's me. Flesh-and-blood Amity Jones." She darted her head from side to side as if seeking something. "If I were dead, who would take care of Spike Jones and Fleezer and Marvel and Jean LaFluff and Kitty Cassatt? And the babies?"

"Babies?" This was a side of Amity he hadn't considered.

"Kittens," she whispered, clutching her belly.

Kittens! Quentin started to tear at his hair when someone tugged at his arm.

"Dutch, it's me. Queenie." She held a steaming cup of coffee out to him.

"Thanks," he said, and took it.

"You've been working real hard." She peered at him. "Maybe too hard?"

He didn't need any more rumors circulating about the state of *Permutation*, especially not stories that said the producer and director were engaged in shouting matches. Not that Queenie couldn't be trusted. "Any couple can have a difference of opinion, Queenie."

She nodded and scratched at her red hair, which despite her calmer lifestyle continued to stick out at odd angles. "But usually when the woman walks away, the man don't stand there and keep on arguing."

Quentin stared at her, then laughed. Amity would be the death of him! "Guess it looked pretty odd, me acting out that scene just now." He hated to tell a story like that to Queenie, both on principle, and because with her country smarts, she'd probably see right through him.

"Looks to me like you was shouting and carryin' on 'cause you couldn't let go of whatever it was you were fighting about." She drained her coffee cup and fastened her birdlike eyes on him.

He sipped his coffee. "Nah, just thinking out loud. I do that sometimes. Matter of fact, that's what got me thrown in jail back in Dalton."

"That day we met?"

He nodded.

"And all this time I thought you was drunk that day."

"So the officer thought, too." Quentin smiled a bit at that memory. That day, Mia had been the invisible woman in his life, and he'd been trying with great frustration to make love to her in a parked car.

"Hmm." Queenie didn't sound too convinced. Then she pointed at the papers in his hand. "Are those the new costume sketches?"

Thankful she'd let the topic drop, and reminding himself to speak to Amity only when unobserved, Quentin gave her the sketches. With all the time he'd spent arguing, he hadn't even glanced at the designs.

Queenie started grinning and nodding.

Quentin pulled the papers back and stared in admiration. Rather than the tongue-in-cheek image of fairy godmother as maid, Amity had whipped out sketches of an outfit that captured the ethereal along with the sexual. Moe the Biker would be caught in a woman's body and garbed in a not-quite-sheer flowing robe that Quentin could see was designed to shift with every movement of the body. Rather than being hidden behind a white bib, the breasts were framed by crisscrossed ties that drifted and floated into the body of the calf-length dress. The feet were bare, something that struck Quentin as especially brilliant. Moe the Biker's feet would be as tough as truck tires and he'd have to adjust to walking barefooted in skin as soft as parachute silk. "These are terrific! Amity, you are brilliant!"

He turned to her, but she'd gone.

He groaned. Queenie patted him on the arm. "The first year of marriage is the toughest. Just take it a day at a time," she said, plucking the papers from his hands. "I don't know who in the devil Amity is, but I do know I've got me some work to do."

12 ⌒

"So, Horace," Mr. G said to the sweetly smiling celestial being hovering across the table from him, "what brings you to my part of the universe?"

"Oh, you know," the blue-eyed angel said, "just things."

Mr. G nodded and puffed air out of his cheeks. "Nobody comes snooping around Purgatory from your part of the globe without a reason. You wanna tell me straight out?"

"Perhaps I could have some cocoa first?"

Mr. G barked a laugh. "Living on the edge there, Horace?" He waved a hand at his housekeeper, who produced a mug of steaming chocolate. "Guess they don't let you have that stuff in heaven."

Horace managed a prim shrug. "We don't really feel the need for stimulants there."

Not for the first time, Mr. G thanked his lucky stars he'd gotten the Purgatory assignment. "So now you wanna tell me what brings you down my way?"

A rim of chocolate on his mouth, Horace said,

"You've been playing fast and loose with one of our special interest subjects."

"Me?" Mr. G laughed, a hearty cackle that shook Horace's flimsy wings.

"Yes, you." Horace patted his mouth with the back of one hand. "You never *did* know when to draw the line."

"Now, wait just a minute. You want to start that argument again?" Mr. G stared at the younger being, wondering how they could have come from the same family.

"Oh, I suppose not. Anyway, I'm here to tell you that you'd better quit breaking the rules where Amity Jones is concerned. Her accidental death occurred while she was engaged in spiritual work, and that puts her under our special-interest watch."

"Guess you guys never took a look at that mural, eh?"

"Judge not, lest ye be judged."

Mr. G rolled his eyes. He hated it when his brother quoted scripture to him. Horace did it only when he couldn't think of a more clever tack. "I don't see why what I'm doing bothers you guys. Every rule I'm bending is designed to help her find her way out."

"But you know as well as I do she has to do it on her own. That's just the way things are."

Mr. G picked up his cigar and planted it between his teeth.

Horace made a face.

"Drink your cocoa. I'm thinking."

As usual, Horace did what Mr. G told him to.

"You're telling me if I interfere too much, Amity's in more trouble than she's in now, wandering around lost with no idea how to save herself?"

Horace nodded.

"Hmmm."

"So you'll behave?"

Mr. G shrugged and lay his cigar back on the table. "When you ask so nicely, what other choice do I have?"

"Good." Horace drained his cup. "Perhaps you're getting more sensible with age."

Mr. G rose and ushered Horace from the table. "Give my best to the old man," he said, pushing Horace gently out the door.

Frowning, he reclaimed his cigar and considered what to do about Amity Jones.

Amity didn't really know where she planned to go. But as her long legs ate up the blacktop lane leading away from the mountainside lodge, she didn't really care.

Clearly she was nothing but a thorn in the side of Quentin and his bride. Amity hated to get in anyone's way. A loner for a long time now, she preferred striking out into the unknown to hanging around the only person who could see her.

So what if she was invisible? That meant she could catch a plane, train, or bus back to New Orleans and no one would be the wiser. She'd learned her lesson last night, with the fiasco over the cash register and she didn't intend to repeat it. No need to steal money; she'd simply help herself to whatever she needed.

"Meeooow!"

Amity stopped in her tracks. Glancing in the direction of the cry, she spotted the cat she'd fed only that morning.

The cat bounded toward her, its fear of her gone.

"Hey, there, you remember me?" Amity bent down by the side of the road and held her hand out. The cat pranced forward.

"You aren't so shy, after all, are you?" Amity stroked the fur, noting the cat needed a good brushing. "Probably a flea dip, too," she murmured.

The cat nudged Amity's ankle with the side of her face.

"Marking me with your scent?"

Suddenly the cat paused and glanced around, ears alert.

Amity made a quick survey of the same territory, but saw nothing to alarm the animal.

"Meow!" The cat cried loudly and arched its back.

Puzzled, Amity looked around again. She knelt down beside the animal and noticed its pupils had widened. "You look like you've seen a ghost."

"Nah, just me." The old guy who'd appeared on the porch steps walked from behind a tree at the edge of the lane.

"I do wish you'd quit following me." She

stroked the cat, realizing the animal didn't mind the man's presence.

The old guy shrugged and pointed at the cat. "You're not going to run off and abandon that scrawny excuse for a feline, are you?"

Amity rose and looked down the lane that led away from the movie location and eventually back to New Orleans. She thought of her animal family, uttering a silent prayer that Breeze was caring for them as she'd promised. August was storm time in New Orleans, and poor Spike Jones would be missing her something awful.

The cat, calmer now, rubbed against her ankle.

Facing the man, her hands on her hips, Amity said, "What's it to you if I do?"

"I don't think you can do it."

Amity looked down at the cat, still rubbing itself back and forth against her ankles. "No, you can't come with me," she whispered.

The kitty mewed softly, and standing on her hind paws, stretched her front paws up toward Amity's knees, looking every bit as if she were asking to be picked up.

Amity looked from the cat back to the old man. Feeling rather foolish, she stuck her tongue out at him, then bent and cuddled the cat to her chest.

The old man smiled. "At least you're consistent."

"Oh, you don't understand anything." Amity glared at the man, wishing he'd go away and leave her alone. As much as she'd longed to be visible, she didn't much care for this guy's company.

"Is it my looks?" he asked.

She stared. "You can read my mind?"

"Or maybe my cigar?" He plucked it from his teeth. "Lotsa people don't like these things. They help me think, though."

Amity backed away. "Who are you?"

The guy shrugged.

And disappeared.

Clutching the cat more tightly, Amity hurried back down the lane. She seemed fated to remain here at least a little while longer.

If Beetle hadn't gone for a run that morning, he'd have collapsed. He'd stayed up most of the night, fighting his frustration and recreating the scene that had flowed so easily the first time he'd written it.

Exercise usually helped to keep him from giving in to fatigue, so even though he'd overslept, he drew on his running clothes and slipped out of his cabin. The scene he'd rewritten wasn't scheduled to be shot until late in the afternoon the day after next, but he needed to go over it with Quentin before that.

Gaining speed and finding the rhythm of his stride, Beetle turned out of the lodge proper and onto the blacktop road that led to the highway. This morning he'd only go down the lane and back, then rush to shower and change. He'd packed light, bringing only black clothing in the vague hope that he'd look very "Hollywood" and fit in with everyone else.

Having only worked on small-budget stuff before, he had to admit he was insecure in the Grandy-Tortelli world. Even though he'd met Mia in McDonald's, his regular stomping grounds, he just knew that had to have been a once-in-a-year dining experience for Mia Tortelli.

It didn't make sense that a woman who produced eighty-million-dollar pictures made a habit of eating fast food or of hanging out with starving writers who dressed in castoffs from the Army-Navy surplus store.

Until he'd gotten the first check for *Permutation*, Beetle had been down to his last $31.26.

Cautious, almost unable to believe the change in his fortune, he'd banked the check, withdrawing only for bare essentials. With all the problems *Permutation* had experienced, Beetle figured he might not see another check of that size again in his life. People in the industry were quite superstitious. Once you were associated with a flop, you could pretty much hang it up. Unless, of course, you just got lucky or your daddy happened to own the production company.

Trying not to think past the immediate moment, Beetle pumped his arms and legs and breathed deeply. The Santa Barbara air filled his lungs and made him wonder how he'd put up with Los Angeles for as long as he had. Surely he could find somewhere else to live and still pursue his dream of writing, writing, writing.

But those were worries for tomorrow, and as one of his wise uncles was fond of saying, "Tomorrow never comes." He threw his head back, feeling freer than he had for days, and drove his legs into a sprint. Flying, flying, he covered the lane in no time at all.

Where the drive met the highway, Beetle slowed, circled, and returned, this time at a more moderate pace. He'd been running so fast the trees and bushes on either side of the lane had been a blur. They were so pretty, it was a shame not to soak in a little of the beauty of the mountainside.

He'd made it about halfway back toward the lodge when he saw the cat.

Naturally, Beetle had read *Alice in Wonderland* and *Through the Looking Glass*. He'd even memorized *The Hunting of the Snark*.

But what faced him, chest high, making its way up the lane without moving a paw, couldn't exactly be called a Cheshire Cat.

Beetle backed away at first. Then his curiosity and scientifically inquiring mind joined forces to drive him forward again.

The cat flattened its ears and hissed.

It struggled, almost as if it were trying to free itself from someone holding it.

The only thing was, the cat hung in mid-air, unsupported.

Breathing a bit heavily, Beetle slowed to a walk and stared at the animal.

He tiptoed closer and the animal spat at him.

Beetle sneezed.

And sneezed again.

The cat flung itself to the ground and hightailed it up the lane, back toward the lodge.

Beetle stopped, scratched his head, and wondered what in the hell had gone wrong with his mind.

Floating money.

Levitating felines.

Hmm. He considered the failure of his computer last night, but rejected the idea some gremlin had been at work there. He, stupidly enough, had neglected to save his work. He'd brought that fiasco down squarely on his own head.

But the cat!

After a glance around, Beetle moved in a slow jog back toward his cabin. Something weird was happening, but something worse would happen to him if he didn't show up in time to discuss the rewrite with Quentin.

Reality ruled over fantasy.

Or whatever tricks his mind had found to play on him.

Mia smelled Randall Hollings before she saw him. He must have bathed in Grey Flannel cologne. Wrinkling her nose, she rose to greet the accountant.

Randall extended an arm clothed properly in lightweight summer wool, with a crisp French cuff peeking out. No one could criticize his blue-and-gray striped tie, but Mia thought his neat, short haircut a trifle too boyish for a man in his mid-forties.

And the cologne!

"Good to see you, Mia," he said, shaking her hand, then settling his briefcase on the floor. He lowered the laptop case from his shoulder and looked about to open it before Mia lay a restraining hand on his arm.

"Let's not get straight to work today, Randall," she said, hoping her olfactory senses would adjust or deaden.

His eyes opened wide and he looked at her as if she'd suggested he dump all his shares in Microsoft. "As the client, you're the boss, but you know my hourly rates."

She did, and the price of teaching Quentin this lesson stung her cost-conscious self. In what she hoped was an appealing gesture, Mia swept a few strands of hair back over her neck and said, "I thought you'd like to visit the set. You work so hard, you rarely get to see moviemaking up close."

She threw in a quick flutter of her lashes, knowing that when it came to flirting, she had little or no practice. She'd been in love with Quentin for so long, she'd never bothered practicing her wiles. And before Quentin had realized he loved her, too, they'd had such a down-to-earth working relationship, Quentin would've thought she'd flipped had she tried to flirt with him.

With a funny, clutching feeling tugging at her heart, Mia remembered that she'd never been

Quentin's type. And reading between the lines of his descriptions of the invisible Amity, Mia had concluded that the artist matched the mold for all the willowy blond bimbos in Quentin's past. Mia gazed into Randall's eyes and fluttered her lashes harder.

He blinked a few times, revealing eyes that weren't bad looking. They were set perhaps a trifle too close together, and the blue lacked intensity, as if someone had washed his eyes and wrung them out too hard, but Randall would do for her purposes.

Mia had to feel just the teeniest bit guilty, because she'd suspected during the time Randall had served as their accountant that he had a slight crush on her. Using him to make Quentin see how unfair it was for him to pay so much attention to Amity might raise hopes in Randall she had no business raising.

Crushing her conscience for the first time in her well-ordered life, Mia took a deep breath, smoothed the skirt of the sleeveless sundress she wore and steered Randall through the door.

At that moment, she experienced a flash of insight into Malcolm X's meaning of the phrase "by any means necessary." He'd been fighting for his life, just as she was fighting for hers.

"The financials are working out well for the last quarter," Randall was saying, as they stepped onto the porch of the lodge.

Mia remained too much of a businesswoman to ignore that statement regarding the corporation

Randall had set up for her and Quentin. "Retained earnings okay?"

He nodded. "I've also brought along a few suggestions on sources of funding for that movie you've been talking about financing."

"*Kriss-Kross*?" She gave him what she hoped was a dazzling smile. "You're brilliant, Randall, darling!"

He blushed. "But I haven't described them to you yet."

Mia wondered how this man ever got a date, as slow as he was on the uptake. She patted his arm. "But I'm sure whatever they are, they're brilliant if you found them."

He looked confused for a second longer, then he practically preened. "Why, thank you, Mia," he added in a deeper voice, uttering her name as if it carried special significance.

At least the fresh air had lessened the impact of his cologne. If he continued to exude that aura by the time they reached the location site, Quentin would know Mia was only trying to get his goat by flirting with Randall. He knew how much she hated overdoses of any fragrance.

Mia managed to prattle about the scenery as she steered Randall in Quentin's direction. She was dying to ask the accountant about the funding for *Kriss-Kross*, but she couldn't bring herself to do that until she'd settled this tiff with Quentin.

Kriss-Kross was their movie, and neither one of them would be bringing it to life if the two of them didn't figure out why they no longer worked together without constant turmoil.

So she chattered on, switching from flora and fauna to Portia Goodhope, whom she described as "rather full of her own importance."

"My mother says Miss Goodhope is the best actress Broadway has ever seen," Randall responded.

"Oh, really?" Mrs. Hollings wrote the theater column for *TinselTown News*. Mia tried to hide her annoyance at hearing this opinion. What did people see in the woman?

Randall nodded. "Oh, yes. Mother says her domination of the stage is absolute."

That sounded like an expression the well-known columnist Penny Hollings would wield.

He cleared his throat. "Would it be an imposition for me to ask for an introduction?"

Mia thought of the way the grande dame looked through her, over her, or around her. "I am the producer," she said, managing a quick smile. "That will be no problem at all. Besides, Randall, your wish is my command."

He slowed his steps, studying her face. "There's something different about you today."

Mia giggled. "Different? How?" Even as she spoke, she hated the way she sounded. Phonier than a fiberfill bra. She despised herself for trying to sink to—no, below—Quentin's level.

Quentin hadn't wished Amity into their lives, hadn't asked to be the only man who could see, and appreciate, her.

"It's not my place to say this," Randall continued, turning to face her, "but are you and Quentin quite happy? I mean," he added, catching her hands and clutching them to his heart, "is it possible I may still have some hope?"

Now she'd done it! Mia tried to ease her hands free, but he'd bent his head and started kissing her knuckles.

"You know you're the woman of my dreams." Kiss, kiss. "You balance your checkbook." Kiss. "You understand mutual fund accounting." Kiss, kiss. "You even understand Rule 10b-5!" Kiss, kiss, kiss.

He gazed into her eyes, his own so much like a sick puppy's that Mia thought she'd be ill.

"It broke my heart when you married Quentin."

"Please," Mia said. "Stop."

"No, no, hear me out!" He dropped to his knees. "I've kept my silence long enough. How can a man like Quentin Grandy make you happy? His head is in the clouds. He'd never make a movie without you guiding him every step of the way. Plus, he's your complete opposite!"

Randall grasped her hands even tighter. In a whisper, he said, "I've no right to ask this, but leave him. Marry me. Just think what two minds like ours can accomplish!"

Mia suddenly had to suppress an urge to laugh. No doubt she'd turned hysterical, but the sight of Randall, his wool trousers planted in the dusty path, a bald spot she'd never seen before glinting in the sunlight, his lips smooching on her knuckles, all added up to a seriocomic scene.

A scene she'd instigated by her plans to use him.

"Randall," she said gently, "please get up. I'm flattered, but I think it's best if we just forget this ever took place."

He sighed and climbed to his feet without releasing her hands.

Mia tugged one hand free. She should have known better than to play such a stupid game. Quentin hadn't even seen her and look at the mess she had created.

"If only I'd spoken sooner," Randall said, gazing woefully at her. "But it's my nature to line up all my ducks in a row before acting."

"Randall, you and I never even went out on a date." Mia was beginning to get frustrated with the man. She'd suspected he had a crush on her, but she'd had no idea he was this smitten.

"I've never been impetuous."

She smiled. He had that right, which was one of the reasons he made such a great accountant. He thought every move through thoroughly. "I know the right woman will come along for you. And you should know I love Quentin . . . with all my heart."

He scowled. "But I'd take care of you. Besides, I need someone to love, to pamper, to idolize!"

She tried slipping her hand free. "I don't need anyone to take care of me. That's not why I love Quentin."

"Then why—" Randall broke off as swift footsteps approached.

Beetle Leonard swung into view. He paused as he came up to them and looked back and forth between Mia and Randall, his expression hidden by dark glasses.

Mia wanted to sink through the ground. Just then, Beetle extended his hand to Randall.

"Jeffrey Leonard. And you are—?"

Randall had no choice but to drop her hands as he introduced himself to Beetle.

Flexing her fingers, Mia threw a smile of thanks at Beetle. Rescued! And she wouldn't be so foolish a second time. She'd march straight up to Quentin and insist on talking things out.

No matter if the delay cost them budget overruns, *Permutation* could wait.

13 ~

The damn frog refused to sit still.

Titters broke out among the crew, and the animal rights representatives cast glares all around. They took their jobs of monitoring animal treatment seriously, an attitude Quentin generally respected.

But at this moment he'd be happy to sauté this frog's legs right out from under him.

The shot shouldn't have taken long. Perhaps they should have done it in the studio, as Mia'd suggested, rather than out here on location. Maybe the contrary critter kept leaping off its mark to go in search of its wild cousins. But Quentin had wanted the shot of the frog taken with the biker gang's hideout in the background.

So much for being a purist. Now Quentin could only mutter curses at the frog and wonder why Friar Johnson couldn't control his animal.

The wizened old man, his features a cross between Apache and African American, had the reputation as the best animal trainer in the business. Now he walked toward Quentin with something that might have been a smile on his weathered face.

"What's the deal?" Quentin snapped the question.

The old man squinted at him and tugged on his ponytail. "Can't say."

Quentin wished Mia were there so she could tell him just how much this juvenile delinquent frog and taciturn old man were costing them.

But no, she'd trundled off to meet with their boy scout of an accountant.

And where was Amity? He'd be willing to bet Amity could coax that frog into sitting still long enough to settle the tiny crown on its head and shoot the creature from three camera angles.

And if she couldn't sweet-talk the frog into it, she could hold him down. Being invisible, as Mia had pointed out during her own undetectable stint in Arkansas, came in handy.

"Take ten," he called, and turned on his heel.

He'd been almost relieved when Amity had disappeared earlier that morning, telling himself that as Mia always said, some things were meant to be, and clearly it had been time for Amity to—poof!—vanish.

But now he wanted her help.

Needed it.

"Amity," he called softly, once he'd made it to a path out of sight of the crew.

"If you're here, come on back. Please!"

No response, not even a rustle of leaves in the still summer air.

Quentin kicked at a stone and missed, nearly tripping.

That was when he heard Mia's voice.

The sound came from just around the bend.

He quickened his step, then halted when he heard a man speaking.

Quentin scowled. He had no reason to; Mia might be speaking with any of the fifty or so men hired by their production company. But their argument, followed by the frog's refusal to cooperate, had put him in a contrary mood.

Tiptoeing forward, he peered through a screen of wild rosemary. His nose filled with the acrid yet somehow sweet scent as he listened to none other than their numbnuts accountant declaring his love to Mia.

His first impulse was to roar forward and knock the man's capped teeth out of his head.

But his pride got to him.

Without waiting to hear another word, he reversed his steps, fuming and cursing. How dare Mia fuss and fret over his being friends with an invisible woman when all the time she and the accountant . . .

This time Quentin kicked a rock bigger than his whole damn foot. "What did you expect, you big jerk?" He smashed one fist against the other, turned to confront the two of them, then swung back toward the set. Mia, with her love of order and figures, rules and budgets, would naturally be happier with a man like Randall.

But with feelings for the man, how could she have married Quentin?

Perhaps she felt she had to, after they'd won a second chance at life. Mia lived with enough superstitions to fill a trunk, and she might have thought she was meant to marry him.

He ground his teeth and wondered how he could worry over filming a frog when his whole life had just fallen apart.

"Dutch?"

Quentin lifted his head. "What, Queenie?"

"I came to show you the costume, but somehow this don't look like such a good time."

"Now's as good a time as any. Let me see the thing."

"As soon as you tell me what's wrong." Queenie stuck her chin out and her red hair bobbed.

"Stubborn old lady, aren't you?"

She bared her front teeth. "When I have to be."

Suddenly Quentin wanted to cry on her shoulder. "It's Mia," he whispered, holding his gut. "She's uh, she's—"

"Ill?"

He shook his head. Lifting a hand, he sketched a slash across his throat.

"Dead!" Queenie looked horrified.

"No, she's not dead. But she's—she's—" He stopped, unable to say the words.

"Now I know the two of you have been having your troubles, but if you're saying she's a-leaving you, I don't believe it for a minute." Queenie rolled up her sleeves. "So why don't you come with me and I'll show you that outfit?"

"I can't think about that now. Not when Mia's running off with Randall."

Queenie wrinkled her nose. "What kind of a name is that?"

"Priss-poor," Quentin said, managing a half-hearted grin.

"Mia's got better sense than that." Queenie pointed. "Look, here she comes now. With two men."

Quentin craned his neck. Sure enough, Mia walked between Beetle and Randall. Had he misheard? Had it been Beetle declaring his undying love? No, surely it had been that scumsucking accountant he'd heard. He shook his head like a heavyweight left too long in the ring.

Queenie prodded him with the toe of her tennis shoe. "If it's true, whatcha going to do about it? Let her run off, or go over there and fight for her?"

"You're right!" Quentin hugged the seamstress, strode over to Mia and the two men, and drew back his fist.

With a roar, he connected his fist with the accountant's nose.

The man dropped like a stuntman playing a corpse.

Quentin glanced back over his shoulder, just to share his moment of triumph with Queenie.

She had her hand over her mouth, eyes wide, shaking her head slowly back and forth.

"Randall!" Mia fell to her knees. Blood gushed from Randall's nose. He groaned, but other than that, didn't move.

Beetle looked from Mia to the fallen man and back to Quentin. "I'll g-go get first aid," he announced.

"Are you out of your mind?" Mia glared at Quentin. "What did you do that for?" She smoothed the short tufts of Randall's hair and Quentin wanted to hit the guy again.

"Just balancing the accounts, Mia," he said, and stormed off, too angry to confront his wife.

Too furious to seek the truth, Quentin reprimanded himself twenty minutes later, as he jogged down the lane away from the location. His haze of anger was finally beginning to clear. He'd told everyone to take an early lunch and gone off to cool down.

In all fairness, he'd only heard Randall declare his feelings. He hadn't heard Mia encourage the creep or even respond to him. A woman as endearing and beautiful and sweet as his wife was bound to have lots of admirers. Randall had been working with her for at least two years before Quentin had awakened to the knowledge that Mia would always be the only woman for him.

Maybe he'd never made a move on her before today.

Maybe Mia had been about to squelch Randall's protestations of love when Quentin had turned away.

He ran faster, trying to force reason, logic, and fairness into his emotional stew.

Then he pictured Mia bent over the fallen accountant, holding a tissue to his nose and staring daggers at Quentin.

Maybe, nothing!

He had to think of something. He wouldn't let her go without a fight.

And that was when he thought of Amity.

Blond, full-breasted, with a laugh that sounded like tinkling silver. Creative, artistic, charming Amity.

What man wouldn't fall for her?

He cut off into the woods, forced to run more slowly to keep from tripping over roots. If only Amity were visible, he'd get her to woo Randall until he forgot all about Mia. He forgot, due to his needs, that he'd pretty much decided Amity was meant to intervene in Portia's life. For now, he needed Amity to distract Randall.

Surely she'd do that for him. She seemed like such a trouper. Hell, he'd make it worth her while. Money, jewels, dog biscuits for all her furry friends. He'd pay her whatever she asked.

There was only one problem with his plan, Quentin acknowledged, slowing to a walk under the sheltering trees.

Amity remained invisible, and that included to Randall. How could a man as earthbound as that numbnuts fall in love with a woman he couldn't see?

Quentin dropped down on a fallen log and considered the dilemma.

He wasn't sure how long he sat there under the leafy trees, listening to the chirps and twitters of the birds. Two squirrels raced down a trunk, sat on their haunches, and chattered at him before chasing each other up another tree.

He heard a scuffling in the underbrush and for a silly moment thought maybe Mia had come to find him, to tell him not to worry, that she loved him and no one else.

Then a four-footed black ball of fluff, marked by a white stripe, tail waving gaily, poked its nose around the fallen log. The animal minced its way past Quentin, who sat holding his breath.

He had enough troubles without returning to work smelling like skunk.

The animal continued on its way, and Quentin relaxed.

Funny, how peaceful nature seemed when he sat and let it flow on its own around him. He closed his eyes and felt the sun on his face as every now and then it reached through the cover of the trees.

Kind of like Mr. G, showing up now and then, he thought, and then his heart stilled.

Mr. G.

That was his answer.

Normally, Quentin wouldn't have considered doing such an un-Quentinlike action, but he had to admit he fell into the desperate category at the moment.

Clearing his throat, he clasped his hands around his knees and said aloud, "I don't know whether you can hear me or not, Mr. G, but I could use some assistance here. I can't say I know much about asking for help, but I guess that's what I'm doing now."

Feeling slightly foolish, and glad the skunk wasn't there to watch him, Quentin wondered what to say next. As a lifelong agnostic, he'd not had much practice with prayer.

"I don't know why I can see Amity. I don't even know where the woman is right now. But if you could just find your way clear to letting her be visible to Randall what's-his-name, I'd be forever grateful."

Quentin slowly opened his eyes to find a thick brown snake making its way across the toe of his shoe. "I sure hope that's not your way of saying 'No way,' Mr. G," he muttered.

"Oh, amen," he added, and as soon as the snake slipped into the underbrush, he rose. Feeling in some odd way as if he'd undergone a monumental experience, Quentin took one last look around the sylvan clearing, inhaled the fragrant pine-scented air, then broke into a jog again.

He had a morning's worth of work to make up.

Mia left Randall in the hands of the first-aid nurse. Quentin had hightailed it from the location, leaving the production staff milling about, nibbling on a lunch for which they'd not yet developed an appetite.

Wondering how long it would take the tabloids to pick up the story of Quentin assaulting Randall, and hoping to high heaven that the accountant didn't sue, Mia kept her chin up and tried to act as if nothing was out of kilter.

When her entire world had gone crazy.

Beetle approached her where she sat in Quentin's director's chair, waiting for him to return so they could work things out.

Silently, he took his own seat.

He sat there, watching her in his own quiet way, not exactly staring, but not avoiding her, either.

"Bad day?" he finally said in a soft voice.

Mia managed a tremulous smile. "That's putting it mildly."

"The kind that makes you want to go back to bed and start the whole darn thing over?"

"Precisely." Mia smiled. What a sensible guy. Since she'd met him that fateful day in McDonald's, she'd always felt at ease with Beetle. "Everything's all mixed up when none of it should have happened."

"Quentin'll be back."

"Oh, I know that!" Mia bobbed her head. "This movie means far too much for him to delay too long." She reached a hand toward Beetle. "Don't worry, we'll get your story told."

He smiled briefly. "I have every confidence." He shifted in his chair, leaning forward and resting his hands on his knees. "You and Quentin, you're newlyweds, aren't you?"

She nodded. Everyone in Hollywood knew that.

"Must be tough, being married and working out all those getting-acquainted kinks in front of so many people."

"What do you mean?"

He shrugged. "It's my understanding that being married takes getting used to."

"When two people love each other, it's just supposed to work."

He kinked his brows, and Mia felt fairly foolish. For someone who made a habit of working at everything, why had she assumed matrimony should be as simple as falling off a log? "Have you been married?" Mia knew from the accounting paperwork that he was single now.

"No."

"Anyone in the wings?"

Beetle frowned a bit, then said, "Only the woman my mother thinks I should marry."

"Ah." Getting her mind off her own troubles made Mia feel better. "And who would you like to marry?"

He shrugged again. "I've never met anyone who made me want to throw in the towel. You know, lose my heart completely, utterly, and hopelessly."

Like she had for Quentin. Mia sighed and determined to keep her attention focused squarely on Beetle's life rather than her own. "What kind of woman would it take?"

He remained silent, then slowly removed his dark glasses. Pointing to his eyes, he said, "A woman who could see into my soul. A woman who also views the world out of eyes very much like my own." He slipped his glasses back on. "If I ever met a woman who looks at a flower and sees a story, or who walks into a bee's nest and runs away fabricating a fable, then I'll know I've met the kind of woman I can share my life with. I don't mean she has to be a writer, but she'd have to have the same sort of vision."

He sighed, then said, "It's funny, what being a writer does to you. Or maybe you're just that way and that's what makes you give up everything else to write. And I imagine living with someone who lives so much inside his head must be a very difficult thing to do."

Mia watched him, rapt. Softly, she said, "Oh, Beetle, I think I understand what you're saying. Quentin is like that, lost to the rest of the world when he's working on a picture."

"You're like that, too, Mia. You just don't see it in yourself." Beetle smiled. "That's the part of you Randall didn't quite grasp."

Mia made a face, thinking of the encounter, regretting her own role in it. "I hope you find your special woman soon."

He nodded and stood up. "I think I'll go back to my cabin and work for a while."

"Work?" Mia stared up at Beetle. The sun, now directly overhead, caught her square in the eyes and framed Beetle's head. She could have sworn she saw a reflected glow around the deep-red hair.

As she blinked her eyes to clear her vision, the idea came full-fledged into her mind.

Beetle.

Amity.

The writer.

The artist.

Her mouth fell open.

"Mia?" Beetle sounded concerned.

She waved him away. "Thanks for talking. You helped me feel better."

He sketched a salute and wandered off, hands in his pockets, totally lost in thought.

Whatever the reason, Amity had crossed their paths. She had no idea of her Intervention assignment, so if the same rules applied to Amity that had applied to Quentin and herself, the artist had no way to win back her life.

Mia didn't hold anything against the woman; she simply wanted her out of Quentin's sights. She also carried the secret belief that she and Quentin must have been meant to help her or she wouldn't be visible to him.

The brightest, most brilliant idea had blossomed in her mind as Beetle had stood over her, the sun shining around him. From everything Quentin had said, Amity would be the perfect woman for Beetle.

Perhaps, if they fell in love, Mr. G would forgive Amity for failing at whatever her original assignment had been. And once forgiven, she'd surely disappear from Quentin's line of sight, and hence from their lives.

Beetle still didn't strike Mia as a man who needed to be rescued, but a man without love could never achieve the same success as a well-loved man. Just think what he could produce, teamed with an artist like Amity! Putting the two of them together was practically as good as solving the mystery of the original Intervention target.

What she needed, then, was a way to get Mr. G's attention. If she could figure out a way to summon him, surely he'd intercede; he'd be the last person in Heaven or on Earth to want Mia and Quentin to end up in divorce court.

Men were visual creatures. Before Beetle could fall in love with Amity, he had to be able to see her.

For that miracle, Mia needed just the teeniest bit of help from Mr. G.

Ignoring the inquiring looks from the crew left twiddling its thumbs, a crew that well knew her aversion to wasted time and money, Mia hurried back to her temporary office in the main building of the Cubby Hole Lodge.

She'd lured Randall to the site of the shooting only to use him to make Quentin jealous. Normally, she had too much work to take care of to hang around the set. And to tell the truth, which she had, of course, shared with Quentin, the agonizingly slow process of capturing a movie on film gave her a headache. Mia wanted things done right, but she hated doing them once, twice, three times. Of course she understood the necessity of the different takes, but when something worked, she hated to have to see it done over.

She really did have things to go over with Randall. As she walked rapidly toward the lodge, she regretted ever having involved the accountant in her personal problems. She should have known better. What would her mother say?

She'd scold her harshly, and Mia would hang her head, knowing she deserved the tongue-lashing. A good wife didn't try to make her husband jealous.

Hmmph. According to her mother, a good wife didn't even complain if her husband strayed from the straight-and-narrow.

There, of course, mother and daughter parted ways.

Thinking of her mother, Mia decided to call her. She couldn't help but remember how tired her ma had looked that morning before Mia had flown to New York to kiss and make up with her husband.

She sighed and trudged up the steps of the lodge. Seemed lately she was always kissing and making up with Quentin.

Mia walked past the entrance to the small bar and cafe, which reminded her of the strange incident with Beetle the evening before. She'd forgotten all about it, talking to Beetle just now. But whatever had come over him to cause him to take money from the register?

Mia knew to the penny how much they'd paid for the rights to *Permutation*. With that hunk of change, Beetle should have been set for quite some time. Unless, of course, Mia thought with a touch of sadness, he'd been living off credit cards and loans from friends from every walk of life.

She'd heard of screenwriters who'd done exactly that, mortgaging everything in the hopes of hitting the bigtime. One novelist she'd read about had owed close to $40,000 when she'd finally sold her first book.

Mia shuddered. She could never live like that. Growing up poor had taught her too well the value of money. And now that she and Quentin were relatively well off, she continued to hold her pocketbook close to her chest. Memories of poverty claimed too much of her mind for her to relax.

Perhaps Beetle had overextended himself. Mia felt she must figure out a discreet way to discover the writer's finances. After all, here she was, powering on her computer and setting out to figure a way to hook him up with Amity.

The least she could do for the talented and charming man was to ensure he didn't have to steal to support the girlfriend she was about to foist on him.

Mia considered her problem, then linked into her Internet search engine.

She knew she could kneel and pray, but prayer didn't seem the appropriate medium for the complicated, and frankly manipulative, request Mia wanted to make.

Mia tapped a finger thoughtfully against her teeth, picturing the state-of-the-art screening room in Purgatory. It was in the Second Chance Room where she and Quentin had found themselves viewing snippets from their target's life after their horrible accident.

The technology had screamed top of the line. Heaven, Mia had a hunch, could show the Earth's high technology a trick or two.

Given that, she found it hard to believe she wouldn't be able to locate Mr. G online.

Stranger miracles than that occurred every day.

Her search turned up no website.

Mia frowned and nibbled on her thumbnail.

Then she smiled, chuckling softly. Mr. G was bound to have an email address. The old coot, as Quentin called him, probably had contacts all over. After all, hadn't he known, almost before Quentin himself, that Quentin would be late for his wedding?

Hadn't he shown up in the nick of time?

Mia furrowed her brow and typed in a test message and an experimental address for Mr. G.

Her output failed to transmit.

Mia stared at her screen, muttering to herself.

She tried a few more variations on Mr. G, Purgatory, and 111.

All unsuccessful.

Then she tried mrgpurg through her usual email provider.

Her computer whirred.

The message bar showed the test text had been sent.

"Hot dog!" Mia exclaimed. She knew in her heart it had to have reached Mr. G.

Bending her head over her laptop, she began to compose her online plea for special assistance.

14 ⁓

"Some days," Mr. G muttered, "you just never know what'll go wrong."

Horace had long since come and gone, and Mr. G continued to mull over what to do about the Amity Jones situation.

Now, puttering in what passed as his kitchen, he stared at his choices. Passing over the hot chocolate, he plucked the last can of Hawaiian Punch from the shelf and popped it open. Mr. G didn't get hungry or thirsty, but some pleasures, like a good old-fashioned Hawaiian Punch, never failed to make him feel better.

Especially when he found himself in something of a pickle.

He knew the rules; knew he'd broken them by allowing Quentin, a former successful visitor to the Second Chance Room, to be able to see the otherwise invisible Amity. And from that point, it had been easy to bend lots of other rules he'd always followed.

Not only had he made Amity visible to Quentin, he'd also swapped her assignment, deftly palming the one that she'd been supposed to receive.

In its place, he'd substituted an assignment no-where near the top of the rotation, an assignment the ditzy artist had managed to lose.

And take materializing on Earth in those silly disguises. At least when he was driving the cab, he met some interesting characters.

"You're getting to be a softie," he said aloud, then popped his cigar into his mouth. "Either she'll work it out or she won't."

But somehow that statement stuck in his craw. He chewed on his cigar and considered what would happen if he just kept on breaking the rules. At least until Amity made it back to that schlocky mural she'd been painting.

There wasn't much precedent on the point. Oh, once, way back when, Lucifer had been a shining star among the angel set. After pushing it too far, he'd fallen from grace and been consigned to the basement. But Mr. G couldn't believe he'd get in that kind of trouble just for trying to help. Lucifer, after all, had done his best to take over the whole ball of wax.

Mr. G swished the dregs of his punch and con-sidered the messages his earnest red-jacketed flun-kies had delivered earlier. First from Quentin, and later Mia.

Yeah, what harm could it do to help 'em out? A tweak here, a tweak there. Besides, Mr. G thought with a grin, watching those two trying to outdo each other was always such fun.

*   *   *

After the traumas of the morning, the afternoon flowed surprisingly well. Quentin sat back in his chair and breathed in the late afternoon air, remarkably fragrant compared to Los Angeles's usual. Thyme and rosemary mingled with the dusty scent of the soil. He glanced around, wanting to share this moment of contentment with Mia, but of course she wasn't there.

Mia hadn't returned to the set all afternoon. That bothered him very much, but with everything else going so smoothly, he figured on carrying over the optimism of the afternoon to his dealings with Mia that evening.

With Amity evidently having gone her own way, he and Mia might even be able to patch up their differences in relative peace.

"Quentin, darling, could you come over here?" Portia's voice beckoned, or rather commanded, and Quentin rose. Watching her perform had quelled his jitters, confirming his instincts that she'd be perfect in the role of Ma Belle.

He grimaced, thinking that had been the last thought in his mind when he'd first witnessed Portia. In her first shot of the afternoon, she'd played to the camera the way she must have played to her theater audiences.

Quentin had taken her aside, held her hand, stroked her ego, all the while murmuring words of praise interjected with gentle instruction on where to stand, where to look, how to repeat her lines for each take.

For all her silly flirting ways, Portia listened.

When they began again, Portia moved as if oiled. Playing a man in a woman's body couldn't be easy for a woman, but Portia had heaved her breasts, staring quizzically at them as if they were poisonous mushrooms sprouted by some evil magic. She'd swaggered, hefting the flowing robes Queenie had sewn based on Amity's sketches as if she'd never worn a flowing silk gown. She'd picked at the ruby rings on her fingers, yet another touch courtesy of Amity's sketches, mumbling she'd never seen such pansy-assed jewelry.

All in all, Portia had been brilliant.

So when she summoned him now, just before the last set-up of the day, Quentin went gladly. If she insisted he go to dinner with her, he'd even do that.

"Darling," Portia said, beckoning the makeup man to pass her his hand mirror, then holding it so she could see over her shoulder, "darling, Quentin, who is that man?"

Glancing over Portia's shoulder, Quentin noted several prop men, two production assistants, and a hairstylist. "Which one?"

Portia affected a pout. "The one who keeps staring at me."

Quentin looked again. That was when he noticed the accountant, not exactly his favorite person, sitting on the ground, his back propped against a tree, a handkerchief still held against his nose.

Sure enough, he did seem to be staring at Portia. Quentin glanced down at Portia, who seemed entranced. That Portia might be interested in the number cruncher had never entered his mind when he'd made his prayer to Mr. G. Wondering whether things might be getting completely out of hand, or were simply starting to come together at last, he said slowly, "That man is our accountant."

Portia practically simpered. "And very well dressed."

Perhaps, Quentin thought, Portia's interest might be a funny sort of answer to his prayers. With Amity missing in action, there could be worse solutions to some of his problems than for Portia to fixate on Randall.

"Oh, very." Quentin gave a gentle squeeze to Portia's shoulder. "Tell you what . . . let's wrap this scene. I'm fairly sure Mia has business to finish with Randall. Why don't the four of us go to dinner?"

Portia batted her lashes. Quentin looked down at the famous face, taking in the taut skin that gave no clue to her actual age. He wondered whether she worried he'd feel overthrown or rejected, but apparently that concept didn't fall within Portia's mental repertoire.

"That would be divine. I do so love to be admired," she murmured, shifting her bustline and swaggering, her shoulders thrown back. Clearly she'd shifted into the role of the biker trapped in the fairy godmother's body. "But not until tomorrow night." She wet her lips. "I do like a man to have to wait a bit. It increases one's appetite. Profoundly."

Thankful to have thrown another man as bait to her preying self, Quentin merely nodded. He didn't want to have dinner with Portia that evening, anyway. He and Mia needed time alone.

Especially after that day. Jeez! It had been first one thing and then another. They'd finally gotten through the frog shot earlier, with the trainer eventually working his magic. Rather than hopping about, tossing off the crown, the amphibian had cocked its head at a jaunty angle, sporting the crown, looking every inch the prince trapped in the frog's body.

Watching Portia swagger, then step on a rock with a bare foot and swear like a sailor, Quentin allowed himself a slight smile. *Permutation* kicked off from the premise of a fairy godmother attempting to rescue a prince she felt certain had been trapped in a frog's body. But as she chanted her spell, she and the frog found themselves set upon by a gang of ruthless bikers.

The spell interrupted, the fairy godmother and the biker chief find themselves in a body swap, the frog remaining in limbo.

It wasn't until the end of the film, when Moe the Biker has discovered the good within himself, and Ma Belle, the Fairy Godmother, has tamed the unruly gang by her example of goodness while disguised in Moe's rough-and-tumble body, that the frog was released.

And the frog, naturally, since *Permutation* was very much a fairy tale, wasn't just any prince, but the prince the fairy godmother had fallen in love with many years ago.

"Beetle?" Quentin turned to the screenwriter, thinking to ask him a question about the next scene to be shot. He saw, surprised, that Beetle's chair had been vacated. The guy was so quiet, he might have been gone for some time for all Quentin knew.

The rewrite he'd done at Quentin's request had been excellent. Quentin made a mental note to find Beetle before dinner and ask him to shore up one of the next day's scenes.

And then, before he knew it, they were done, with him calling for the last time that day, "That's a wrap. Print it!"

Portia surged toward him, still somewhat in character, shoveling her shoulders and speaking out of the side of her mouth, "So didcha ask the goy to dinner for tomorraw?"

Then she winked, and said, in Portia's voice, "Dinner at eight, darling?"

Quentin paused. Did she mean that night or the next? He waited a beat, and she didn't disappoint him.

"You don't expect your star to dine alone in her room, do you?" She arched her brows.

He should have figured. He'd do it, but not one-on-one. "Mia and I will meet you at your hotel."

"Oh, well, if you must bring your chaperone, all right," she said, and sauntered off, beckoning with an imperious finger to her maid, who had been holding Mr. Pish on a leash.

Suddenly, before the maid could react, the otherwise quiescent Mr. Pish yelped and broke free. Howling in a most unpedigreed fashion, the schnauzer launched itself after a cat streaking across the open space where they'd just shot the Ma Belle scene.

Portia, naturally, went ballistic. "My baby," she cried, clutching her throat. "He's not up to such exertions!"

Quentin figured he'd better at least pretend to go after the dog. The way the actress worshiped the pooch, he'd be up a creek without a paddle if anything happened to it. And with everything going so smoothly now, he hated even to consider that.

Thrusting himself from his chair, he jogged after the dog, who turned to snarl at him.

"Oh, my," Portia cried. "I thought he liked you."

Without Amity nearby, Quentin knew the dog would never approach him. Kicking himself for ever having wished her gone, Quentin slowed his steps and switched his strategy to shooing the cat away.

The cat, however, had different ideas entirely. She arched her back, then, sitting still, began to lick one front paw, swiping it slowly over her face before wetting it again.

Mr. Pish, his leash caught on a branch, howled.

"Just bring him back to me," Portia called.

"Yeah, right," he muttered, and circled around the dog. To his surprise, the leash landed in his hand and Mr. Pish trotted obediently up to him. Quentin glanced over his shoulder. Amity! She had to be close by, but for the life of him he couldn't see her.

"My darling baby!" Portia held out her hands and Quentin delivered the dog to her.

"It's just so-so-so-bad you're married," Portia murmured, glancing at Quentin across the schnauzer's silvery head. Then she looked across the clearing, toward the tree where Randall had sat earlier. "But I suppose there are consolations in life."

Kissing the dog, she strolled off. The last words Quentin heard from her were, "You must do what Mommy tells you and not cause trouble."

At that, Quentin rolled his eyes.

Again he looked around for Amity.

Had it been his imagination? Had the dog finally accepted him, or had it merely wanted to go to the trailer for its supper?

Seeing no signs of the artist, Quentin shrugged and decided his imagination had taken control of him. Or perhaps the dog had merely grown used to him.

His stomach growled, reminding him he'd skipped lunch. As the crew cleared and packed up for the evening, Quentin slipped off, down the path to their cabin. The routine end-of-day production details could wait until after dinner.

Now all he wanted to do was talk to Mia.

*   *   *

"Excuse me, miss." The short-haired man, sitting with his back against a tree, garbed in a white dress shirt and dark trousers, contrasted sharply with the casual cast and crew. Amity paused, noticing most everyone had scattered as soon as Quentin had called it a wrap for the day. Looking around, she couldn't see anyone else he might be speaking to.

"Are you talking to me?"

The man, staring straight at her, looked at her as if she'd said something less than intelligent. "Yes."

She tapped herself on the chest. "You're talking to me? Me!" He could see her!

He nodded and stood up, clutching a soiled hanky to his nose.

"Oh, you're hurt!" Amity steadied the stranger's shoulders. "Let me take a look at that face," she murmured, lowering her voice the way she did when she handled an injured animal.

"You're too kind," the man said, his words muffled a bit by the hanky. "I'm afraid it's not a pretty sight."

"I'm sure I've seen worse." All the bloody noses in the world couldn't bother her right now. Visible again! Back to normal, which meant she could go back to New Orleans. Too bad everyone else had scattered. She wanted to throw herself about, shouting something silly like, "Look at me, I'm Amity again!"

Instead, she studied the man's nose, tracing it gently with her fingers. She knew quite a bit about anatomy from her sketch work. "Bloodied, but not broken," she said cheerfully. "You should put some ice on this, though."

"Ice. Of course." The man was gazing up into her eyes. "You're an angel to help me." Lifting a hand he touched her hair where it fell above her breast. "A very beautiful angel, too."

Amity removed his hand. "Nonsense. I'm as much flesh and blood as you are." Under her breath, she added, "At least, now I am."

The man continued to stare at her as if he'd never seen a woman before, and Amity wondered what alignment of forces had returned her to normalcy. It must have happened just as she walked in this man's direction.

That she'd been invisible all afternoon she'd have bet money on. After deciding she couldn't abandon the cat that had adopted her, she'd returned to the production site. She'd remained all afternoon, even though Quentin had pointedly ignored her. All things considered, that was just as well, as Amity had no wish to cause trouble for him and his bride.

She'd had fun helping out. It hadn't taken her two seconds, after she'd quit laughing hysterically at their efforts to film the frog, to know they'd never put the frog through its paces without her invisible assistance.

So she'd soothed the jumpy amphibian and held his crown on, adjusting it at a much jauntier angle.

Quentin had been pleased, but when Amity had

turned to him and given him a thumbs-up after they'd finished the shot, he'd had his back to her and was talking to several people.

"You wouldn't want to have dinner with me, would you?"

Amity started. She'd almost forgotten about this unassuming man. Returning his look, she took in his neat clothing, the thick band on his gold watch, a band that didn't look like the kind that would turn his wrist green. She measured the plodding intelligence in his eyes and checked with a quick peek the condition of the heels of his shoes. Not worn at all.

She thought of her string of boyfriends, losers all. Oh, talented in their own way, but not a one of them had the wherewithal or desire ever to settle down and raise a family, let alone earn two cents to rub together. No, they'd all been too busy drinking, smoking, and dreaming of their own glory to produce anything.

He had French cuffs, too, with gold cufflinks.

"Well?" He sounded pretty insecure.

"What do you do?"

A flicker of annoyance, or maybe frustration, crossed his battered face. He looked up into her eyes. "Does the answer determine whether you'll have dinner with me?"

Amity nodded. She was through going down the path with guys who didn't have their act together. Some might say it was only dinner, but Amity knew better. Guys had a way of falling for her, and if she didn't say no in the beginning, she was too soft-hearted to break it off until they'd really pushed her to the limit.

"I'm a, a—uh," the man trailed off. Then he threw back his shoulders and puffed out his chest. "Why, I'm Randall the Magnificent." He seemed very pleased with his announcement.

"A magician." Distaste dripped from her tongue as the word crossed her lips. That was even worse than an actor, artist, or writer. What was it with her? Why must she always attract lunatics and losers? What ever happened to nice normal bankers and accountants?

She fingered the ends of her hair, smoothed the flowing lines of her purple smock. "Do I look like the kind of woman who'd go to dinner with a guy who pulls rabbits from hats?"

"Oh, yes!" His eyes shone.

Amity peered more closely at the man. The sun had dropped toward the ocean and evening had claimed the light, leaving only shadows. Something on the front of his shirt caught her eye. "Since when do magicians carry pens and mechanical pencils in their pockets?"

He smiled weakly. "Perhaps I'm a modern magician?"

Amity shook her head. "I think you're a bullshit specialist."

She moved away, but the guy fell to his knees and grasped her hands.

"Please don't go. I'll tell you the truth! I'm really an accountant, but women always find that so boring. I can see their eyes glaze over when they find that out. And after the horrible day I had, I thought it would be nice to pretend to be someone flamboyant. You know, the kind of guy who gets the girl." His last words carried more than a hint of bitterness. "But my name really is Randall. Randall Hollings."

Amity tugged him to a standing position. "Amity Jones. And you can tell me all about your horrible day over dinner."

"Do you mean it?" He skipped a step or two and Amity almost changed her mind. But she was getting awfully hungry, and now that she'd become visible again, stealing supper would be risky.

A meal ticket. The phrase entered her head and she grimaced. Here she was, regarding this man as a means to an end. Rather than answering him, she started down the path toward the lodge. It was one thing to seek a stable sort of man in her life, another to use someone.

Halfway back to the lodge, Randall paused and pointed to a spot on the ground. Rather dramatically, he said, "This is the place I learned a very hard lesson."

Amity looked at the dusty path, the bushes surrounding it, mottled now in the approaching dusk. Her stomach growled. "I said I wanted to hear all about it. Over dinner," she added, in the voice she used to rein in her dogs.

Randall held his hand briefly against his heart, then started walking again. When they reached the parking lot, he nodded toward a sleek black

Lexus, the kind of car rarely seen in Amity's neighborhood. He held open the door for her and she smiled up at him, thinking a meal ticket might not be the worst thing in the world.

As he drove away from the lodge, Randall said, "There's a hotel near here that provides food at an excellent cost/value ratio. I thought we'd go there. Is that okay with you?"

Amity, being a New Orleanian, found that a very odd way to describe food. Food and drink were the nectars of life. Any disaster, large or small, merely provided an excuse for people to eat, drink, and gather together. Hurricane parties, wakes, weddings, you name it; in New Orleans, good food and drink found themselves combined with life, death, and every occasion in between.

Still mulling over her mercenary reactions to this man, Amity only nodded. If she didn't see something she liked on the menu, she'd speak with the chef and between them they'd rustle up something worthy of her burgeoning appetite.

Settling against the cushy leather seat, Amity said, "Why don't you tell me about what happened today?"

He smiled, almost bristling with pride. "Just wait till she sees me with you," he said under his breath. Amity wasn't sure she'd caught that right, so she waited for more. He added, "For several years I've suffered unrequited, one-sided love for one of my clients. Mia Tortelli, to be exact."

"Quentin's wife?"

He frowned. "Exactly. All the while I've been

working to get my ducks in a row. Financially, that is. And what does she do but go off and marry that nutty director! I had it all planned. First the pension plan, the house in the country, the college savings accounts for our son and daughter—"

"Savings accounts!" Amity inched nearer, not even marveling over the revelation that he and Quentin's wife had had children together. She didn't even possess a checkbook. Then, to be polite, she asked, "How old are the children?"

"There are no children, silly. I, as usual, was planning ahead."

"Oh." Well, that made sense, given the man's pedantic nature. Amity wondered suddenly if every stable man had to be boring. She found herself wishing she were in a car like this one with a guy like, well, for instance, Beetle Leonard. He didn't give the impression he'd slow down just because a road sign indicated 25 mph.

No, Beetle looked like a guy who'd accelerate into the curve.

Which is what Amity would do. Her fingers itched to get at the wheel of Randall's luxury automobile. She forced her attention back to his troubles, though they didn't seem like much to her.

"Anyway," Randall was saying mournfully, "today I revealed my feelings to Mia. My long-dampened, hidden away feelings. For all the good it did me."

"She hit you?"

"Oh, no, not *Mia*."

Amity wondered if he realized he'd spoken her name with such reverence.

"Quentin, that loose cannon. He overheard me."

Ooh, no wonder Quentin had been in such a weird mood this afternoon. "You can't really blame him, though, can you? She *is* his wife."

Randall seemed to undergo an inner struggle. Eventually he said, "True, and I'd like to think I'd hit anyone who expressed affection to my wife." With that, he looked sideways at Amity.

She wondered if he knew how unappealing it was to a woman to be wooed on the rebound. Noting the calf look in his eyes, she figured he didn't have a clue. Still, she fingered the buttery soft leather of the seat and wondered what it would be like to have anything she wanted in the world, wondered what it would be like not to have to scrape together pennies and whip out paintings for Jackson Square tourists to pay for her pets' inoculations.

"So the lesson you've learned today is?" Feeling a little like the sisters at the foundling home, Amity prompted Randall to wind up his tale.

He caught one of her hands to his lips. "The lesson I've learned, my dear, is to act!" He released her hand, then returned both hands to his cautious grip on the wheel.

Amity pondered her position. Here she was, obviously being wooed by the first halfway stable man she'd ever met. Stable, and judging by the car and the talk of pension plans and country homes, rich to boot.

Still, gazing at him she felt a lot like she did on the rare occasions when she visited her dentist . . . not at all excited by the occasion, wondering why people insisted on telling her it was good for her.

The image of Beetle striding from his bathroom last night, the still damp hairs of his chest glistening in the light from his desk lamp, crowded her mind. Beetle didn't make her think of the dentist. She shivered. When Randall reached over and patted her hand with a dampish palm, she managed a smile.

Dinner and out, she told herself.

Just then, Randall pulled into a courtyard sparkling with tiny white lights planted among the trees. Two valets, dressed in toreador uniforms, scurried in their direction. When one opened the driver's door, Amity inhaled wafting scents of citrus from the nearby foliage. With her spirits buoyed as she reacted to the fragrant scent, she smiled.

She had nothing to feel guilty about. Randall had asked her to dinner; she'd accepted. That was that, she said, sitting there, waiting for the valet to open her door and forgetting all about the lecture she'd given herself earlier about how, to a man, dinner always meant something else, something more.

15 ~

"**W**hat do you mean you don't want to have dinner?" Quentin scowled and Mia wished she could go to him and have him open his arms and enfold her.

Instead, she fixed her hands on the keyboard of her computer, poised to continue her work, still fuming that Quentin had actually believed she could have been involved with Randall, or could at least have encouraged the guy! Her chin trembled and the figures on her screen jumped and wobbled as she blinked furiously.

"Mia, we need to talk."

She nodded. "That's true, but I don't think now would be a very constructive time. Besides, I'm sure Portia expects you to take her to dinner."

"Portia be damned!" Quentin covered the few feet between them and lifted her hands from the keys. "Look at me, Mia, and tell me what's wrong."

Mia kept her eyes fixed on their joined hands. Where could she start? So much crowded her mind she didn't know what to say first. She heard the phrases tumbling in her head. *Quentin, I love*

*you, let's just forget all this silliness. How could you
even think I'm interested in Randall? What's wrong
with me, worrying about our love when I should believe
in us? Why is Amity upsetting me so much? Why is
the work we do not fun for me anymore? Why is it,
now that I have the only man I've wanted, I'm messing
things up?*

She licked her lips and kept her eyes down.
Miserable with herself for not simply letting go of
all the chaff circulating in her mind, she simply
shook her head and said, "I don't think I understand myself right now."

Quentin blew air through his cheeks as if he'd
been holding his breath. "Oh, is that all?" The sar-
casm stung her, but she couldn't really blame him
for it.

He tipped her chin toward him. In a soft voice,
he said, "I'm sorry for jumping to conclusions
about Randall, but what's a man supposed to
think when he hears a guy declaring his love for
his wife? And I think you'll be happy to know
Amity seems to have split."

"Really?" She couldn't keep the pleasure out of
her voice.

"I haven't seen her since—" He knit his thick
brows together, as if remembering something.

"Since when?"

"Oh, midday." He smiled a smile out of pro-
portion to his words.

Mia knew him well enough to realize something important had happened and he had re-
frained from sharing it with her. With a sigh, she

slipped her hands from his. "Well, I hope things worked out for her."

"It's okay to be concerned, now that she's not around me?"

"Quentin, you make me sound so selfish."

"If the shoe fits, why not wear it?" He threw up his hands. "I just don't get it. You were the first person to say she'd been sent to us for a reason and the last to help figure out what that reason might be. Why? Simply because I made the mistake of complimenting her once in a while?"

Mia felt like retorting, "You mean, every five minutes," but she held her tongue. She'd treated Amity badly, and Quentin, too. Ever ready to accept her own guilt, Mia didn't see any point in continuing their nonproductive exchange. Summoning a proper smile, she said, "I'm sorry for my behavior. Why don't we go to dinner now?"

Quentin stared at her as if she'd suggested he give away one of his Oscars. "Now? Now you want to go to dinner?" He backed toward the door of the temporary office. "Right now I'd rather face Portia on my own."

Mia watched as he strode out of the room. Clearly there was a lot more to being married than simply being in love.

And for once in her orderly and logic-driven life, she didn't have a book or a plan to tell her how to make the thing work.

She dropped her chin into her hands and wondered what to do. Her ma would tell her to get off her butt and run after Quentin. Letting your husband eat dinner with another woman, even if she was fifty-nine years old—no, her ma would say, "That's a mistake, a big mistake."

He'd come in prepared to talk things over, ready to apologize for jumping to conclusions over Randall. And she'd rebuffed him completely. What an idiot. She'd never have done such a bad job of a contract negotiation, yet with her own marriage she'd let her temper and hurt feelings rule.

As her ma would say, she'd better get over that.

Mia felt her thumb creep between her lips. She nibbled, reverting to a habit she thought she'd long since left behind. As she gnawed on her nail, she fretted.

Perhaps she hadn't been meant to marry Quentin. Perhaps she wasn't cut out for making a marriage work. The harder she worked on her thumb, the darker her emotions grew, until Mia had both destroyed her thumbnail and convinced herself her destiny held no Quentin in the future.

Quentin huffed out of Mia's temporary production office more lonely than mad. Now he'd have to spend another dinner with Portia, due to his own stubbornness.

"Idiot," he said to himself, as he pushed open the door of the Cubby Hole. He'd have a beer and cool down. Maybe Mia would change her mind and come to find him. He took a seat at the fallen log bar and ordered a beer.

Without saying anything to him, the bartender

set Quentin's drink before him and then turned around and started playing with the remote control.

Quentin shook his head. Well, it had been his idea to shift production here, and Mia had worked a miracle, making the deal in as short a time as she had. No point in complaining over a lack of niceties.

The door creaked open and closed.

"I thought I told you to make yourself scarce."

Quentin looked up to find the bartender glaring at Beetle.

Beetle stared back, his dark glasses absent from his face.

"Chill out," Quentin said. "This guy stays, or the whole production walks."

"Says who?" The guy pushed up the sleeves of his none-too-white T-shirt.

Quentin tapped his chest.

The guy stared at him, working through the statement. With a shrug he turned back to his remote control.

"Thanks," Beetle said, taking the stool next to Quentin.

"It's nothing." Quentin gave the screenwriter a grin. He'd come to like the guy and hoped to work with him again. Beetle was that rare gem— an original thinker and a genius at rewrites. He had his own ideas so clearly in mind that he didn't get his back up when Quentin suggested ways their delivery might be improved. Yeah, Quentin could stand to work with a writer like Beetle several times over.

"Give my friend a beer," Quentin said.

A mug slid its way down the bar.

"What's he got against you?"

"Uh—" Beetle took a swig of his beer. "Mia didn't tell you?"

Quentin frowned. "No, Mia didn't tell me."

"This guy thought I took some m-money from him."

"Why would he think a stupid thing like that?"

"Because he caught me with my hand in his till."

"Aren't we paying you enough?"

"It's not that!" Beetle blushed a fierce red.

Quentin felt sorry for the guy. "Just a joke, man," he said. "But what happened?"

"I swear I saw money floating out of that drawer the other night. When I went to investigate, that guy"—he jerked a thumb toward the bartender, who'd moved to the far end of the bar—"caught me."

"And no one else was within sight?"

"Nope."

"Amity."

"Excuse me?"

Quentin shook his head. How could he explain the presence of the invisible artist to Beetle? Where would he start? "Nothing."

Beetle took another swig. "Strange things have been happening to me. The floating money is only one of 'em."

"Oh?" Maybe he should give Beetle a hint. He wouldn't want the guy thinking he was going nuts. "You ever consider there are creatures who live right alongside of us, only exist on some other kind of plane?"

Beetle shrugged. "Aren't we making a movie about a fairy godmother and a prince in a frog's body?"

"Good point. Well, if I were making a similar yet different movie, I think I'd feature a gorgeous blond artist, really built"—Quentin sketched a sumptuous figure with his hands—"and she'd be caught between life and death and trying to figure out what she's got to do to pass Go and collect two hundred dollars."

Beetle was staring at him as if he'd said something really stupid. "Uh-huh. And then what?"

"Forget it. I'm not in a creative mood right now." Maybe he'd try to explain it another time. Somehow, with Mia sulking and with him facing another night with Portia Goodhope, Quentin didn't feel like exploring the mysteries of the state between life and death.

"You waiting for Mia?"

Quentin scowled. "No, I'm having dinner with Portia."

"Oh." Beetle studied his beer. "Maybe I'd better get going. I have some writing I want to do."

"Are you always working?"

Beetle flashed a grin. "Mostly."

"All work and no play—"

"When I find the right woman, like you've done, then maybe I won't work so much. Your wife's a gem. She even fed me supper the other night."

"Supper?" Quentin's voice lowered. Chalk up two little things Mia hadn't mentioned.

"Cup of soup." Beetle tossed a couple of dollars on the bar. "Tasty, too. See you later." He strolled out of the Cubby Hole, an absent expression on his face, his mind clearly already at work on whatever project he had going.

Quentin finished his beer and stalked off to the cabin. No Mia. He showered and changed, wishing he weren't quite so stubborn. He ought to go back to the production office and beg her on bended knee to join him for dinner.

Instead, he left a message as to his whereabouts and drove off down the mountainside toward Portia's hotel.

A knock on the door saved Mia from completely annihilating her thumb.

With the interruption, she forced a semblance of calm. "Come in," she said, staring woefully at the thumbnail she'd sacrificed to her worrywart tendencies. As she heard Quentin's voice in her head calling her his little worrywart, Mia's face crumpled.

"Something wrong?" Beetle spoke from the doorway.

"No, no, everything's fine." She noted he'd put away the dark glasses; he gazed at her with concern in his deep blue eyes—at least, she hoped it was concern. Just what she'd need, another man after her! Mia smiled at that irony. She'd spent years head over heels in love with an oblivious Quentin, during which time she'd never noticed whether other men were interested in her or not.

Married two months, and now two new guys were sweet on her. What a record. Then she chastised herself for letting her imagination get the better of her.

"Rough day?" Beetle asked.

She looked closely at him. Concern, yes. Relieved, she said, "Par for the course, I guess. How about you?"

He laughed ruefully. "Stayed up half the night redoing a scene I lost in a computer crash, then today I was so blottoed from lack of sleep I imagined I saw a cat walking in mid-air. Not exactly par for the course."

"A cat?" Mia sat up. Quentin had described Amity with a cat that morning. He'd also been positive Amity had gone. "What time did you see, I mean, what time did you suffer that hallucination?"

"Probably late morning."

Quentin said she'd been gone since midday. What had happened to chase her away? Now her curiosity had kicked in, mixing with a tiny dose of guilt. What if something bad had happened to Amity?

Mia rose, found her purse, and walked toward where Beetle stood near the doorway. "I wouldn't worry too much about the cat," she said. "It's probably a side effect of creative stress. I heard

Quentin mumbling something to that effect this morning."

"He saw a cat in mid-air, too?" Beetle sounded as if he didn't believe a word of what she'd just said. For that, Mia didn't blame him. But what could she do, simply announce an invisible woman had been visiting them from Purgatory?

Mia shook her head, thinking only she and Quentin could ever understand a line like that. That thought gave her a pang of missing Quentin.

"Didn't think so," Beetle said.

She'd go to him. He would have left word of his dinner destination, something they always did while working on location. Glancing at her purse, she realized how rude it would be to rush off and abandon the screenwriter.

"Beetle," she said, "how would you like to join me for dinner?" Thinking of the money he'd taken from the cash register, she added, "My treat."

Gazing out the panoramic windows overlooking the valley, Quentin left a smile in place and wondered what had possessed him to show up for dinner with Portia Goodhope.

Being miffed at Mia didn't mean he had to punish himself!

Crooking her little finger, Portia lifted her wineglass, filled with Italian mineral water, and took a dainty sip. She played with the stem of the glass, then looked straight at Quentin.

Rather than the coy voice and flirtatious tone she'd employed during the past half hour, she said, "You're a lost cause, aren't you, Quentin Grandy?"

"How's that?" He quit checking out the scenery. She had his full attention now.

A half-lift of her shoulder, a graceful upturning of her palm on the table—these were the actress's motions to accompany her wistful words. "When I throw myself at a man the way I've done with you, and get not even a teensy-weensy rise"—she wagged a finger at him, a rueful smile on her lush lips—"there are only two possibilities. And the one I'm betting on is that you're very much in love with your wife, aren't you?"

Pleased to see this much less artificial side to Portia Goodhope, Quentin smiled and said softly, "Oh, yes, I love my wife."

She nodded, gracious in her defeat. "She's a lucky woman." Portia tapped a long red nail against her glass. "Where is she tonight?"

"Working." His response came out clipped and he knew he'd answered too quickly.

"Ah." She nodded as if he'd revealed a long-kept secret. "Working." She turned the word into at least three syllables, fluttering her lashes in an echo of her earlier flirtatiousness. Pushing up a diamond bracelet banding one wrist, she murmured, "Perhaps I gave up on you too soon."

Quentin couldn't tell whether she was teasing or trying to hint at some motherly advice.

"Oh, look, there's that man again." Portia fastened her gaze on a point across the crowded dining room.

Sitting with his back to the rest of the diners, Quentin, of course, couldn't see the subject of Portia's scrutiny. He couldn't help but note she lost no time in finding another subject for her interest, though.

Observing his blank expression, she said, "You know, the man I asked you about."

"Randall?" He spat out the accountant's name.

"What a lovely name." Portia ran her tongue over her upper lip. "Manly."

Quentin experienced a vision of her sharpening her claws for her new prey. If Randall hadn't overstepped his bounds with Mia, he might have felt sorry for the guy. "Who's he with?" He had to ask the question, even as he vowed to himself that there was no way he even thought Mia would appear at the side of that numbnuts numbercruncher.

Portia studied the room. "Hmm, it would appear he's all by his lonesome."

"Shall I ask him to join us?" With luck, she'd leap at the offer, then fawn over Randall, leaving Quentin free to excuse himself early. He ought never to have come; he belonged with Mia, even if they ate hotdogs at the Cubby Hole Lodge while she slaved over her budget projections, or whatever the hell it was she insisted she had to do that kept her working. Or maybe she'd saved some of the cup of soup after feeding Beetle last night.

Odd, but Quentin didn't remember Mia staying in the office so late on their other movies. Only lately had she insisted she had more to do than could be done within the confines of their usual work days.

He frowned. Only since they'd begun work on *Permutation*. Sometimes he wished she'd never bumped into Beetle Leonard and that he'd never heard the word *Permutation*.

Maybe some movies were cursed. What had the clerk at Tiffany's said? Not every movie was a godchild? He sighed, glad that Portia seemed amply distracted by studying her victim from a distance. Since the day Mia had come home from her accidental meeting with Beetle Leonard, her face aglow as she'd talked about the writer she'd met and a screenplay Quentin just had to read, nothing had gone right.

Well, not exactly nothing. He'd married the woman he loved.

Now he had to figure out how to keep her happy.

"I think," Portia said, "it would be better if we don't ask him to dine with us." She toyed with the stem of her glass with a sensuous motion of her tapered fingers.

Quentin noticed she'd shifted her body and crossed her legs. The cleverly placed slit in her narrow skirt revealed legs a thirty-year-old would be proud to sport.

Getting into the spirit of the hunt, and enjoying the idea of flinging the accountant into Portia the Barracuda's path, Quentin scooted his chair around enough so he could view most of the dining area, leaving it in a position to allow Randall a clear line of vision featuring Portia's shapely leg.

He noted with satisfaction the man's swollen nose and bruised cheek. Looking more closely, he observed that Randall appeared to be talking to himself. Maybe he shouldn't have hit him quite so hard; nah, he should've hit him harder. Turning back to Portia, Quentin said, "He's fairly well fixed, you know."

She lifted her finely drawn brows and waggled a finger at a waiter. The maitre d' materialized at her side.

"A bottle of Dom Perignon for the gentleman at that table." She indicated where he was with a tip of her head. Not much of an indication, but as Randall was the only gentleman dining alone, Quentin figured the maitre d' wouldn't have any trouble interpreting the request.

For a second, Quentin pictured her in her heyday, conquering every suitor in sight, then he shook himself free of the image.

He thought instead how sexy Mia, with her quick smile and perky self, would be when she reached Portia's age. Mia, with her love of life, would never have to dress like a teenager to make him look twice at her.

He started to rise. He needed to go to her and to quit wasting his life playing stupid games. Thinking again of the present from Tiffany's he'd not yet given her, he felt it burning a figurative hole in his pocket, even though he had it safely stashed in his locked briefcase.

Wishing he'd given the necklace to her the night

she'd crept into his bed in New York, he began to make his excuses to Portia, thinking he'd insist on inviting Randall over so the actress wouldn't dine alone. Her room was at the hotel, so there'd be no problem about her getting safely home.

"Portia, will you—" he began, but stopped as she put a finger dramatically to her lips.

"Don't look now," the actress said, "but I do believe I see your bride."

"Mia?" Quentin pushed his chair back. She'd come looking for him. Smiling, he began once again to excuse himself.

"And she's with that hunky screenwriter. What's his name? Skeeter or Lizard, or some such?"

"Beetle," Quentin said, the name coming automatically. Beetle, who'd been on his way back to his cabin to write.

Portia leaned over and patted Quentin's arm. "There, there, the first year of marriage is always the toughest. I ought to know, I've been married five times. Ah, they're taking him the champagne now."

Quentin remained in his chair, unable to rise, unable to go to Mia. What was she doing with Beetle?

"The waiter is pouring two glasses." Portia narrowed her eyes. "I didn't send him that champagne so he could drink it with some bimbo. Quentin, darling, jump up this very minute and ask him to join us."

"Are you—" he swallowed the word *crazy*.

He'd wooed Portia to *Permutation* and he had to continue to pay the price. But what was Mia doing with Beetle? Feeding him supper—again? The question bounced around in his mind, causing his emotions to boomerang from reason to jealousy and back again.

Feeling like a man hoist on his own petard, Quentin scraped his chair back one more time and stood.

And turned smack into Mia, Beetle very much in tow, a shit-eating grin on his face, his dark glasses nowhere in sight.

"Mia, what a surprise. Work all caught up?" he said. "And Beetle, did writer's block make you hungry?"

Mia heard the caustic note in Quentin's voice, loud and clear. Well, she'd have to be deaf not to, she thought, the smile on her lips fading. "I came to join you," she said.

"And brought Beetle with you?"

She inclined her head in Portia's direction. "Four is so much better company than three, don't you think?

"There's nothing more boring than other people's lives," Portia said, in a voice that carried straight to Mia's sensible self.

"Shall we stay or shall we leave?" Mia asked Quentin in a low voice.

"By all means, join us," Quentin said. "Portia and I don't mind playing chaperone, do we?"

Portia produced a tiny shrug, then, in her imperious style, flagged down the maitre d' and requested he add three places to their table.

That he had to rearrange the diners next to them didn't seem to matter to the actress. Mia almost admired her assumption that nothing could possibly be too much trouble for Portia Goodhope. Sometimes she wished she had that kind of gumption.

Only of course she didn't. And the actress continued to look straight through her. Mia wondered what it would take to make someone like that sit up and take notice of her. She'd love to figure it out before Portia finished her role in *Permutation*. Men, of course, always got the actress's attention. Wondering if Quentin would be impressed with her if she were more commanding, Mia shot a quick glance at him before she said, "Beetle, have you met Miss Goodhope?"

The screenwriter bowed over Portia's hand. She fawned and made a show of fussing over his manners, while the waiters busily wrestled the chairs into place.

Quentin offered Mia his chair, which she accepted politely. A distance greater than the eight or ten inches between them mounted a barrier Mia felt hopeless to bridge. She'd rushed off after him, thinking to dump Beetle in Portia's hands and whisk Quentin off so they could talk ... really talk.

On the drive over, Mia had taken her mind off her own troubles long enough to tell Beetle all about a friend she and Quentin expected to be visiting the set any day now: Amity, a friend of

Quentin's from New Orleans. An up-and-coming artist, Amity possessed the sensitive soul Beetle sought in a lover. Mia had said so many wonderful things about Amity she almost felt driven to find a priest and confess her hypocrisy.

Mia could tell Beetle's interest had been aroused. He'd been especially interested in the name, repeating "Amity" as if he'd heard the unusual name somewhere before.

He was definitely intrigued, and now, Mr. G had to come through with his end of the deal. Glancing at Quentin glaring at her in his polite company manner, Mia sure hoped Mr. G would hurry.

Mia suddenly noticed the staff had laid one too many places and brought a fifth chair. "Are we expecting someone else?"

Quentin didn't respond. Beetle sat silent. Only Portia spoke, in that "don't brook me" voice of hers. "Quentin, darling, run along on your errand."

Mia replayed the pushy request in her head, wondering how the woman had gotten away with being so bossy for so long. She looked at Quentin, curious to see what he'd do.

Sure enough, he rose and crossed the room. As Mia followed his progress, she spotted Randall, and also saw her husband had headed straight for the accountant. "Oh, no," she said, "how embarrassing."

Portia looked down her nose at Mia. "A word of advice: nothing is embarrassing unless one lets

it be." Then she ran a finger along Beetle's fore-
arm. "You're awfully strong for a writer. Do you
lift those big, heavy, manly weights?"

Mia knew she'd owe Beetle one after this evening. She caught his eye and saw the humor there.
He'd agreed to play up to Portia so Mia could
escape with Quentin, and she could tell he'd keep
his part of the bargain.

Right now she'd best run interference between
Quentin and Randall. "I'll be right back," she said,
rising and making her way toward the accountant's table. She couldn't let Quentin rough Randall up in public. The last thing they needed for
Permutation's health was another layer to add to
their scandal.

But the two were talking cordially enough as
Mia rushed up. She couldn't help but see the
hopeful look fan into Randall's face at her approach; naturally, she experienced a twinge of
guilt at having used him earlier.

Randall rose and took her hand. "No hard feelings, I hope," he said softly.

Mia sensed Quentin shooting daggers at them.
She shook her head, and taking his hand and
squeezing lightly, said, "Right, Quentin?"

He nodded, looking down at her with an expression she couldn't quite decipher, something
most unusual for this man she knew inside and
out. Or thought she did.

Worrying her lip a bit, Mia noticed the magnum
of champagne. From their business dealings and

occasional dinner parties, Mia knew Randall scarcely touched alcohol of any kind.

"I'd like you to meet my date," Randall said. "She just popped off to the powder room."

Popped off? Mia stared at the staid accountant. The Randall she did business with never spoke that way, never looked quite so jolly. Then she looked down. The glass at Randall's place sat empty.

Just then the waiter appeared and replenished his glass. "Two more glasses," Randall said. "We're modern people. Let's just drink a toast to the one that got away."

"Actually, Randall, I came over to convey a message from Miss Goodhope."

"Portia Goodhope?" Randall's eyes bugged. "She's here, in this room?"

Mia remembered him waxing eloquent over the actress. "Oh, yes, over by the windows," she said. "And she really would like you to join her. And your date, too."

When Quentin issued the invitation, Mia had to swallow a laugh at the look on his face. The last thing Portia Goodhope would want would be Randall's date sitting at her table, drinking her champagne. But what nerve to send a magnum over when he'd actually gotten lucky enough to have a woman out with him. Of course, Portia had no way of knowing a date for Randall was a once-in-a-century event.

Glancing toward the tables in front of the window, Randall lifted his glass in a toast to Portia, then drained it.

His face had turned a beety tone. "Where is that girl?"

Mia worried her lip yet again. Some of the other diners had started to glance in their direction. No doubt people recognized Quentin. At least he hadn't "popped over" to bash Randall in the nose again.

"Ah, here she comes!" Randall half-rose from his seat, tottering slightly.

Mia thought they'd better take his car keys from him as soon as they had him settled with Portia. Beetle could drive him to his hotel in her car, as she planned to return to the Cubby Hole with the only man who mattered in her life.

Still holding Quentin's hand, she gave him another, gentler caress. Her heart leaped when he smiled at her, an upward tug of his lips that promised that once more they'd work out whatever misunderstanding they were having.

"Sweetest," Randall said, extending his hand, "I'd like you to meet Mia Tortelli and Quentin Grandy. She's quite a famous producer and Quentin directs movies."

Mia and Quentin stared across the table at Randall, holding hands with thin air.

"How do you do?" Quentin answered first.

Mia kept staring. Quentin never should have coldcocked the guy. Now he'd lost his marbles, or maybe it was simply too much alcohol following the knock on the nose that had caused Randall to drop over the edge.

Then she felt Quentin nudge her and nod toward the empty space next to Randall.

Amity!

Mia's stomach dropped. Amity was back, and both Quentin and Randall could see her!

Obviously pleased at Mia's stunned reaction, Randall said with the pride of a blue-ribbon winner at the county fair, "She's something, isn't she?" He pinched the air and stroked his hand downward, then filled four glasses.

"A toast," he proclaimed, "to love at first sight."

Despite her dislike of the way the bubbles in champagne always made her sneeze, Mia drank. And as she did, she watched the fourth glass waft upward, then empty itself into nothingness.

16 ∾

Amity knew she should make herself scarce.

Without delay.

She'd been so caught up in her thoughts, and in keeping Randall's wandering hands off her body, that she hadn't paid much attention to people's reactions. When Randall had requested a table for two, the maitre d' hadn't blinked an eye.

When Randall ordered two drinks, and the waiter delivered them, she'd noticed nothing to cause her to think she'd gone invisible again.

But the blank look on Quentin's face had keyed her in immediately. She'd smiled, waved, said how nice to see you again. He'd responded to Randall's cues but not at all to her presence.

His wife couldn't see her, either, but that Quentin could no longer make her out gave her a sense of having been abandoned, as if she were now lost to the world in a way she hadn't been before. Orphaned all over again.

Quentin had been her friend, had tried to help her.

Randall only wanted to get into her pants. She could imagine explaining to the bottom line man that she'd dropped in from goodness knew where and no one else could see her. He'd laugh and chuck her under the chin, all the while drooling on her.

Using Randall's besottedness to her advantage now, Amity rubbed up against the front of his chest and slipped one hand around his waist. She hated to leave such quality champagne behind, not to mention the dinner she hadn't even had a chance to order. Her tummy growled, but she told herself she'd have to wait.

"My big, handsome Randall," she said, forcing a pout to her lips, and thinking she deserved this humiliation for considering, even for a moment, of taking on a man like this simply because he had a few lousy dollars in the bank. "Your friends are very nice, but I think the champagne is making me the teeniest bit unwell."

Easing her hand free, Amity kept her arm hidden behind Randall. While she didn't think Quentin could see her, she wasn't taking any chances. Remembering Beetle and the floating money made her cautious.

He stroked her nose. "You don't want to get sick. Not tonight." He sounded almost desperate. "Why don't you go back to the powder room and put a cool cloth on your precious face?"

She smooched her lips at him, and one hand tucked into the pocket of her smock, she weaved her way from the table.

At the end of the room, she turned toward the ladies room, then kept on walking.

She passed through the kitchen, her nostrils flaring at the wonderful aromas filling the air. She almost stopped to help herself to a to-go carton, but decided caution best served her interests.

After all, since Randall could still see her, he might come after her. She patted the pocket of her smock. Randall's wallet looked mighty thick. She'd catch some dinner for herself and splurge on Fancy Feast for Fate, the name she'd bestowed on the cat at the Cubby Hole.

And if Randall acted true to the cautious nature of most money counters, he might even carry a spare key to that lux car.

"Beetle, most divine, do skip over there and see what's keeping Randall."

Happy to escape the carnivorous actress, Beetle rose and made his way across the dining room. It seemed the grande dame had set her sights on the accountant, an observation that relieved Beetle. He'd agreed to help Mia, but ten minutes with Portia was worse than fifty of listening to his mother expound on Sheila's virtues as a prospective wife.

The three of them appeared to be toasting—to what, Beetle could only guess. Of course, since he was a writer, ideas crowded into his head. A funny world, Hollywood, where a guy could bash another guy's face in at noon, then drink with him at dinner.

As soon as he walked up to them, Quentin said, "I take it Portia is growing impatient?" He spoke lightly, but Beetle noticed the director looked at him in a none-too-friendly way.

"Who's this?" The man of Portia's immediate dreams swayed and plied the air with his glass.

Drunk.

Beetle despised drunks. Even the times he'd gotten rip-roaring roasted, he'd despised himself. "Jeffrey Leonard. We, er, met earlier today," he said in reply. He cast a look of entreaty at Mia, which unfortunately Quentin intercepted.

And misinterpreted.

The director pointed to Randall's swollen nose. "I'd advise you to keep your mitts off my wife."

"Quentin!" Mia gasped and let go of his hand. "You're being rude."

"And most unnecessarily," Beetle threw in. All he needed was to be bounced from *Permutation*. "Not that I don't find your wife charming, attractive, and intelligent, all qualities I admire in a woman."

"You know what I admire in a woman?" Randall asked, and without waiting to see if anyone cared at all, continued, "A butt shaped like a pear." Glass still in hand, he fashioned a shape in mid-air.

"You've got one, Mia," he said, with something close to a leer, "and so does Amity."

"Amity?" Beetle stiffened. The woman Mia had described to him had had the same name, a most unusual name. That was also the word Quentin had said in response to his tale of the levitating cash.

Mia groaned, and for the oddest moment, Beetle thought both she and Quentin were about to burst out laughing.

"Do you know someone named Amity?" Mia directed the question to Beetle, a look of anticipation on her face.

"No." Truthfully, he hadn't met any such woman. And from Mia's glowing description, he had half a doubt she even existed. If he ever did meet a woman as creative, insightful, quixotic, and gorgeous as Mia had pictured her, he'd be pretty sure he'd died and gone to Heaven.

Especially if the woman paid him any attention. Not that he didn't have lots of women fawning over him. More than enough for any man. But somehow they always seemed to be the pretty-but-halfwit type, attracted by his brawn rather than his art. Or the bookish ones like Sheila, who thought it their duty to convince him to give up writing, and to settle down and teach.

"Well, I do." Randall refilled his glass, glanced at the other glasses, but stopped short of offering them more. He settled the magnum carefully into the wine stand. "And she's the most bee-yoo-tiful woman on the face of the Earth."

"Or Purgatory."

Quentin murmured this phrase into Mia's ear, but Beetle heard him.

Beetle glanced over his shoulder and saw Portia had risen. He really hated to be part of the growing scene. From the corner of his eye, he'd seen a man scribbling in what Beetle recognized as a reporter's notebook. Maybe he was a fool, because wiser heads than his would probably say any publicity was good publicity, but Beetle decided to take matters into his own hands.

"Randall," he said, "Portia Goodhope sent me over to invite you to her table. Why don't you follow me over there?"

"P-Portia?"

As the man stuttered her name, Beetle winced. Then he realized he hadn't stuttered all evening. What a miracle!

"What about Amity?" he said, obediently rising, pausing only to collect the champagne bottle.

"She can join us, too," Beetle said, in the voice he and his parents used when they visited his great-aunt Hilda in the nursing home.

Mia and Quentin stood back as Beetle led the accountant across the room. He saw them glance at each other and smile, and knew he'd played his part well.

And as soon as he'd delivered the tipsy Randall into the solicitous arms of Portia Goodhope, Beetle made his excuses and headed outside. Mia had given him the keys to her car and the valet ticket, confident she'd be leaving with Quentin.

With a smile playing on his lips and a hope in his heart that one day he'd find a love as solid as theirs, Beetle requested the car and wondered when Quentin's friend Amity from New Orleans would appear on the scene.

*   *   *

Even the wallet stuffed with twenties and fifties couldn't console Amity.

Invisible again!

She'd tried to hitch a ride, and from her failure to interest any driver, Amity had to conclude that somehow she'd definitely slipped back into her funny nonbeing state. Then she'd walked right up to two of the parking attendants at the hotel and tickled them under their chins. They'd kept on talking about the Dodgers' chances in the pennant race.

She'd sighed and plopped down in the circular drive, prepared to wait for someone she knew to exit. She'd hop into their car with them and hitch-hike back to the movie location sight. It felt like the only safe place to go, plus, she couldn't bear to abandon Fate.

If only Randall had kept a spare key in his wallet, she'd gladly have borrowed his Lexus. He'd been getting rapidly intoxicated, so the way Amity figured, she would have been doing him a good Samaritan sort of service by keeping him from driving.

Mia and Quentin walked out of the restaurant hand in hand. Amity rose, then halted. The two of them appeared to be well on the way to making up after their earlier misunderstandings. What if she became visible to Quentin again? No, she'd wait. Beetle or Randall would show up eventually. And if Randall tried to summon his car, she would let him collect it, then slip behind the wheel and take control. Even if it meant sitting on the mug's lap.

Fortunately, Beetle walked outside, looking fairly satisfied with himself. He no longer sported those dark glasses, even though he still wore his uniform of black turtleneck, black pants. Plus a black jacket, probably added for the occasion.

As he waited for his car, Amity watched him. He didn't strike her as the kind of man who was used to eating at restaurants where the appetizers cost more than ordinary people's complete dinners.

For that matter, she wasn't that kind of woman, either.

She appreciated the finer things in life; unfortunately, she could rarely afford them. Probably, she mused, knowing she was trying to justify her earlier behavior, that was why she'd accepted Randall Hollings' dinner invitation.

Now she shuddered, wondering how she could have fixated on the man's money for even a millisecond. Thank Heaven she'd been saved from herself!

Beetle headed for a late model Buick and Amity edged up behind him. She'd figured out enough about this invisibleness to know if she opened the door, that action would be apparent to anyone paying attention. Only her body and clothing appeared invisible to others, as long as what she wore remained on her body.

Hustling into the car while he turned to tip the

valet, Amity scooted to the passenger side of the seat. Beetle carried some weight on him, and she didn't want to be squished. Though, eyeing him as he slid behind the wheel, she knew he had the kind of body she wouldn't mind lying beneath.

Only she wouldn't lie still. Amity smiled. Despite her weird state and impossibly unbelievable situation, she found herself fantasizing about the man next to her. If only she had her sketchbook, she'd love to capture the firm line of his arms, the angle of his head, the slight curve to his lips.

Full, well-formed lips that beckoned kisses.

Shivering a bit at the deliciousness of that thought, Amity settled against the seat. Since she didn't have her sketchbook, she'd have to let her thoughts and Beetle's satisfying presence keep her company during the ride back to the Cubby Hole.

Watching him, comfortably in command of the car, humming softly as they sped through the night, Amity almost forgot that once again, she'd be going to bed on an empty stomach. Keep this adventure up, and she'd be down to skin and bones.

Like poor Spike Jones, she thought suddenly, the vision of her dear dog coming to mind. She pictured how thin he'd been when she'd found him, abused and abandoned by some cruel monster who'd chained him to a stake in the middle of a concrete parking lot and left him without shade or water in the middle of a New Orleans July day.

Spike, who'd knocked down the scaffolding, and sent her into this misadventure.

Smiling softly and looking out the window to the darkness, Amity whispered, "Hang in there. I love you, Spike." Somehow, she'd find her way back to her family of dogs and cats.

Glancing at Beetle who'd reached out to tune the radio, smiling as he settled on a jazz station, she wondered whether Spike hadn't known what he'd been doing that stormy day in New Orleans.

Mia rested her head on Quentin's shoulder and gazed out the window at the dark road rushing by.

Quentin ruffled the top of her hair, grateful she'd warmed up to him from the moment he'd convinced her he hadn't been able to see Amity with Randall. They still needed to talk, and he had a confession of his own to make, but for the moment, he savored their peace. "Penny for your thoughts," he said, knowing in his heart she'd feel the same.

"I feel as if I've gotten my life back," she said.

"Or at least your husband?" Quentin stroked the tip of her nose.

"You are my life, you know."

She sounded so serious it made Quentin nervous. "If something happened to me, you'd find yourself with a trail of suitors wagging their tails like eager puppies."

She shook her head, in effect rubbing it against his shoulder. "That's never happened to me, and even if it did, I'd pay no attention to them." She traced the outline of a heart on the front of his shirt.

"Just don't replace me with a guy like Randall," Quentin said. "My ego couldn't take it."

Mia laughed. "It was very bad of you to bash him in the nose."

"What? That didn't impress you? Hero to the rescue, and all that?"

Mia wrinkled her nose. "That's not my definition of a hero."

Quentin turned off the main highway onto the lane leading to the lodge. He slowed the car, found a suitable spot to park, and maneuvered off the road. Pulling Mia into his arms, he said, "Want to tell me your definition?"

Her lips hovering near his, Mia whispered, "My idea of a hero is a man who understands me even when I don't understand myself. Someone who forgives me when I've been selfish or prickly." She kissed him lightly on the lips, then added, "Someone who loves me so much he can't help but go nuts when he hears another man telling me he wants me."

She drew back slightly. Little light filtered into the lane, but his eyes had grown used to the night, enough so that he could see she was looking into his eyes as if searching for some sign, some indication.

"What is it, sweetheart?"

"You do love me that much, don't you?" She sat up, free of his arms. "That is why you knocked him out, not out of some macho tendency to play king of the hill?"

"Frankly, I did it for both reasons." He pulled her back. "Men are like that, Mia."

"Even heroes?"

"*Especially* heroes," he said, slanting his lips over hers. She parted her lips and greedily sucked in his tongue. He groaned and shifted one hand to her buttocks to draw her closer.

Closer wasn't good enough. Mia was plumbing the depths of his mouth, dancing her tongue over and around his, swaying with him in an erotic dance. Inside. Deep inside. He gripped her bottom.

Mia gasped and broke their kiss. Placing a hand on her backside, she said, "Pear-shaped!"

Intent on easing up her skirt, Quentin barely heard her.

She stilled his hand. "Randall said I had a pear-shaped butt."

"So?" How could she think of Randall at a time like this?

"He said Amity did, too." Her eyes had gone wide and dark, and Quentin would happily drown in them. If only she'd quit talking about Randall.

"Why could he see her? What does it mean?"

Randall and Amity.

Quentin shifted on the seat, easing Mia onto the seat beside him. "Mean?" He knew he sounded stupid, but he couldn't help it. His body screamed for release. He wanted to bury himself in Mia, for-

get all about the horrible day, and wake up tomorrow, his arms wrapped around the woman he
loved.

"I mean, why did Amity become visible to
Randall, of all people? He's an excellent accountant, don't get me wrong, but he lacks imagination. I can't believe he'd be of one second's use to
Amity in achieving her mission."

Quentin almost blurted out the truth, almost
shared that he'd prayed to Mr. G to ask for exactly
that reality. But he felt suddenly shy, almost embarrassed, to admit he'd asked for help from the
old coot. Even to Mia, who believed in such in-
tercession, he couldn't say it. Plus, listening to
Mia, he wondered why he'd thought for a second
Amity would hit it off with Randall. So he merely
mumbled, "Maybe Randall's her target."

"Are you nuts?" Mia drew back and studied
him as if passion had cost him his reason. "You
were in the Second Chance Room. You know the
rules. No direct contact with the target."

"Maybe Randall could help her," Quentin suggested hopefully. "He's got a good brain, didn't
you say?"

"For figures."

"Well—" He shut up before he made the mistake of saying Amity had a figure worthy of Randall's interest.

"He's her total opposite. Staid, boring and re-
spectable. According to you, she's footloose, an ac-
complished petty thief, and absolutely unsuited to
hold a conversation with a man like Randall."

"You don't have to glorify the guy."

"And you don't have to make Amity out to be Mother Teresa."

Quentin held up his hands. "Listen to us. Mia, sweetheart, no matter what the reason is for Randall being able to see Amity, let's not let it come between us."

Her face softened and she leaned over and kissed him on the lips, a kiss as whispery as the wings of a butterfly closing over his mouth. "Thank you," Mia whispered. "That's one more reason why you're my hero." Snuggling against him, she tapped the steering wheel. "Now, let's go home and go to bed."

Quentin started the car, then slipped his arm back around his wife's shoulders. She smiled up at him and his heart caught. She trusted him completely, implicitly. And an essential ingredient to the trust that nurtured love was sharing and communicating.

Holding her more tightly, he pictured how she'd feel if she found out he'd engineered the deal with Randall and Amity. Why didn't you tell me, she'd ask.

And, kick himself as he might, he really couldn't answer that question.

Because he should have told her.

Mia snuggled against Quentin, her mind racing to answer what had backfired in her message to Mr. G. Had she mistakenly typed in Randall's name rather than Beetle's? Surely she couldn't have made such a monumental mistake.

Glancing up at Quentin, seeing the love in his eyes, she almost told him that she'd summoned help from Mr. G. But she felt embarrassed; not only had she muffed it somehow, but her motivation for asking for help had been so selfish.

She'd wanted Amity safely out of their way, and she supposed it served her right that the artist had turned up in their midst again. Her ma had always told them, as little kids, that prayers were meant to be used to ask for things bigger than yourself.

Mia could still remember the time her ma had smacked her brother Michael when she'd heard him praying for a shiny yellow dump truck for Christmas.

She'd made him carry out their arthritic neighbor's trash for a week, plus forbidden him dessert for a month.

But on Christmas, the shiny yellow dump truck had been under the tree, wrapped in a big red ribbon.

So why, if even selfish prayers were answered, could Randall, rather than Beetle, see Amity?

17 ✑

By the time Beetle parked the car at the lodge, Amity had decided two things. One, she definitely wanted to get to know Beetle better. And two, she'd been born a fool and would probably die a fool, if that hadn't already happened.

Amity slipped out the door before Beetle turned to close it, ruing her penchant for falling for men who floated, drifted, meandered or otherwise wandered through life.

What was it about Beetle that attracted her?

Was it his body?

Keeping pace with him as he strode down the path toward his cabin, she cast a sidelong glance.

Certainly physical attraction played a role here. Amity liked to think of it as the artist in her that got her into situations with impossibly gorgeous guys who had absolutely no potential.

Why, she'd let Tuggle Breaux sleep on her couch because she fell for the way he quirked his brows when regaling their friends with stories of silly tourists who paid him to create his balloon animals. If they'd known how much fun Tuggle made of them, not one would have paid him the mere dollar he advertised as his minimum.

Of course, Amity hadn't gone as far as sleeping with Tuggle Breaux, and she liked to pride herself on her self-control, but the truth was, she'd been about to consider it the day she'd come home early and found him violating her no smoking policy.

And that had been the end of Tuggle.

There were others, more than she cared to remember, who'd had broad shoulders, marvelously developed pecs, legs as muscled as Olympians', and chests that tapered to waistlines any Southern belle would have envied.

Beetle had all that.

But he had something more.

He had presence, a way of seeing the world, of assessing. He'd also completed a screenplay, now in production, rather than sitting around talking about doing so, an accomplishment that ranked him head and shoulders over all those other guys.

Her hormones, naturally, didn't much care about those additional qualities. Her heart, however, felt differently.

So what was it? Something on a higher plane, perhaps? His creative self mirroring her own?

Cocking her head, she considered that possibility, thinking as she did so that she'd love to slip her hand into his and study his palm. But so far, she'd only been able to connect with inanimate objects, and animals. Anything human she could not seem to feel or interact with. Except for Randall, but she'd already dismissed him from her mind. And Quentin, of course.

As a writer, Beetle seemed to have done an admirable job in concocting *Permutation*. She liked the story, enjoyed the humor and pathos of the premise of a bad guy trapped in the body of a fairy godmother and vice versa. She particularly liked the way the characters developed.

The only thing she'd disapproved of had been the love scene she'd attempted to tamper with, but after analyzing the story further, she'd realized something that had made her very, very sorry she'd tampered with Beetle's computer.

What had upset her was the love scene she'd seen on the computer screen, the one where the woman had said, "Do me now." In between moments of helping out with the frog shot, she'd overheard enough to realize that she'd come across a love scene involving Moe the Biker in Portia's body. So it'd been Moe's voice, speaking from Portia's body, saying those words.

Which made a lot of sense. It was a clever way of pointing out some basic male-female differences in the whole sex scenario.

But, oh, no, Amity had to jump in with both feet and mess things up for Beetle—who, all along, had been doing something she thought brilliant, now that she understood.

Ah, nothing like getting the big picture.

The other thing Amity liked about *Permutation* was that the story ended happily ever after.

Which was something, Amity thought, as she watched Beetle unlock his cabin door and prepare to go in and shut her out, that would more than likely never happen in her own life.

Wishing for what she couldn't have, Amity hesitated, but only for a second. What harm would it do to follow him into his room? What trouble could she cause? He'd be none the wiser, and she had to sleep somewhere. She was invisible, for Pete's sake.

Beetle stepped inside his room, leaving the door ajar. That gave her time to peek in and see him strip his jacket off and toss it on the bed. Strolling back to the doorway, he braced his arms against the frame and gazed out into the night.

He'd not switched the light on in his room. From her vantage point, teetering on the edge of the postage stamp of a porch, only inches from him, Amity gazed at him, admiring the way his body stretched across the doorway. She appreciated the hungry look in his eyes as he scanned the stars twinkling overhead.

It seemed to her overactive imagination that he appealed to the stars for a special sort of evening. He communed with the beauty of darkness, lit only by the echo of light from hundreds of thousands of miles away. But maybe she saw only what lay in her own heart.

Amity knew she tended to picture things that never existed, one of the reasons she could produce abstract paintings as well as her bread-and-butter landscapes and tourist portraits. But

honestly, standing there, watching Beetle absorb
the beauty of the evening, she could have sworn
she heard the whisper of a prayer from his soul.

All of which made her shiver.

All of which made her even more determined
to slip into his room before he retreated and
closed the door behind him.

And then Fate stepped in.

Or rather, padded up, tail at half-mast.

The cat moved in a cautious half-circle, one eye
pasted on Beetle in the doorway, the other clearly
making a beeline toward where Amity stood. Obviously deciding she was safe as long as she
stayed close to her protector, the cat braved her
way to the top step, then rubbed against Amity's
calves. Amity knelt and stroked her head. The ensuing purr was reward in and of itself.

Purr motor still going at full blast, the cat nosed
at the pockets of her smock and Amity laughed.
"You learn fast, don't you, Fate?"

"*Meeoooowwwww!*" The cat let out its hunger
cry, the call that had first attracted Amity's attention that morning.

Beetle, his stargazing abruptly interrupted,
looked down.

And sneezed.

The cat edged back a few steps, and Amity
placed a comforting hand on its back.

Beetle sneezed again, and Amity heard the echo
of that sneeze from that morning. Only that morning? She'd been cruising down the lane, the only
thought on her mind to put space between her

and this Cubby Hole Lodge. It was the cat that had dragged her back to where Beetle was. In fine form, he'd been jogging down the lane, bare-chested.

As soon as he'd gotten within five feet of Fate, he'd sneezed.

Amity's heart dropped.

He couldn't be allergic to cats.

Not Beetle. Not the man she'd decided to throw her lot in with.

Fate shifted her nose forward, scenting the wind.

Beetle stooped down and held out a hand. "Hello, fella," he said. "I like cats. It's not my fault I'm al—"

The ensuing sneeze blew the cat backward and Amity had to scramble to calm Fate to keep her from running away and wounding Beetle's feelings.

He was right. It wasn't his fault he was allergic.

Plenty of people who loved animals found they were allergic.

But in Amity's experience, such allergies could be overcome.

By love.

She stroked Fate, whispering to her, letting her know she was safe. Secure. Loved.

Beetle sat down on the top step. Amity scooted over a bit, which was kind of silly, since Beetle couldn't see or feel her. But invisible or not, she didn't want to get squished.

Calmed by Amity's soothing strokes, Fate sat

back on her haunches, studying Beetle.

Beetle pulled a tissue from a pocket of his pants and wiped at his eyes. Speaking in a low voice, he said, "Sorry not to be more welcoming, but I'm as allergic as hell to cats. Dogs, too, so it's nothing personal."

"There," he said, "at least you're not running away from me. I actually like cats." He sneezed. "A lot. When I was nine, I begged my parents for a kitten."

Beetle leaned against the rickety porch railing, one hand still outstretched to the cat, the other pressed against his nostrils.

"Hey, there, you didn't run away from me, fella," Beetle murmured, and reached to pet the cat.

The cat drew back and hissed. Beetle laughed and stood up. "Not on the first date, huh?"

He left his hand extended past his thigh, studying the cat, wondering, between sneezes, why it had decided to adopt him.

Trying once more, he stretched out his hand and felt a surge of satisfaction as the cat allowed him to stroke the soft fur of its back, if only for a moment.

"That's not so bad, is it?"

Beetle no more had the words out of his mouth than he exploded into a crescendo of sneezing.

Lifting his shoulders apologetically, he said, "You see my problem."

"I've tried everything," he said, wiping at his eyes and nose. "After my parents finally gave in and got me a kitten, a little black-and-white spit-fire, all I did was swell and itch and sneeze. My mother finally took the cat away, and to this day, she swears she found it a good home."

The cat, ears cocked at an angle that made Beetle feel as if it actually were listening, stared intently at him.

"And you know what? I still wonder if she didn't just take the cat to the pound. She won't admit to it, and she'd never tell me that, but I'm just not sure."

The cat stared, unblinking, at him.

It crossed Beetle's mind that most of his friends would think he'd flipped. Here he was, sitting on a porch, under the stars on an incredibly beautiful evening, talking to a cat. With only a minimum of effort, Beetle knew he could have had any number of the cute young things on the production set entwined in his arms at this point, yet he sat there alone, except for the cat.

The cat, he reminded himself, that had thrown him into this agony of sneezing.

"So you know what I did?"

The cat continued to stare, something Beetle had always liked about felines. They watched, they listened, and only sometimes did they speak their minds. But when they did, they always had something to say.

Behavior from which a writer could learn a good lesson.

"I went to an allergist. I had a million shots. Then I went to the pound. And within ten minutes,

I was sneezing so badly, I had to fight my way out. Blinded."

He hung his head, thinking of his failure.

No wonder he'd gotten the nickname *Beetle*. He'd finally given up on cats or dogs or other cuddly creatures, and taken to lizards as pets.

Not, of course, that lizards were beetles, but somehow his insect collections and his pet iguanas had all gotten rolled into one, and the nickname stuck.

The cat, after a cautious sniffing of the night air, edged its front feet closer. Its body relaxed a micrometer.

Beetle smiled.

"I thought I'd redeem the kitten my mother had probably sent to its death, but instead I was driven out, a victim of these goddamn allergies."

His voice must have risen, because the cat had drawn back in alarm.

"Sorry," Beetle said. "But if I had my way, I'd have a houseful of cats. And dogs. And not to get maudlin, but a couple of kids skipping around would be nice, too."

He leaned his head against the railing, thinking of Mia and Quentin, and how contented the two of them seemed together. When they weren't arguing, that was. But even when the two had their differences, their love shone like an arc, covering the very air between them.

Ah, what he wouldn't give for a love like that.

A love, he knew, he'd never even begin to hint

at with Sheila, his mother's candidate for Mrs. Jeffrey "Beetle" Leonard.

He sneezed again. With a final longing look at the now quite friendly cat, Beetle rose and backed into his cabin.

Amity, her eyes moist, gave Fate a quick pat to the head and whispered, "Sorry," before she whipped into the room after Beetle.

He yawned and stretched again, then collected the jacket he'd shed earlier and turned to hang it up on the bar that served as his clothes closet.

So the writer had neatnik qualities. Amity smiled. Her life could do with some of that influence. So what if they'd both be poor vagabonds living from creation to creation. She'd paint, he'd scribble. Together they'd make masterpieces.

From the other side of the door, the cat mewed plaintively, demanding attention. Amity stared from Beetle toward the window, willing him to walk over and slide it open. She didn't want Fate to be left out.

And he did.

She smiled. What a hero. Any man who could read her mind when he didn't even know she existed was Heaven sent! Then, she remembered the last man she'd found to fix her interests on, the last man she'd thought destined to turn around her weirdly empty (for someone so busy) life. Amity's smile faded. He'd been an even greater flake than Tuggle Breaux, though on the surface he'd seemed fairly harmless.

Lance what-was-his-name? Amity sank down

on the edge of the bed close to the door. She'd met him at the Tomato Festival, swaying along with the rest of the raucous crowd lining the streets around the French Market. In New Orleans, any event provided an excuse for a parade, for a party, for an opportunity to turn strangers into friends.

Over oysters Rockefeller, blocks from the Tomato Festival where they'd bumped into one another, Lance had explained to her that he was in town on a consulting job—a job, he'd hinted, that meant a lot to a very important but unnamed company. Very hush-hush, he'd said, slurping the last of his Hurricane through a straw.

Rats! What a fool she was.

When the police came and hauled him away the next morning, she'd had to answer endless questions. And that morning, in between trying to sort out exactly what manner of scam Lance had been running, Amity had promised herself she'd never be taken in again.

Yet only tonight she'd gone off to dinner with Randall.

Why is it, she asked herself, *you think every man you meet is Mr. Perfect? What if just once in your life you studied the lay of the land before diving in? Or whatever the unmixed metaphor might be?* Her shoulders slumped.

Pivoting away from the window, Beetle tugged his turtleneck from his pants, stripped it off, and dropped it onto the bed. It landed half on and half off Amity's lap.

Looking down at the shirt, she froze. Knowing enough about her situation, Amity realized that if she shifted, the shirt would appear to move of its own accord.

She tipped her head around and froze all over again.

Beetle's bare chest looked even sexier tonight than last night.

She wet her lips. What she wouldn't give to run her fingers over those beautifully formed pecs, trace the hairs that spread from navel to clavicle. She could do it, too, and he'd never know.

Being invisible had a few things going for it.

Then she caught sight of the shirt in her lap and remembered she couldn't move.

Kind of like the time she'd been playing doctor in the confessional with one of the gardener's sons and lost all track of time. When the priest opened the door, Tommy had snatched his pants and run before the old man could grab him.

Amity's blouse had snagged on something in the fusty old cubicle and Father Fitzmorris had nabbed her.

Despite the browbeating Father had delivered and the nasty stings of the sisters' favorite switch, Tommy's name had not passed Amity's lips. She explained her stubborn refusal to name her accomplice as doctor-patient privilege, an answer that got her sent to bed without supper after a final denunciation as not only a sinner but a smart-mouth.

Beetle crossed the small room, pausing at the

foot of the bed. He looked from his computer to the bathroom and back. With a sigh, he walked into the bathroom and Amity heard the faucets of the tub squeak on.

Immediately she slipped from beneath the turtleneck, leaving it jumbled on the bed. As soon as she heard Beetle step into the shower, she slipped over to the window.

Fate sat below the windowsill, washing her face. When Amity appeared, she stopped and looked up.

"Want to come in?"

The cat glanced toward the window, sat back on its haunches, and glanced upward, then back to where it sat several times.

Amity patted the windowsill. She wanted Beetle to make friends with Fate, too.

The cat twitched its tail, gathered its body, then sprang. Rubbing her body against Amity's hand, she strolled back and forth on the sill, purring.

The water stopped. In a few minutes, Beetle reappeared, toweling himself dry.

Amity swallowed. Her throat constricted, as she suddenly considered to what degree she'd invaded this man's privacy. How would she like some strange man sneaking peeks at her?

Well, Amity answered herself, that would depend on the man.

As usual, it was a little past time for rethinking her actions, but Amity decided to concentrate on scratching Fate under the chin, her back to Beetle, until he put some clothes on.

As much as she appreciated the male form and all its attributes, having lived so many years of her life in the foundling home where the pursuit of privacy had ranked right up there with fibbing as a venial sin, Amity thought better of robbing Beetle completely of his.

She heard him walk back to the bathroom. A man who hung his jacket would no doubt leave his towel neatly on the bar, rather than tossing it on the floor, as Amity had been known to do more than once.

She gave him several more minutes, during which time she heard him rifling about in a suitcase. Surely he'd put some clothes on. Finally, when even Fate had gotten enough of her under-the-chin rub, Amity edged around.

"Oh, my," she said, "oh, my."

Beetle finally found his journal. The bag he'd bought at the Army-Navy store had so many zippered compartments he had to look in every last one of them before he unearthed his notebook.

"That's what you get for neglecting it so long," he muttered. At one point in his life, when he'd been knee-deep in science and academia, the personal writing he'd done in his journal had been his salvation.

Now, with the writing he'd done for his film work, the journal often lay neglected for days and even weeks on end.

Not good.

Feeling refreshed from his brief shower and glad to be free of his clothes, Beetle found a pen and carried it and his notebook to the lumpy bed.

He stacked the two scrawny pillows as well as he could and climbed into bed.

He opened the journal, studied the inscription he'd penned on the first sheet, then closed it again and got back out of bed.

Returning to his makeshift desk, he collected the papers Queenie had given him earlier that day, then got into bed again.

Queenie hadn't known who had sketched the remake of Portia's costume. Quentin had given them to her, and Beetle had figured out quickly that in Queenie's eyes, the director could do no wrong. But it had been Mia, according to Queenie, who'd instructed her to make sure Beetle saw the sketches.

What amazed Beetle about the drawings of flowing, lighter-than-air fabric that somehow also conveyed depth and texture was the similarity between the designs and his own conception of how the fairy godmother would appear.

Not, of course, that Beetle, a mere writer, had ever expected to be asked about wardrobe.

But this unknown artist had captured his own vision, almost as if she'd been putting into pictures the thoughts in his head.

Plus the artist had written on the paper in bold strokes, "They've done her up for comedy, rather than for theme."

Words Beetle thought perfectly described the hideous maid's getup Portia had first appeared in. No matter her other faults, and whether or not her objections had stemmed from vanity, Portia had his vote on holding out against a look that had been totally, completely wrong.

Beetle lay the sketches beside him on the bed and opened his journal. He saw the last entry had been the day he'd met Mia Tortelli at McDonald's. Spurred on by the length of time he'd neglected his once nightly recordings, he began to write.

Earlier tonight my head was filled with this beauty Mia Tortelli promises to introduce me to. She senses, I think, the lonely part of me that longs to find its other half. But as I look at these Ma Belle sketches, I think that their designer must surely be a woman, and even if that woman should turn out to be as ugly as a frog, I would fall in love with her.

Beetle sighed and wished he'd grow out of being a hopeless romantic. Perhaps he should go home and marry Sheila and produce two-point-five bouncing babies who'd grow up to wear spectacles and never venture outside the boundaries of the Land of Lincoln.

Fact: you have no idea who drew these sketches. For that matter, it's probably Quentin, and he just didn't tell Queenie. So much for falling in love with the artist.

Beetle heard a rustle of paper and glanced up from his notebook. His eyes widened as he watched the sketches levitate. Without thinking, he grabbed at them. They tugged back, then abruptly fell into his hands. He let them drop to the covers again and continued to stare, his heart beating quickly.

Amity could have kicked herself. When she'd

turned and gotten an eyeful of his gorgeous, muscle-rippled, utterly naked body, she'd whipped back around. She'd almost whispered a prayer to calm her pulse. Then she'd remained at the window until she was positive he'd settled himself under the covers.

Yet when she'd turned from the window at last to find him gazing at her sketches, she'd completely forgotten what happened when she interacted with objects. All she wanted to understand at this moment was why Beetle Leonard held her costume sketches in his hands.

Feeling very cross, as if he'd invaded her privacy, Amity sat down on the bed and drew her knees to her chest. He continued to stare at the drawings as if he'd seen a ghost.

She chuckled. In a way, he had. Then she quickly sobered, lurking thoughts of her unsettled state crowding into her head. Thankful that Beetle had left the lights on, Amity lay her cheek on her knee and waited for Beetle to go back to whatever he was writing.

Maybe she'd get some insight into this man who gazed at her sketches. It was as if he could truly appreciate the beauty of the images she'd given birth to in her mind and then released to life on paper.

Maybe, with that knowledge of him, she could finally get some sleep.

She glanced over to the window, where Fate still perched on the sill, blended into the shadows. Amity didn't think the cat would brave its way into the room, which was just as well. She hated to think of listening to Beetle sneeze all night long. Sitting quite as still as Fate, Amity poised on the edge of the bed, waiting for Beetle to quit worrying over the presence of ghosts.

At last he returned to the notebook. Amity crept closer, careful not to rearrange anything on the bed as she peered at the page he'd begun to fill.

I do not believe I am being visited by spirits.

Glancing at the line he'd written, Beetle went back and added parentheses around the sentence. After all, these illusions he'd been experiencing couldn't have too much relation to the rest of his life.

A life that's been fairly straightforward. If I met this unseen/unknown artist, would she find me boring? Too prosaic?

"Someone better suited to teaching?" Beetle muttered. Finding himself fairly uninspired, he closed his journal. Gathering the sketches, he inserted them in the notebook, then lay it on the floor. He reached over and turned off the light.

"Ooh," Amity breathed, turning his words over in her mind, feeling as if some fate, far greater than her latest cat adoptee, had to be at work. If only she could tell him who she was, that she existed!

Sorrow touched her as she realized the two of them would be nothing but two ships passing unobserved on a dark and silent night.

He admired her artist's insights, even seemed to understand them. She felt, for the first time she could remember, as if potential existed for another human being to understand and appreciate her.

Not just Amity the ditz, Amity the trouble-maker.

But the Amity who viewed the world through a child's eyes and saw miracles where others saw clouds.

She sighed, wishing she could tell him how important he might have been in her life.

Then she realized she could. If she waited until he fell asleep, she could tiptoe off the bed and make her own entry in his journal. Enough light filtered in the window. As long as she was quiet as a mouse, he wouldn't awaken.

And then, after she'd shared her heart with Beetle, she'd slip under the covers.

She wasn't one to miss a chance to embrace her destiny.

18 ～

As soon as they reached their cabin, Quentin spotted the message tacked on the door. Luckily, he found it first. In the glare of the bare bulb of the porch light he recognized his assistant director's scrawl.

Palming the note, he turned and scooped Mia into his arms, lifting her easily. Good news or bad, it could wait until he made love to his wife.

"May I carry you over the threshold?"

Tucked against his chest, smiling up at him with one of her impish looks he loved so much, Mia said, "If I didn't know you better, Quentin Grandy, I'd say you were quite the hopeless romantic."

"Let me show you," he said, and reached for the door. Unfortunately, he lost his dashing effect as he couldn't quite manage the key with Mia in his arms.

Laughing, she said, "Let me help." In a flash, she had the door opened.

"What would I do without you?" he asked as he carried her into the cabin.

Mia clung to him, her breasts cozied against his

chest in a way that drove him wild. Reaching for a light switch, he swung his foot into the base of the chair and swore.

"You're hurt," Mia said.

"Oh, I'm hurting, all right, but it's not my toe I'm particularly concerned about."

He kissed her lightly and started to set her on her feet.

"Wait," Mia said, a spark in her eyes that delighted Quentin. "Let's do this nice"—she brushed a fingertip over his lips—"and slow." Still in his arms, she unfastened the top button on his shirt. "And easy," she murmured, placing a kiss on his chest, then reaching for the next button.

"Nice and slow and easy." Quentin wondered what he'd done in his life to deserve Mia. It must have been in a past life, or Mr. G had taken pity on him.

Mia wriggled slightly, and Quentin realized she was reaching for the buttons at the shoulders of her dress.

"What a clever design that is," he said, as the bodice of her sleeveless dress fell forward, revealing the scrap of lace that Mia called a bra.

Cupping her breasts, Mia offered herself to him.

Inspired by this lovely game, Quentin lifted Mia closer to his now very greedy mouth. Unable to use his hands, he claimed her breasts with his tongue.

"Nice. And slow." Mia lulled him in a low voice, her hands playing with the back of his neck, twining through his hair, as she breathed in wispy moans that drove him even wilder.

With his teeth, he pulled free the lace that restrained her breasts and lapped at her nipples. She seemed to forget herself as she caught her breath and writhed against him. With a funny little smile, she said, "I may just die of too much pleasure."

"No such thing." He captured her lips, seeking her mouth, seeking to bury his tongue, to devour and be devoured. The minx was turning him into a hopeless romantic, he thought, then forgot to think as Mia reached between her legs and found the buckle of his belt.

He came up for air. "Can I put you down yet?"

She'd started to tug on the zipper. "Oh, no, I don't think just yet."

"Mia, you're—you're—" He groaned. She had both her hands wrapped around his shaft. "Oh, God."

She tipped her head up. "Kiss me," she said.

He did, and it was all Quentin could do to remain standing and not drop her as she stroked, first slowly, then more rapidly. Breathing raggedly, he staggered, then propped himself against the bar separating that room from the kitchen.

He was seeing red and about to explode when he realized he wanted to play more of this game before it came to an end.

Lifting his lips from hers, he said, "Mia, Mia, now I have something for you."

"You do?" She slowed her hands but kept them wrapped around his throbbing shaft.

"Hmm, yes, yes, I do." He eased around, then settled her gently on the bar top. The maneuver caused her to have to let go of him. She looked disappointed, which made him chuckle.

Then, as he kissed her and edged her dress up, she began to smile. She tossed her head back, stretching out on the counter. "Ooh, Quentin, you're naughty," she whispered, then helped him raise her dress to her waist.

He had to laugh. "I think that's the pot calling the kettle black," he said, and lowered his mouth to inch down the scrap of lace and satin that stood in his way.

Quentin teased her tender inner lips with his tongue. She sighed and lifted her hips, offering herself to him. He tasted, sucking and nibbling, about to explode himself as she started those breathy moans. Watching him love her, she massaged her breast in sensuous circles.

That image, which he caught out of the corner of his eye, almost sent him over the edge. Mia, Mia, who would have thought his practical beauty hid so much sensuality?

Then, once again he lost all train of thought. He delved and then gently, softly, exactly the way he knew she loved, lapped her most sensitive spot.

She cried out and shuddered, and Quentin filled himself with her, thrilled and humbled to be the man to share this woman's loving.

"Oh, Quentin," she said after a long moment, "I'll never move again."

He smiled. "Shall I lift you down and carry you to bed?"

She nodded, but when she slid to her feet, she kept going, kneeling in front of him, taking him in her mouth.

And Quentin knew exactly what Mia meant about dying from too much pleasure.

A long, long, long time later, lying on the bed with Mia in his arms, Quentin said, "I have a surprise for you."

Her eyes widened. He smiled. "No, I mean a gift."

"A present for me?"

He nodded. Easing free of their arm-in-arm embrace, he said, "I'll be right back."

Mia lay on the bed and stretched her arms lazily over her head. Quentin was the most wonderful husband and lover in the whole world. And a present, too!

She lay naked, the covers having been tossed off the bed at some point in their lovemaking. Smiling naughtily, Mia marveled at her lack of inhibitions. Running a hand from her breast to her hip, it occurred to her that for the first time in her life, she felt beautiful.

That thought hit her with a jolt.

Mia Tortelli, with her turned-up nose, her tendency to freckle in the sun, and a penchant for pragmatism, had never been described as "beautiful."

Wondering if loving Quentin had somehow changed her, Mia slipped from the bed and went over to the mirrored dresser. In the dim light from the bedside lamp, she studied herself.

Still Mia.

But there was a certain something that seemed different about her.

Quentin walked up behind her and she jumped. Embarrassed at being caught looking at herself naked in the mirror, she turned to hop back on the bed.

He caught her hand and swiveled her back around to face the mirror. She noticed he kept one hand behind his back.

Standing behind her, he said, "I'd love to have a portrait of you like this."

She started to blush.

"You're exquisite."

Mia glanced back at him, surprised at his word choice. Wistfully, she said, "Not really. Cute, maybe, but no more than average."

"No?" Still standing behind her, he reached around and traced the line of her jaw, the slope of her nose, the outline of her lips. "Beauty," Quentin said, "shows in so many ways. In Hollywood we sometimes forget the grace of the soul, the appeal of the intellect, the attraction of the spirit that won't give in to wrong. You have all those qualities, Mia."

"Thank you, Quentin. For saying that, for loving me." Mia's heart filled in a way that she knew she wouldn't have felt had he simply said, "You're beautiful, babe." She started to turn and put her arms around him.

"Present first," he said, keeping her facing forward. "Close your eyes."

She did, eager to see what he'd gotten for her.

"No, open them first."

His arms around her, Quentin held in front of her an eggshell blue box with a white satin ribbon. She saw the name Tiffany & Co., but knew the telltale package immediately. She received their catalogs, but practical, economical Mia had never purchased anything from them.

"Oh, Quentin!"

"And don't say I shouldn't have."

For once, she agreed.

"Now, close your eyes," he said. "Normally you get to open your own presents, but this one requires special handling.

Almost hopping from foot to foot in anticipation, Mia closed her eyes, scrunching them tight. "It's like Christmas, only better," she said, as she listened to him opening the box. "Better, because I didn't know I was getting a present."

Quentin laughed slightly and kissed the back of her neck. "I bought this for you in New York, the afternoon I went to see Portia. I missed you terribly and wanted to give you something special to show you how much I missed you."

That had been the afternoon she'd been stuck at O'Hare, the afternoon she'd prayed to Mr. G about their marriage.

"And then, you little minx, you slipped in my room and performed that sexy striptease, and I forgot all about the gift."

Mia felt something icy cold and solid in a very pleasing way tease her neck, settling just above her collarbone. A necklace!

Quentin worked at a clasp, then whispered, "Open your eyes, Mia."

Slowly, dying to know what he'd gotten her, Mia opened her eyes.

And gasped.

"Quentin! Are these diamonds?"

"And that's a sapphire in the center." His reflection in the mirror showed him looking very pleased with himself.

Mia touched the sparkling gems cautiously. Two circles of diamonds glittered around a dark oval stone that reminded her of Quentin's eyes, dark with passion. "I don't know what to say," she whispered.

He smiled and circled her waist with his arms. Leaning around, he kissed her.

In the middle of the kiss, Mia broke off and said, "I'm so overwhelmed, I forgot to say thank you."

"You say thank you every day in a million ways," Quentin said, and pulled her into his arms and carried her back to the bed.

Lying on his side, gazing down at her, Quentin said, "I'm afraid the clerk in Tiffany's thought I was bonkers."

"Why?"

He circled her breasts with his fingertips, then trailed them lower.

With a grin, he said, "You might say I was fairly

distracted. I kept thinking of how you'd look wearing only this necklace while we were making love."

"Ah," Mia said. Touching the stones, she said, "Want to make that picture now?"

An hour later, having put the necklace carefully to bed in its white satin nest, Mia lay fingering the dark hairs on Quentin's chest, her head nestled in the crook of his shoulder. "Quentin, there's something I need to tell you."

"What's that?"

He sounded sleepy, and for a second, Mia thought of murmuring "I love you" and letting him drift off to sleep without any further discussion.

But telling him tomorrow or the next day would only be more difficult. And right now, after this very special evening, they were so emotionally bonded she didn't want to keep a secret from him.

"I'm pretty sure I know why Randall could see Amity."

"Oh?" He answered in a much less sleepy voice.

"It's because of me. Because of something I did, or rather, tried to do." She forged ahead, wondering whether Quentin the perpetual agnostic could ever understand the part of her that prompted her to pray to Mr. G for help in their marriage.

But she knew one very important truth. If she didn't share her actions with him, he'd never come to understand them.

Stilling her hand, but leaving it clasped against

his chest, she said, "I sent a message to Mr. G, asking him to let Amity be visible to Beetle, only I may have been distracted and typed 'Randall' by mistake."

"You what?" Quentin shot up in bed. He stared at her. Then, in a gentler voice, he said, "What do you mean, you sent him a message?"

"Well, it was going to be a prayer, but I was online at the time, so I typed in some addresses, and one of them worked for a Mr. G in Purgatory."

"So you're telling me Mr. G surfs the Net?"

She couldn't miss the dry tone to his question. "I know it sounds crazy," she said, "but it's exactly what happened."

"Then you can go back and check your outbox and see whether you typed 'Randall' or 'Beetle,' can't you?"

"Why does that matter?"

Quentin had reached for the bedside light, snapped it on, and grabbed his robe. "Let's check now."

"But that's not the point of what I'm trying to tell you," Mia said, feeling as if a strong wind had swept by and done away with her sense of purpose. Funny, but Quentin didn't seem to think it odd she'd sent a message to Mr. G; he only wanted to know whether she'd typed in the wrong name.

"Does it bother you that I might have had Randall on my mind and put his name in by mistake?" With her arms folded across her naked chest, she asked the question rather than hopping out of bed and joining Quentin in his flight to her laptop.

"That's the least of my worries, Mia." Quentin held his hand out to her. "Come on, I just want to know."

"Tell me why," she said, her voice low but determined.

He looked from her to the door and obviously could tell she meant business, because he seated himself on the side of the bed. Not quite looking at her, he mumbled into his hands, "I've got my reasons."

"Quentin, don't you see the whole point of my bringing this up is to share with you what I did? In effect, I prayed to Mr. G to let Beetle be able to see Amity so maybe they'd fall in love and then she'd go away and leave us alone and then we could be happy again."

He stared at her, and to her annoyance, began to laugh.

"My dearest Mia," he said, leaning close and brushing a kiss over her lips, "I don't know what I'd do without you. I, too, have a confession to make. For the first time in my life, I prayed. I asked Mr. G to make Randall able to see Amity, so maybe they'd fall in love and he'd whisk her away so she wouldn't be around to drive you nuts."

"You did that?"

He nodded.

"For me?"

He nodded again.

She skipped forward and encircled him in her arms. "I love you," she said.

When Quentin at last raised his lips from hers, he edged them both back into bed and pulled the covers around them. "Mia," he said, determined to make a few more things right, "we both asked Mr. G for something, but I think we asked only for ourselves."

Mia sat up, her eyes wide. "Forgetting all about helping Amity."

He nodded. "And somehow, I think this whole episode is about our lending her a hand. About figuring out the unknown Intervention target."

Mia cupped her chin in her hands, a study in reflection.

That's when Quentin noticed her thumbnail. Gently he lifted her hand. "When did you do this?" He pointed to the nail she'd chewed away.

"Oh." Mia tugged at her hand, but he held it firmly. "Earlier tonight."

Quentin kissed her fingertips. "And it was probably my fault." He let go of her hand and stroked the top of her spiky hair. "Sweetheart, you don't have to worry quite so much, you know."

Mia smiled. "Sometimes I can't help myself. But right now we'd better worry about Amity."

"I figure her target's got to be someone involved with the film."

"Because of the timing." Mia plumped her pillows, then settled back against the headboard. "I wanted it to be Beetle. And I wanted to beat you to a solution."

"Competitive minx, aren't you?" Quentin grinned at her, but the truth was, he'd wanted to solve it himself, too. "Two heads are better than one, agreed?"

Mia nodded. "But I can't find anything about Beetle that needs fixing."

"Must be nice to be so perfect."

Mia tickled his ribs. "Don't get jealous. You know you're the only man for me."

"And I have a feeling Beetle might be the only man for Amity."

"Oh, Quentin, I do, too! That's the other reason I wanted Beetle to be able to see her."

"Portia's my number one candidate," Quentin said. "Her life's pretty screwy."

"But she is a good actress." Mia played with the sheet. "I guess I should tell you now that I think you were right about her for Ma Belle."

Quentin leaned close and kissed the tip of Mia's nose. "Thank you for that," he said, pulling her close. "Maybe we should revisit this problem in the morning."

Mia snuggled into his arms. "Maybe if we both prayed to Mr. G at the same time, we'd come up with a solution."

Quentin made a face. Mia had a point, but he wasn't sure he could go that far on this faith thing. Sleepily, he said, "If we haven't figured it out by tomorrow, I'll go along with that, okay?"

Mia smiled.

*   *   *

Sometime during the night, when the stars had gone to bed along with the rest of the sky, Amity awakened. She lay on her side, one strong arm wrapped around her waist, a purring cat at her feet.

She smiled and brushed her fingertips over Beetle's arm. As she shifted in the bed, she realized she'd somehow shed her smock and slept in only the sheer knee-length chemise she wore under it.

Ever since the day the nuns had assured the solemn assemblage of twelve-year-old girls they could get into trouble if they forgot to wear their underwear, Amity had sworn off panties.

Feeling secure and protected, Amity snuggled against Beetle. Fate raised her head, as if to check whether she should go on alert, but Amity soothed her with a murmured "Go back to sleep, kitty."

And then she followed her own advice, drifting off on a peaceful cloud of dreams.

Beetle hadn't had such sweet dreams in years. He groaned and shifted, rolling the nymph he held in his arms onto his chest. This creation of his subconscious was blessed with perfect breasts, heavy and full and crowned with nipples that pearled against his hand as he reached and cupped them close.

The only flaw to his dream, other than that it wasn't reality, was the thin fabric that met his flesh. Anxious to feel her skin unfettered, he grasped the fabric at her neckline and ripped it swiftly in two, freeing her body.

All mine, he murmured, and sucked greedily on one nipple. He heard pants and moans and smiled as the beauty shifted to offer him her other nipple, which he took, tugging with his lips before flicking his tongue, his hot, panting, needy tongue, over the rock-hard tip.

God, what a dream! Beetle writhed against the lumps in the mattress, caught now between sleep and waking and the horror of opening his eyes to find only bleak solitude awaiting him.

So he kept his eyes closed and willed sleep to rule his mind and leave him to dream.

He sent one hand lower to seek excited, glorious release, and found his dream nymph worked her magic there. Two hands wrapped around his shaft and captured him, turning the heat back on itself. Swiftly she stroked him, then suddenly stopped.

Beetle almost opened his eyes, figuring reality had intruded at last.

Then, he realized the nymph had paused only to tease him with a strand of her hair, then lowered herself to catch him between her breasts and rock him gently, then faster and faster.

"Oh, God!" He'd died and gone to heaven.

Eyes gripped tight, he passed over the edge and gave himself up.

Dazed, triumphant, and wondering what in the hell had gotten into him, Beetle slowly opened his eyes.

And promptly sneezed.

Once, twice, three times, quickly, all in a row, one atop another.

He'd blinded himself. Feeling for a pillow, he pulled the case off and dabbed at his watering eyes. Then, with a dawning sense of unreality, he realized someone was patting at his lower body with a swath of the bed sheet.

He started to sit up, then fell back against his one remaining pillow and gave in to another bout of sneezing.

As he opened his eyes again, he saw two things at once. One, a cat streaking from his bed toward the open window, and two, a blond with long, tousled hair and breasts exactly like those of the nymph in his dream, perched across his feet, a smile not unlike those of the angels lighting her face.

One of the advantages to being invisible, Amity decided, smiling down at the very satisfied-looking Beetle, was that she could do truly outrageous things and no one would ever be the wiser.

Maybe she'd remain invisible forever. As long as she had her cats and dogs for company and could spend nights with Beetle, she didn't think she'd mind at all. She could still paint; she'd merely have to have a front man to sell her work.

She smiled and lifted her arms over her head, feeling not only pleased with herself, but incredibly aroused, too.

Glancing back at Beetle, she realized his eyes

were fixed on her face. He'd been having the most incredible sneezing fit, so it was a good thing Fate had decided to jump through the window.

"Who are you?" Beetle's lips moved, so Amity knew he'd asked the question.

She pointed a finger at herself, then noticed her breasts were bare. She smiled, remembering what an animal Beetle had been, ripping her chemise from her body. Then his question registered in her sex-starved brain.

"Who am I?" Amity began backing from the bed, searching for her smock. If he had asked that question, then he could see her!

He sat bolt upright in bed. "You're that friend of Mia and Quentin's, aren't you? My God, what were they thinking, introducing us in bed?"

"Mia and Quentin?" Amity squeaked the names. She made a grab for her smock and pulled it on over her head. Beetle would think she was some floozy who slept with just any guy. And that wasn't the case at all. She felt bound to him, as if their souls had already known one another for years and years.

"What is this, some sort of life-in-the-fast-lane joke?" Beetle jumped from the bed. He grabbed at the bedspread and pulled it around him.

"I wouldn't do that if I were you," Amity said.

"Too modest for you?" Beetle said, then sneezed.

"I tried to tell you not to do that. The cat slept on the bed."

He flung the spread to the floor. Hands on his hips, he glared at her.

Despite her embarrassment, Amity had to admire Beetle's body. He possessed that miracle of anatomy, the perfect male body, with broad shoulders that tapered to narrow hips and a generous endowment that even now, in the midst of this craziness, stood at attention.

Her blood stirred. *Don't be a fool*, Amity said to herself. *Invisible you might have had a chance, but he'll never come near you now.*

Beetle advanced on her. "Mind you, I've nothing against great sex with a woman I hardly know." He halted and swiped at a pair of shorts, which, to Amity's mingled relief and disappointment, he drew on.

"But I'd at least like to know I've been invited to the party and who my partner is." He held out a hand. "My name's Beetle. What's yours?"

She thought he was being sarcastic, but she couldn't quite tell. Digging her toe into the frayed carpeting, she said, "Amity."

"Amity." He nodded as if digesting the name, then sneezed again. "And I suppose that's your cat?"

It was her turn to nod. "Her name's Fate."

He laughed and took another step closer. To her surprise, he caught her by the shoulders and drew her to him. "Now that we've been introduced, do you want to finish what you started?"

Amity swallowed. "Wh-what do you mean?"

He cupped her bottom and swiveled his hips

against her and she knew exactly what he meant.

"Oh, I don't think that would be a good idea. Not now." Amity tried to tug free, but he wasn't having any of that.

He brushed her hair back from her face and stared into her eyes, a dangerous glint showing in his own. "Come on, you can tell me. You're a girl who gets paid to do this, aren't you? Why else would you be in my room, doing what you were doing? Did you get paid to go only so far, and that's that?"

"How can you say such mean things?" Amity struggled, then remembered how foolish that was against a stronger force. Instead, she let herself go limp against him, leaning into his chest. "Oh, all right, maybe some of it's true."

"Hey, what's this?" Beetle had reached into one of the pockets of her smock and pulled out a wallet.

Amity's heart sank. "My wallet?"

Beetle, one firm hand holding her wrists, flicked open the black leather. "Randall Hollings, CPA," he read. He flung the wallet on the bed. "You're a thief, too," he said, sounding as sorrowful as he did accusatory.

"I'm lots of things, but I'm not a thief. I only take items I absolutely need." Amity stomped on the back of his foot and went for the back of his arms with her teeth, a technique she'd used against some of her less friendly compatriots in the foundling home.

Beetle yelled and loosened his grip. Amity

broke free. She made a grab for Randall's wallet, nabbed it, then hightailed it out the door, Beetle in pursuit.

Tucked out of sight behind a nearby oleander bush, Amity watched as Beetle halted a few feet outside his cabin. He looked down at his bare feet, then dashed back inside.

Figuring he'd return pronto, clothed and shod, she scampered off to hide from him. Even as she fled, knowing he thought her a thief, Amity admitted she'd be disappointed if he didn't come looking for her.

Mr. G hunched over a table in the Second Chance Room, watching as the last grains of sand in the egg timer dropped to build the growing cone-shaped pile in the bottom. He then beetled his brows and glared at the picture displayed on the wall-sized monitor.

"Bah," he said, looking back and forth from the screen to the egg timer.

A Second Chance assignment had to be completed before the last sand joined the rest. Everyone knew that rule.

On the screen, Amity ran, fleet-footed, with Beetle in fast pursuit.

Mr. G had a feeling he wouldn't catch her in time. Especially when the guy paused, then disappeared back into his room.

He sighed.

He'd done what he could to rectify the situation. He'd canceled out Quentin's vision of her, thinking to work a little damage control by correcting at least that degree of rule-bending. And Mia hadn't yet discovered the card he'd left in her possession when he had, against every rule, visited the Big Apple and kindly driven their taxi.

So maybe not all had been lost.

But Amity, bless her pointed little head, was too much of a scamp for him to be able to sit back and watch her miss out on a second chance at life. The good in her heart outweighed all the naughty habits she'd acquired in her school of hard knocks. Her animals would certainly agree with that judgment, and Mr. G had seen enough of the universe to be able to state that most times animals showed a great deal more horse sense than their two-legged keepers.

Only three grains of sand left. . . .

Mr. G wondered whether Amity would be having this problem if he hadn't swapped her assignment. If he'd treated her exactly like every other person to pass through the Second Chance Room, and not interfered or tried to help, perhaps she'd have read her assignment, followed through, and right now be back in New Orleans with her happy menagerie.

Two grains left.

His cheek twitched and he clamped down hard on his cold cigar.

If only he hadn't had such a soft spot in his heart for Mia, too, Amity might be safely home.

One grain to go.

Aw, what the heck. He'd broken so many rules

already, what harm could one more infraction cause?

Mr. G grabbed the egg timer and gave it a violent shake. Sand swirled top to bottom and back again. He plunked it back on the table with a grunt of satisfaction.

"If you fools can't work it out now, I wash my hands of you," he said, and rose to leave.

As he headed for the door, it swung open, revealing another of his messenger boys, this one grim-faced and holding forth an envelope bearing the Heavenly Seal.

Mr. G grunted again. He guessed he'd been expecting some sort of summons.

"Okay, okay," he muttered. "Hold your horses, I'm coming."

19 ~

Mia smiled and waved another kiss at Quentin as he left their cabin. He was shooting one of the scenes with all the bikers today and had risen early, with only a minimum of grumbling, to prepare.

The roar of the arriving Harleys filtered to her ears. They'd been pouring in for the last half hour, ever since Mia and Quentin had been walking back from the lodge, where they'd eaten breakfast together.

It was on the way back that they'd seen Beetle racing by, speeding as if the bulls were running in Pamplona. They'd waved, but Beetle had seemed pretty much lost in his thoughts, something they took for granted in creative types.

Curious about the biker culture, Mia planned to visit the set that morning.

But first, she wanted to phone her mother.

Eireen had been on her mind since she visited with her, and this morning, having awakened with the feeling that things were beginning to look up, Mia wanted to let her mother know she had at least one child she didn't need to worry about.

Using her cell phone, Mia punched in the numbers, numbers she'd had trouble memorizing after her parents had moved from the neighborhood of Mia's childhood. It was almost as if she thought if she didn't learn the new phone number, the move never would have really taken place.

Silly her. She tapped her foot, listening to the phone ring, and sighed a sentimental little sigh. Since last night's rhapsodic lovemaking and their heart-to-heart talk, Mia almost believed, despite all her worrying, that everything between Quentin and herself would be okay.

Though if she were pressed on the point, she'd have to admit that a little knot of doubt remained lodged in her heart. How would she feel if Amity was still hanging out with Quentin? Could she feel secure only in spurts? She'd promised she'd be the best wife ever, but somehow, the harder she tried, the more she worried, the more she found to fail at, the more to fret over.

Because there'd be the next Amity, or the next casting couch lovely, and she'd start the worry cycle all over again.

Feeling much less cheerful, Mia almost switched off the phone. She hadn't called her mother to seek comfort, but rather to offer it.

"Hello."

Mia paused, her finger poised over the off switch. "Hey, Ma, it's me, Mia."

"You think I don't know your voice after this many years? What's wrong?"

Mia gave a little laugh. Her mother's predictability was comforting. "Nothing. I called to say hi, that's all."

"That's all?"

Mia shrugged. "Sure. How's Dad?"

"He's down at the store, getting us some more milk. The last carton went bad and it wasn't even up to the date stamped on it. I think I'm going to take it back."

"So everything's okay, is it?"

"Your brother and his wife finally got some sense in their heads."

"They're back together?"

"They're going to counseling. What they need with a counselor when they've got a priest I'll never know, but at least he saw the light and she took him back."

"Are they happy?"

Her mother made a noise that Mia assumed indicated disgust with Mia's question. "They have a good marriage and their family isn't going to suffer. I thank God they came to their senses now, rather than later."

"Well, being married isn't easy, you know."

"You want to tell your ma what's wrong?"

"Nothing's wrong." Then Mia felt her shoulders sag and she said, "I love Quentin and he loves me, and I try so hard to be this perfect wife and make everything beautiful, but then things happen and we have words and I feel like—a—failure." She sobbed the last word and suddenly realized that the feeling of failure was what had been bothering her for days and days and days.

Because she should be happy. Quentin was.

"I feel this pressure to make things right all the time," she said, ending again in a stifled sob.

"There, there," her mother said, "you always were one to have to make straight A's."

"What do you mean?"

"I mean you couldn't make an art project, you had to create a museum. You couldn't put together a bug collection, you had to build one of those insectariums."

"What are you saying?"

"Perfection is a recipe for misery." Her mother repeated the phrase, rolling it off her tongue.

Mia gave a little hiccup into the phone.

"Does that husband of yours treat you right?"

"Oh, yes."

"And he seems happy enough?"

"Oh, yes."

Mia heard her mother *tch-tching*. "Sometimes I don't know how I raised such opposite children. You're a little worrywart and your brother is Mr. Easy Come, Easy Go. At least your sister's somewhere in the middle. Here's your father, back with the milk. Go find your husband. If he gives you straight As, then give them to yourself."

"Ma?"

"What?"

"You're pretty smart."

"Hah! You're a good daughter," her mother said, sounding quite cheerful. "Your father's back, and right now he wants his breakfast."

The line went dead.

Mia switched off her phone and stood staring at it, not seeing it, seeing instead the worn face of her mother, talking commonsense and waiting for her father to bring home the milk so they could have their Raisin Bran together.

For forty years, her parents had eaten Raisin Bran for breakfast.

Comforted by that continuity and by her mother's words, Mia decided she'd give in to her desire to slip over and see Quentin before she settled down to her own work.

If she didn't quit fussing over her marriage, she'd have a lot more to worry about. She had tons of work to do relative to the marketing and advertising of *Permutation*. And now, with Portia Goodhope in the cast, and acquitting herself beautifully (in front of the cameras, anyway), Mia needed to consider pushing that publicity angle.

She'd voted against her; she'd been wrong.

Mia rummaged through her clothing, looking for a light wrap. The early morning mountain air was cool, even in August, and she'd shivered a bit coming back from breakfast.

Spotting the same linen jacket she'd worn the day she and Quentin had visited Portia and stumbled across Amity, Mia smiled and slipped it on.

Something rustled in one of the pockets. On her way out the door, Mia checked the pocket and pulled out a business card.

She paused to read it and saw that it belonged to a cab company. She started to drop it back in the pocket, to use as a business expense receipt, when

the name of the cab company sounded in her brain.
G Whiz.

"G Whiz," she whispered, the image of the
grumpy old cab driver filling her vision. Fingering
the card, she read the fine print on the bottom line:
This Card Good For One Wish Of Absolutely Any Kind.

Mia shivered, then laughed. Good old Mr. G,
he'd been there all along for them, and all she'd
had to do was look in her pocket.

They could have wished for Amity to remember
her target or to be visible. Or, Mia thought, she
could have wished happiness always for herself
and Quentin.

It sounded kind of selfish when she turned over
the idea in her mind, but tempting, too. And what
was wrong with being happy? What had her
mother said? If he gives you straight As, give 'em
to yourself. Wishing for happiness always was
kind of an extension of that.

Only Mia didn't quite buy that argument.

She stroked the face of the card, then slipped it
back in her pocket. She'd begun to learn enough
about marriage to know she didn't want to make
a wish until she'd shared this touch of magic with
Quentin. Together, they'd decide.

Once again, almost to the door, she turned back.
A smile playing on her lips, she unlocked her trav-
eling safe and pulled out the Tiffany's box.

Her face heated as she thought of Quentin placing the necklace around her throat last night, loving her as if she herself were a priceless jewel.

Mia opened the satin-lined box and gazed at the

diamonds reflecting the light overhead.

Her heart danced along with the light in the facets, and for once in her life, she let her impulses rule her mind.

In a snap, she pulled the necklace from the case and placed it around her throat. The stones felt both cool and hot at the same time, or did she feel hot from thinking of Quentin selecting this gift for her, of Quentin fastening the clasp?

She buttoned her blouse all the way to the tiny button hidden below the collar. That way, the extravagant jewelry wasn't visible. Mia smiled, thinking she'd find a moment to pull Quentin aside, and in private, play last night's love scene with the necklace once again.

Picturing how Quentin's face would light up when she let him see she wore his beautiful gift, Mia hurried to the door, and this time made it out without turning back.

Beetle gave up on Amity. He'd scoured the grounds and found no trace of her or that darn cat. Disgusted with himself, he stomped back to his cabin and took a quick shower.

Even if the girl had been a thief and a prostitute, he'd had no call to frighten her and run after her that way. He'd received more pleasure than irritation at her hands, and if he was a little more honest with himself, he'd admit he'd struck out at her because he'd feared the depth of his reaction to her.

Dressing quickly in his screenwriter get-up, he

pulled on his dark glasses, grabbed his journal, and headed out the door.

During the tedium of the filming process, he'd find plenty of opportunity to examine his reaction by describing it in his notebook.

At some point during his shower, it had occurred to him that there were thousands of long-legged blondes in California and he had no real grounds to assume the woman in his cabin had been Mia and Quentin's friend from New Orleans. More than likely, one of the crew had played a trick on him. As standoffish as he was, he probably deserved it. He couldn't expect the crew to understand it was only his insecurity that led him to keep to himself.

Suddenly anxious to get to the set, Beetle focused himself into a calmer frame of mind. When they did introduce him to their friend, he didn't want to be frothing at the mouth.

Walking down the path toward the set-up for the biker gang scene, Beetle was assailed by the roar of motorcycle engines. They must have arranged for hundreds of extras for this shoot. Dust swirled as he rounded the bend toward the broad clearing where the bikers had gathered.

His journal tucked under his arm, Beetle paused a moment and reflected on the sketches inserted into the pages of his book. Or rather, on the artist who had rendered them.

Dwelling on those thoughts kept his wayward mind from returning, as it seemed determined to do, to the nymph who'd stolen into his dreams and then made them come true, if only for a few fleeting moments.

Spotting Quentin, Beetle strode forward.

The cinematographer got to Quentin first, and Beetle hung back, still unsure of his place in the pecking order.

Soon, though, Quentin turned to him and said, "Good run this morning, Beetle?"

Beetle flushed. Quentin had seen him chasing the blond pickpocket. "G-good," he said, wanting to die when he stuttered his response.

Quentin glanced at his playback monitor, then the few feet over to the rows of bikes where the motors had all been stilled.

"I'm a runner myself," he said. "Ever done a marathon?"

"N-no. 10K, though," Beetle managed.

"Those are fun, but I'm thinking a marathon might be an interesting challenge." Quentin said something to an assistant standing by his side and the woman scooted away. "Not that I like to get up early to train. I was impressed to see you running this morning at the crack of dawn."

It hadn't been that early, although Beetle did like to rise before the sun. He found his mind clear, his thoughts untroubled by concerns of where his next meal would come from or whether his mother might call and ask about Sheila. The later the day grew, the harder it was for him to sit at his keyboard, marshalling fantasy into reality.

"I—er—needed to run," he said at last. Was it possible Quentin had seen him, but not the object of his pursuit? "Could I ask you a question?"

"Shoot." Quentin glanced around, but Beetle didn't get the impression he was in a hurry to proceed. The wardrobe and make-up people were examining the bikers.

"About these sketches," Beetle said, opening his journal.

"Yes?"

Beetle stared down at the pages of his journal. No sketches. He held the book by the spiral binding and shook it. No papers floated free.

"The sketches for Portia's costume. Queenie showed them to me," Beetle said, still staring at his journal.

"Good, weren't they?"

"M-much better than the originals. Can you tell me who did them?"

Quentin stared at him, and Beetle met his gaze, wondering whether he'd asked some question he wasn't supposed to ask. There were so many rules of behavior in this business, it was hard to learn them all at once. He still remembered the time he'd picked up a chair and moved it out of the sun. He'd been scolded by one of the assistant directors for violating union regulations. Only prop people, it seemed, moved chairs about.

"Why do you want to know?"

"Why? Well, because they're exactly what I had in mind when I wrote the role, and I have to admit I'm curious to meet the person who could read my mind."

"Ah." Quentin kept staring at him, then said,

"You want the truth, the whole truth, and nothing but the truth?"

Beetle nodded.

"Wait right there," Quentin said, then hurried off.

Beetle closed his journal and remained rooted to his spot. Perhaps Quentin had gone to get the person who'd drawn the sketches. His heart racing the tiniest bit, he gazed around him, safe from the rest of the world behind his dark glasses.

Amity confirmed what she'd feared. For some strange reason, she'd become visible to Randall, and then to Beetle. But no one in the kitchen of the Cubby Hole gave any indication that they were aware of her presence.

So she helped herself to breakfast and wondered what to do next. Beetle hadn't found her, somewhat to her regret. After she finished her scrambled eggs, she slipped two dollars from Randall's wallet and left them under her plate.

The very idea of Beetle calling her a thief rankled. She'd bet he'd never been cold and hungry and without a dime to his name. And she'd been able to tell quickly enough that he thought her not only the thief he called her, but a whore, too.

A trace of a tear smeared her vision and Amity dashed her hand across her eyes. "Forget it," she said, "the last thing you're going to do is feel sorry for yourself."

She marched out of the kitchen and bumped smack into Fate. The cat meowed piteously and

Amity did an about-face. Finding what she sought in the kitchen, she returned and watched as Fate feasted on chopped ham washed down with a dab of milk.

As the cat ate, then licked its paws and cleaned its face, Amity sat in the sun on the back steps of the lodge and considered her choices.

Assuming she had been trapped in some after-life puzzle, what she had to do was figure out the answer. And if she was dead, she figured some-one or other would come along soon enough and pronounce judgement.

Quentin had questioned her about her experi-ences in a place he called the Second Chance Room. She thought of it as a boudoir done in really bad taste, unrelieved red velvet, but she figured they'd described the same place. He had seemed to think it important that she remember some assignment given to her by the old codger shouting at her from the front of the room.

At the time, she'd laughed at him. After all the screaming she'd endured at the hands of Sister Ig-natius, that old guy couldn't begin to frighten her. So Amity had gazed around the room, at the man.

He'd had a most interesting face, especially his nose. Something about him was ageless, timeless. Amity had thought at the time about an article she'd read in the dentist's office about old souls and had immediately set about deciding how she'd capture him on canvas.

Someone had given her a piece of paper and

she'd sketched on it, using a pencil still lodged in the pocket of her smock.

Fate quit bathing and glanced at Amity, as if asking, "What's next?"

Amity scrunched her eyes shut tight and tried to remember whether she'd read the name on the paper before she turned it over to sketch on the back. Her head didn't throb anymore when she tried to recall the moment.

A few letters drifted into her mind, but Amity rejected them. Initials, nothing more, nothing less.

"Oh, Fate," Amity said, catching up the cat and hugging her close, "if only I could figure it out, we could go home."

Quentin rounded the bend in the path and bumped into Mia.

"Quentin," she cried happily, "I'm on my way to see you."

He kissed her, then said, "Same for me. Beetle asked me who drew the sketches, and I really didn't know what to tell him."

"Hmm." Mia kept her hand in her pocket. She'd answer Quentin's question first, then share her story.

"Let's walk while we talk," Quentin said, steering them back to the set. "We're almost ready to start the first biker scene. We're starting with a long pan of the bikes, all empty, ready and waiting."

Mia nodded, but Quentin could tell her mind was still on his original question. "Why not tell him the truth?"

"About her being invisible, stuck between life and death?"

"Yes."

Quentin laughed. "Not even Beetle would believe that, and he's got quite an imagination."

"He also possesses a very sensitive soul, and I think he would believe it."

"Would you?"

She nodded.

"Well, if it hadn't happened to me, there's no way I'd sit still during a cock-and-bull story like that."

Mia sighed.

He bent over and kissed her. "Sorry, Mia, but not everyone has your faith in the unseen."

She stopped just shy of the jumble of cameras, people, and bikes. "You prayed."

"Yes, I did."

"Why?"

Quentin thought he'd rather be getting a tooth pulled than discuss his foray into the religious. Scuffing the ground with his shoe, he said, "Because of you. Because I'd do anything to keep you happy."

Mia smiled and reached up and brushed a finger across his heart. "Thank you, Quentin. And I think I've learned something from this whole Amity experience. I've learned—"

A tremendous metallic crashing noise hurtled against their ears.

Quentin swung around, then, horrified by what he saw, raced ahead.

20 ⟢

Beetle hadn't spotted the cat until it was too late.

He sneezed, and sneezed again.

"Oh, dear," the voice of his nighttime nymph spoke from behind him and he whirled around.

"It's you," he said, wiping at his eyes. "I thought you'd have gone back to wherever you came from by now."

"If only I could," she said. The cat wound itself in between and around the woman's legs.

"Who are you?"

"I told you, my name is Amity."

Beetle sneezed. "More like Calamity," he said, wanting to turn from her but finding it quite impossible. Despite the agony of his sinuses, he found himself captivated. "At least tell me why you were in my bed this morning."

"I like you," she said, "though right now I can't quite remember why."

He sneezed. "Does that darn cat go everywhere you go?"

She nodded. "The cat's the reason I'm still here."

"You're nuts, aren't you?" He swiped at his

eyes with the back of the sleeve of his turtleneck.

"Oh, I daresay I am," she said, stooping gracefully to stroke the cat. "I don't know why else I'd bother talking to a man who called me a thief."

The wallet! His allergies had driven it from his mind. "Return it to him and I won't report your theft."

"Why don't I hand it over to you, and you can deliver it?"

"Why would I do that?"

She looked at him with her big violet eyes and Beetle held out his hand. "Give me the damn wallet."

"There's no need to swear." Amity pulled Randall's wallet from one of her pockets.

"You are a strange one, aren't you?"

"What makes you say that?"

Beetle gestured around them. Someone was buffing the chrome on the front Harley of a long line, stacked like metallic dominoes. A woman with a shaved head and a nose ring was talking earnestly with the leading man; two men, their eyes locked on one another, sipped coffee together.

"You fit right in with the kind of crazies a movie crew attracts. What's your job, anyway?" Beetle knew he was annoyed with her partly because she did fit in, and deep in his heart, he knew he'd always be a child of the Midwest. White bread, Hershey's chocolate syrup in his hot cocoa, and red, green, blue, and orange bulbs on his Christmas tree.

To a point, boringly normal.

"Um, I don't really work here."

He sneezed again, then three more times. Swiping at his eyes, he cried, "Can't you get your cat to go chase a squirrel for a while?" He stumbled, blinded, then sneezed again.

He never knew at what point he tripped into the first gleaming Harley and set off the chain reaction, sending every last one of the bikes crashing into the next, until not a one remained standing.

"Oh, my," Mia said, surveying the fallen bikes and the glowering expression on Quentin's face. Beetle, looking very much like the proverbial boy with his hand caught in the cookie jar, sat on the ground by the front bike, his head buried in his hands.

His shoulders quaked rhythmically. Mia hurried to him and saw that he sneezed repeatedly. Quentin, too, along with half the crew, rushed to the screenwriter's side. Staring down, he said, "You want to tell me what happened?"

Beetle finally lifted his head and Mia saw his red, watery eyes. "I'm allergic to cats," he said, and sneezed again.

"Is that all? Let's move away and get this reset," Quentin said, looking disgusted.

Beetle got up and Mia led him a few feet away. Quentin loomed behind them, making slashes across his throat behind Beetle's back. Mia knew Quentin had to be furious with the hapless writer; for her part, she hoped and prayed none of the

Harley owners sued them for damage to the bikes. Luckily, all forty bikers were being fed breakfast back at the Cubby Hole at this very moment.

Suddenly, Quentin turned around, accepted a piece of paper from someone Mia didn't notice, then turned back to her. "Well, would you look at this?" He held it out to her.

Don't be mad at Beetle. It's my fault, or rather, my cat's, I guess. Scrawled next to these words was Amity's name, followed by a smiley face.

"Amity's still here?" Mia, knowing how fruitless the movement was, looked around.

"Of course she is," Beetle said. "That Amity is a one-woman disaster team. I asked her to keep that cat away from me."

"You can see her!" Mia clapped her hands together, then quickly stuck one back in her pocket. She meant to hold on to that wish card until she and Quentin were able to decide what to do with it. "Oh, Quentin, that's marvelous."

"It means Mr. G heard both of us, doesn't it?" He looked bemused.

Around them, the prop people were busy righting the bikes. "Check those for any scratches," Quentin called.

Beetle sneezed. "Who's Mr. G?"

Mia and Quentin shared a glance. "You may as well tell him," Mia said.

Beetle began sneezing again.

Mia, without thinking, said, "I wish you'd never sneeze again!"

Beetle stopped in mid-sneeze. He blinked his

eyes; they'd dried, and the red had disappeared. "What a miracle," he muttered.

Mia looked from Beetle to Quentin and back again. She fingered the card in her pocket, then gasped in horror.

"I wished your sneezing away!"

Quentin looked at her as if she'd lost her marbles.

"Oh, I can't believe what I've just done," Mia said.

"However you did it, I'm forever grateful," said the dry-eyed Beetle. "I'm very sorry for the disaster I've caused. I'll do whatever is necessary to rectify the situation. Feel free to send me a bill if any of the bikes were damaged."

"Forget it," Quentin said. "Beetle, you did say you wanted to know the truth, the whole truth, and nothing but the truth?"

Beetle nodded, glancing around him. Members of the crew stared at him, some none too friendly. He'd delayed the whole day's production, so Quentin couldn't blame them for giving the writer the evil eye.

"Mia, will you excuse me for a few minutes?" Quentin threw her a wink, then drew an arm around Beetle's shoulders, leading him away from the fallen bikes.

As Beetle walked off with Quentin, he caught sight of Amity, the cat cradled in her arms. She watched him, a look he recognized as longing in her eyes. For the life of him, he didn't know how this one-woman disaster team had so affected him, but he knew he'd come back to her side. Just as soon as he heard what Quentin had to say.

Quentin had lowered his arm and thrust his hands into his pockets. The two of them stopped in almost the same point on the path where Quentin had coldcocked Randall the day before.

Kicking at a cluster of dried pine needles, Quentin said, "Do you remember what gave you the idea for *Permutation*?"

Beetle wondered what the question had to do with the explanation he expected to hear. But having faith in Quentin's vision, and hoping the brilliant director wouldn't be disappointed in his answer, he said, "Actually, no. Ma Belle appeared, full form, in my mind, and the story unfolded around her."

"Exactly!" Quentin slapped his hands together. "And sometimes life is exactly like a movie or a book. Things happen and logic doesn't always apply."

"And this philosophical insight relates to Amity?" Beetle hesitated, then added, "To a woman who appears from nowhere and just happens to meet me for the first time in my bed?"

"Not exactly." Quentin scratched the back of his neck. "I mean, yes, the insight applies, but I'm not so sure that's the first time she met you."

Beetle waved a hand, signaling for Quentin to continue his explanation.

"Let me put it this way: if I were going to make a movie about a gorgeous female artist caught between life and death, I'd make her someone who rescues animals and has a whimsical penchant for causing trouble. Then I'd make sure I cast her opposite a guy who views the world just a little bit more creatively than your average joe."

Beetle tapped a finger on his chest. "A writer, perhaps? No, don't tell me—a screenwriter!"

Quentin nodded. "And in this same movie, I'd give the artist a problem greater than herself." He tipped his head back, appearing to draw his next sentence from the clouds drifting overhead. "For instance, a soul she's been assigned to help by some ruler of the afterlife, and if she succeeds— and only if, she'll win a second chance at life."

"Don't forget to throw in that she also wins the heart of the lonely guy." Beetle chuckled. Quentin should be writing as well as directing. "Just one thing—how in the world did you come up with that bit about the second chance at life?"

Quentin winked. "Remember, life is always stranger than fiction."

Beetle thought of Amity, appearing from nowhere. He remembered, too, the floating money, the levitating cat, the sketches moving about above his bed last night. He relived Amity loving him awake that morning.

And Beetle knew Quentin meant every word of the yarn he'd just spun, knew what he was being told was the only tale that explained Amity's presence.

"She and I have met several times before, haven't we?"

Quentin nodded.

"What does she—I mean, what would this character—have to do to get back to life?"

Quentin stared at him. "Say that again. No, never mind!" He jabbed a finger at Beetle's chest. "That's the secret! Think of the puzzle as a film and decide how I would solve it for the story line!" He dashed a hand against his forehead. "Why didn't I think of that before?"

Beetle shrugged. "So who's she supposed to rescue?"

"The woman who couldn't see her. The woman driven to face her own insecurities as a result of the artist's presence around her husband, who can see her!"

"You can see Amity, too?"

Quentin nodded.

"She's beautiful, isn't she?"

"Oh, she's not my type. But with a woman like her, you'll never be bored!" He grabbed Beetle's hands. "Thanks for your help." Then he turned and raced back toward the location site, a grin on his face.

"Mia, may I see you alone for a moment?" A strange light danced in Quentin's eyes.

"I thought you'd never ask. There's something I'm dying to tell you!"

"Me first!" Quentin grabbed Mia's hand and hustled her toward Portia Goodhope's trailer. The actress wasn't scheduled on the set until afternoon, and Quentin figured it would be empty of occupants.

He flung open the door and drew Mia in after him. He felt like a kid about to burst from waiting for Christmas morning to finally arrive. What he wanted to share with her couldn't wait for them to trek all the way back to their cabin.

"I think—" he began.

"Who's there?" called a male voice from the back of the trailer.

Quentin shut up. To Mia, he mouthed, "Who is that?"

She started to shake her head, then said aloud, "Randall!"

Sure enough, the accountant, shrugging on a red silk robe trimmed with feathers, marched toward them. "What are you doing in Portia's trailer?"

"We could ask you the same question," Quentin said.

"Darling, Mr. Pish needs to go out for a walk," Portia called. "Could you do that before you bring me my toast and tea, dearest pumpkin?"

The schnauzer bounded toward them. With a yelp, he threw himself on Quentin's ankle and sank his teeth in.

"Goddamn dog!" Quentin lifted his leg and tried to shake the animal off.

Randall made a grab for him, and the schnauzer treated him to a show of teeth. "I think I'll take him out for a walk," the accountant said, snatching the dog by the collar.

Mia knelt to check his ankle, but Quentin said,

"I think he only got my pants. Thankfully. Little beast."

Portia appeared in the doorway leading to the back room. Her hair was tousled and she wore a simple black peignoir and no makeup. Quentin thought he'd never seen her looking better.

"We're not seeing visitors," she said sweetly, then handed the leash to Randall. "Do remember I like my toast dry," she said, then turned and made her exit.

Quentin decided to follow suit. He reached for Mia's hand. At the door, he paused and said over his shoulder to Randall, "If I were you, I'd slip into something a little more suitable for dogwalking."

They dashed out the door and both burst out laughing.

"Have you ever seen anything as silly as Randall in red silk?" Mia held her sides.

"No, but Portia did look happy, didn't she?"

Mia stopped laughing. "You're right, Quentin. Her face positively glowed. And you know, she looked both older and younger in a very pretty way."

"Good," Quentin said offhandedly, his mind elsewhere. "Come on, there's still something I have to say to you." Quentin led her to the wardrobe trailer.

"Queenie," he called, poking his head in, "You here?"

The red-haired seamstress bustled up, a black leather vest in her hands. "That you, Dutch?"

"Yeah, me and Mia."

Queenie smiled at both of them. "It's good to see you both looking so happy."

"Thank you, Queenie." He leaned over and whispered in her ear, "Would you mind if we borrowed your trailer for a moment alone?"

She winked and put the vest down on a work table. "Lola," she called over her shoulder, "Come on, we're taking a break."

When they'd left, Quentin turned to Mia, then pointed to the dressing table. "Please be seated," he said formally.

Obviously in the spirit of things, though she couldn't know what was in his mind, Mia settled herself regally on the stool in front of the mirrored table. She ruined the image just a bit by bouncing around, as if she, too, were dying to share a secret.

Quentin stood behind her, stooping slightly so the mirror framed them both. Smoothing his hands gently over her shoulders, he said, "I needed a mirror to say what I have to say."

Then he saw the wink of the sapphires from the neckline of Mia's blouse. "You're wearing the necklace!"

She nodded. Reaching back, she stroked his hand. "It's ridiculously extravagant, but I wanted to wear it this morning, because I think I finally figured something out."

"About us?"

She nodded.

Quentin tapped on the mirror. "And I think I figured out Amity's assignment."

"You did!"

"Yep."

"Oh, Quentin! But before you tell me, I want you to know I've decided to quit worrying about our marriage." She turned to face him and tilted her head up, gazing straight at him with those dark eyes of hers that managed to see right into his heart. "I love you, and more important, I'm going to trust our love to work things out."

He lowered his head and kissed her softly on the lips, then edged her back around to face the mirror.

Mia looked into the glass, felt Quentin's arms around her. Slowly, feeling as if she were reading his mind, she smiled into the mirror and flitted her gaze from her reflection to Quentin's.

"You think it's me, don't you?" Mia said the words, marveling that Quentin had reached that conclusion, one that suddenly struck her as the only possible solution.

"Yes, I do," Quentin said.

"I did say a prayer to Mr. G, on my way to New York. I never mentioned it, because I knew you weren't as worried about our marriage as I was."

Quentin kissed the top of her head, bussing the spiky tops of her hair until they danced. Mia smiled. "You think I'm a worrywart, but I'm trying to tell you I've learned not to worry."

"So Mr. G has worked another miracle, hasn't he?" Quentin spoke in a low voice, not at all teasing.

"If you're right, then yes." Mia gazed into the

mirror and smiled up at the man she loved. "I feel very humble. I mean, why would Mr. G bother so much about me?"

"You're the one who believes in answered prayers, and you're asking me that question?"

He had her there.

Quentin leaned over her shoulder and started unfastening her blouse.

Mia's pulse stirred. She tipped her lips back for a kiss.

Quentin flicked his tongue across her lips, then plunged it in, claiming her with a fierce kiss. Then, abruptly, he let go and returned to unbuttoning her blouse and relieving her of her jacket.

"Wait," Mia said. "I forgot to tell you about the wishing card."

Quentin had her blouse unfastened and her bra unhooked. Lowering his lips to hers, he whispered, "Tell me later."

She twisted around to face him. He dropped to his knees, then captured her by the waist and lowered her to the floor. She whispered, "Why don't I tell you later?"

Beetle walked back to his cabin, Quentin's ingenuous story of an invisible woman trying to win a second chance at life filling his mind. Inside, he switched on his computer and stared at the blank screen and the blinking cursor.

Images of Amity filled his mind, chasing all other thoughts away. Was it true? Did she exist, only on a plane where he couldn't reach her—at least, not until she met some sort of challenge?

He groaned, and pushed back from his work space. Grabbing his journal and a pen, he flopped down on the bed. Opening to last night's entry, he glanced in surprise at the sketch of himself seated at the dresser, hunched over his laptop.

Turning the page, he found a series of well-executed cartoon drawings, featuring a woman with long hair garbed in a flowing dress. In one frame, Beetle recognized the scene in the Cubby Hole when he'd been accused of taking cash from the drawer.

In the sketch, the woman, drawn in feathery strokes so that the image shimmered, had her hand in the register.

Another cartoon featured the same woman in front of a cottage surrounded by five dogs, four cats, and three gamboling kittens. An easel sat in the yard.

Beetle shook his head. Obviously, Amity had drawn these pictures last night, sometime after she'd entered his room.

There were more sketches, many featuring a man he clearly recognized as himself. In the last frame, he sat hunched over his laptop, in the cottage garden, the woman standing at the easel nearby.

At the bottom of that page, she'd added a bit of text. He read, puzzling over her words and Quentin's hypothetical film. How could she be caught between life and death when she'd been flesh and blood in his bed only that morning?

What had Quentin said? *Life is stranger than fiction*. The woman who'd shared his bed had been more real than any other woman he'd ever known.

Beetle slapped the journal closed, then held it to his chest. His heart beat rapidly, and he knew he had to find Amity Jones. Whether her story made any sense or not he didn't care, he only knew losing her would be the worst mistake of his life.

Inside the trailer, locked in one another's arms, both Mia and Quentin tried to ignore the knocks that sounded sharply on the door.

Mia whimpered and Quentin groaned. Lifting his head, he called, "Go away."

"I can't."

"That's Beetle," Mia said.

"What do you want?"

"The truth."

"There's a lot of truth-seeking going on around here today," Quentin mumbled.

Mia smiled and smoothed the hair back from his forehead. "Answer him and he'll go away," she said, knowing she wouldn't have Quentin alone for long. The necklace lay cool and heavy on her throat. She pictured herself wearing only the jewelry, leaning over Quentin, driving him wild with pleasure. "Hurry," she said, "tell him anything he wants to know."

Quentin got to his feet and cracked open the door. "Truth about what?"

"Amity. I found a passage in my journal, all about how she's caught between life and death and she recognizes me as her kindred spirit, only she'll never get to meet me. Yet I woke up this morning and she was in my bed."

Mia heard the frustration loud and clear.

"And then I find these sketches, which I sure as heck didn't draw, telling a story about an artist with a family of animals and answering a lot of questions I've had about some screwy things that have been going on. And they're signed by Amity, and there's even an address penciled in on a mail-box next to the cottage, a New Orleans address."

Quentin whooped.

Mia shook her head and called, "What are you waiting for? Go find her."

"She's nowhere around. I've searched the entire area. There's no sight of her, or that cat."

Mia and Quentin exchanged a long look. They smiled. "She's made it back to life, hasn't she, Quentin?" Mia whispered.

He nodded. "She's played her role."

Quentin called, "You'd better catch a plane. To New Orleans."

"But she was here this morning. There's no way she can be in New Orleans now."

Quentin began to edge the door shut. Before he did, he said, "Beetle, I'm only going to say this once, so listen. Miracles do happen. Go to New Orleans; she'll be there. *Permutation* will get by without you."

Then he slammed the door and lowered himself to the carpeted floor.

"Now," he murmured, gazing into her eyes, "where were we?"

"Right here," Mia said, touching her heart and opening her arms to her husband.

Amity huddled in the center of the room, the cheesy one done all in red velvet. She didn't crouch out of fear, but rather to protect Fate, who she'd captured in her arms to keep her safe.

Which was the last thing she remembered before opening her eyes to find herself standing back in this hall Quentin had called the Second Chance Room.

She glanced around, but the old man with the bulbous nose wasn't there. Instead, a sweet-faced man wearing a white robe stood behind a lectern.

"Don't be afraid," he called. "My name is Horace, and I'm here to finish up the assignment Mr. G gave you."

"Assignment?" Suddenly, the letters she'd been trying to remember formed in her mind. She saw the M, then an I, and then an A. "You mean Mia?"

The man checked a clipboard. "Yes, that would be the name of the target. And you made it just in time, too, if I may say so. The timer's almost completely out of sand." He made a *tch-tch* noise. "Only one teensy grain left."

Amity stared at him. He wasn't nearly as interesting as the original guy in the red velvet room.

"What happened to the man who was here before?"

Horace pressed his hands together and looked upward.

Amity glanced at the ceiling.

The ceiling!

As she stared, the red velvet disappeared. She blinked and found herself staring up at the mural of the chapel.

Spike Jones stood over her, licking her face.

Then he barked. Amity looked down. Fate struggled in her arms, then broke free. Spike woofed and bounded forward, scenting the cat. Fate turned, and slapped Spike sharply on the nose, then frisked back to Amity.

Properly chastised, Spike ambled to her side, keeping a respectful distance from this new family member.

"Oh, Spike Jones," Amity said, feeling the back of her head and tousling his fur, "I'm home again."

Mr. G stood in the Heavenly Presence Hall, turning the summons over and over in his gnarled hands, awaiting his fate. Mindful of the No Smoking sign posted at the entrance, he'd tucked his cigar into the breast pocket of his crimson silk dressing gown.

Suddenly, the booming voice he hadn't heard in ages filled every corner of the room. "Look at you! You've broken just about every rule we ever came up with!"

Mr. G nodded. He was pretty proud of his inventive ways.

"You're not afraid of authority!"

Well, they had him there. No denying that point.

"You'll go the limit to help someone you believe in!"

Mr. G thought of some of the people who'd found happiness from some of his finagling ways. He pictured Mia and Quentin on their wedding day. He saw the glow in Gemini Dailey's eyes as she taught yoga to her husband, Alexander Graham Winston. He thought of Amity, and how pleased she'd be, reunited with her dogs and cats now that Mia had learned the lesson she needed out of that almost bungled assignment. And, too, he pictured the thrill she'd experience when Beetle showed up on the doorstep of her studio-cum-menagerie, cured of his allergies.

And if he hadn't meddled, hadn't gone the limit, hadn't broken a few rules here and there, none of it would have happened.

Mr. G wished he'd left his cigar planted between his teeth. He could use a good chomp on it right now. "So what's the verdict here? You gonna shoot me, or what?"

"Shoot you?" The voice boomed even louder. "No way! But I am thinking of giving you a very special assignment." The booming voice laughed heartily.

Mr. G hoped the old man was enjoying himself. All he'd ever wanted was to be left alone to run

Purgatory his own way. He'd done just fine for a long, long time.

"No, we're sending you back to Earth!"

"You're *what*? " Mr. G sank to his knees. Bony as they were, the floor hurt like heck, but to avoid a fate worse than death, he'd beg. "Whaddya want to do that for?"

"You're a special case. And Earth needs help, can use a man who isn't afraid to shake up the status quo and stir up a bit of creative trouble. Every so often, the state of affairs of the universe calls for an old soul to return and lend a hand. You fit the bill, and you deserve the honor."

"But I bucked the system, broke the rules!"

"Pay attention! That's my whole point."

"Fine," Mr. G yelled, "go ahead and make your point, but send someone else. Send Horace!"

Laughter filled the chamber room. "Horace! That's a good one. He's a good son, but he'd live a quiet sixty years, stuck in middle management, and never make any waves."

Mr. G climbed to his feet. He might as well meet his punishment like a man, if that's what the future held in store for him. But he wasn't too proud to beg. "Look," he said, "all I'm asking is that you give me another chance."

Silence answered him.

He pulled a crimson silk hanky from a pocket and mopped at his forehead. Rather than press his luck, he held his tongue. He didn't want to go to Earth. He wanted to go back to Purgatory, back to doing what he did best, identifying clever people who, courtesy of the Second Chance Room, made a difference in other people's lives.

"You won't break any more rules?"

One hand deep in the pocket of his dressing gown, Mr. G crossed his fingers. As solemnly as possible, he said, "No way, José."

"Why is it I have trouble believing that?"

Mr. G produced a grin. Had he pulled it off?

From the corners of the room, a chuckle sounded.

Supremely satisfied with himself, Mr. G nodded and planted his cigar between his teeth.

Epilogue ~

Nine months later

"**O**h, look, Quentin," Mia said, waving a card at him. "A postcard from Amity."

Quentin looked up from his computer, where he was putting the finishing touches on the rewrites of *Kriss-Kross*. With the successful release of *Permutation*, including an Oscar nomination for Portia Goodhope, now known to her intimates as Mrs. Randall Hollings, Mia had had little trouble arranging financing for the film.

"What does she say?"

"She's going to teach an art class at the foundling home, and oh, guess what!" Mia looked up excitedly. "Beetle sold a novel—for quite a nice sum, she's thrilled to report."

"That's great." Quentin smiled, thinking he knew what Mia would say next.

"Oh, Quentin, let's get a copy of the manuscript from his agent. It might be good movie material."

His smile broadened. Mia never missed a beat.

"I'm glad they're happy." Mia opened another

envelope. "This one's a birth announcement," she said, her voice softening.

"Who's it from?" he remembered to ask, still watching his cursor blink.

"Chelsea and Luke." Quentin smiled, thinking of the couple he and Mia had met in their first otherworldly adventure. Thanks to Mia's belief in the power of love, a belief he'd come to share fully, she'd added the sexy pastor to their plan to turn around the selfish and suicidal actress.

When Chelsea Jordan had renounced stardom to marry the Arkansas pastor, *TinselTown News* had run the banner headline, "Preacher Plucks Ex-Porn Star from Filmdom."

Mia crossed the room and held out the card to him. "They had a little boy. Look at him, isn't he cute?"

Quentin glanced at the red-faced infant. "Looks a bit like a monkey, don't you think?"

"Oh, Quentin, he's beautiful. And any baby lucky enough to have Chelsea and Luke for parents, Timmy for a big brother, and Ely for a great-great-uncle will be a most special child."

He smiled at her. In the past months, Mia had bloomed. They continued to debate production issues, they still occasionally resorted to their tradition of pulling straws to determine some of their decisions, and they made sweet, sweet love every night.

And Mia didn't worry.

"I'm happy for them," he said. "What did they name the baby?"

Mia smiled. "Ely G Quentin Miller. Isn't that precious?"

Quentin nodded.

"Wherever Mr. G is right now," Mia said, "I just know he's smiling."

Forgetting about *Kriss-Kross* for the moment, Quentin pulled Mia onto his lap. Whispering, he said, "If we make a baby, do we have to name him after Mr. G, too?"

"What do you mean, if?"

Quentin felt his jaw drop. "Are you telling me what I think you're telling me?"

Mia nodded. "I found out for sure today."

He started to leap from his chair, but realized he held her in his lap. Settling her carefully on the ground, he jumped up. Running his hands through his hair, more excited than he'd ever been in his life, he exclaimed, "A baby! What do we do first?"

Always practical, Mia stood on tiptoe and whispered, "Kiss me."